ADVENTURES OF A WHITE TRASH WEDDING PLANNER

By

Diane Mettler

To Delores
Diane Mettler

Chapter 1

The zoo's security alarm was blaring, and the wedding guests were screaming, running for the back gate. After flinging my heels into a bush to make better time, I was sprinting too. I had to get everyone out before the lovestruck chimpanzee or the zoo security guards got to them first.

The damp, short-clipped grass felt kind of good under my feet, but my chest burned, and I could hear my ragged breath pounding in my ears. I would have to get in better shape, if I was going to continue being a wedding planner.

I caught a glimpse of the sun setting over Puget Sound and the evening's pink glow on Mount Rainier. It would have made the perfect background for a wedding photo.

The wedding guests who were more fit (or more terrified), and those who had gotten a head start, had already made it out to safety. Good for them. I was still fifty yards from the gate.

"Help me!" someone yelled, as I almost fell over a woman who had stumbled and was sitting on the grass holding her ankle.

"Sorry," I said, jumping over her. But I was panting so hard, my words came out as more of a cough.

I would have to feel guilty about that some other time. My first duty to get the gate before the chimp.

I could see the gate ahead of me. Then I turned and saw Daisy, the chimpanzee, cresting a knoll. Daisy was big—like straight out of Planet of the Apes big. Her eyes were frantic, looking for a mate. She let out a piercing cry that was louder than the zoo's alarm. Daisy's cry set off a new wave of screams from the wedding guests.

Daisy was fast. And if my heart wasn't pounding hard enough from sprinting, the thoughts of what would happen if got out of the zoo doubled my heart rate.

My plan was to reach the eight-foot back gate, get everyone through, and then shut the gate before Daisy arrived.

I tried to judge the shortening distance between the gate, the wedding guests and myself. Daisy was quickly closing the gap. It was going to be close.

With my lungs burning, I dug deep for any last bit of energy. I gave one more push, jumped over another fallen family member, and raced harder toward the gate.

It was at this moment that I wondered if I was cut out for wedding planning. How many weddings end with deafening alarms, security guards in hot pursuit, and an amorous chimpanzee? Not many, was my guess. Where did I go wrong? Was it at the bride's interview? Should I be more selective? Maybe steer her toward a different theme?

Daisy screamed again, obliterating my thoughts. She was much closer. Too close. This time, I screamed too.

Less than a week earlier, I had interviewed Cheyenne at my workplace—a construction site in Benston, Washington—an armpit of a town lying in a lower income area between Seattle and Tacoma.

"Sheila, I can't believe this is where you meet with your brides now. It sucks," said Cheyenne, judging me from behind mascara-laden lashes and thick, cherry-colored lips. Cheyenne was twenty-six, slim, and long-legged. And she could pull off a mint-green tube top and denim short-shorts better than anyone I knew.

"You said it couldn't wait," I responded. "You're lucky Charlie even let me use his office."

She was right, though. My boss's beat-up, portable office—what most would call a shed—did suck. I normally didn't meet future brides in a room with a desk covered in papers and receipts, miscellaneous tools strewn around, and a garbage can teaming with flies and overflowing with fast-food wrappers and empty water bottles. To top it off, a fan buzzed in the corner, moving around a gritty layer of dust.

"I'm getting married again," said Cheyenne.

"I kind of guessed. Congratulations."

"Thanks," she said, adjusting her tube top for the third time since we'd walked in.

"What's the problem?" I asked. "You look worried."

"This is my third wedding. I need this one to stick."

"I'm a wedding planner. I don't have a lot of control after the vows."

"Well, I figured, since you did the last two, you could make this one really different. Special."

Cheyenne's marriages were legendary. Her first wedding was to Buddy, three years ago. That marriage only lasted about two months before he ran off with Cheyenne's mother. Cheyenne and her mom looked so much alike, and Buddy was so dumb, I always wondered if he just grabbed the wrong one. Cheyenne and her mom haven't been too close since.

Her second husband, Garth, raced cars on the weekends. Unfortunately, he didn't have a knack for driving. Last year, he ran off the track and crashed into a power pole. Electricity went out all over town, and it made the cover of the papers, with headlines like "Man Dies and Town Goes Down Too." At the age of twenty-six, Cheyenne had become the first widow from our high school graduating class.

"This husband is going to be different," she said, leaning in. "His name is Tony. He's smoking hot, and he's got a cool apartment outside of town."

Cheyenne paused and tapped one of her blue-and-turquoise-painted nails on my red wedding planner book—the place where she knew I kept all my wedding information.

"Sheila, aren't you going to ask me the questions?"

"Give me a second," I said, rummaging through the top drawer of Charlie's desk, pushing aside screws, a stapler, and a few photos of a very attractive woman, until I finally found a pen. I grabbed it and opened my book.

Just opening my red wedding book made me smile. It was filled with all my notes from past weddings—the colors, dress patterns, centerpieces, and themes. I flipped past the previous month's pie-themed wedding I did for Big Amie, and the butterfly wedding I'd planned for Sandra and Pete. It was just page after page of romance and happiness.

Usually I started off asking some general questions, but since this was wedding number three for Cheyenne, I jumped right to the important stuff.

"Do you have your colors and theme picked out?"

"Yes. My colors are yellow and white, and the theme is monkeys."

I paused. "Seriously? Monkeys?"

She nodded, and I jotted it down. My motto is that the bride is always right, but unfortunately the bride isn't always sane.

In Cheyenne's case, it turned out it was the groom with the loose screw. "Tony says he has a connection with them," she said proudly. "On our honeymoon, he's going to take me to the San Diego Zoo to see them."

Cheyenne rolled her engagement ring around her finger. The

diamond was huge—and fake. I could tell, even from across the desk. I wondered if she knew.

"What's the budget?" I asked.

"That's the thing," she said, her smile fading.

My heart sank.

She pulled out two one-hundred dollar bills from a tiny, green rhinestone clutch and laid them on top of a pile of papers on the desk. "It's all I've got right now. And I figured I should get a bulk rate, since this is number three."

"It doesn't work that way," I said. "I don't do them for less than $400 now."

"I'm thinking something classy," she continued, ignoring my price. "And make sure you get a white dress. This wedding needs to be the real thing."

I set down my pen. "You don't even have a dress?"

"That's what the wedding planner does," she said.

"Not for $200 they don't." I tried to keep my voice professional, but I could feel it rising.

Cheyenne pointed her painted nail at my red book again. "I saw the dress you did for Big Amie's wedding. I want something even better."

"She paid me extra for that."

"But I don't have any extra," Cheyenne clamped her bony hand around my wrist and squeezed. "Sheila. You have to help me. This is wedding number three. It's got to be stellar. I need this one to last."

I knew I'd regret it. For $200 I'd be lucky to break even, let alone pocket any money for myself. "OK," I sighed. "Just let go of me so I can write."

Cheyenne smiled, showing off a set of big, incredibly white teeth. I wondered if she used those Crest Whitestrips.

I skipped to the last question. "Have you guys set a date?"

"Saturday, July 23."

I dropped my pen. "Today is Monday, the eighteenth. No way. It's impossible."

I was about to tell her that any respectable wedding took at least three weeks to plan, when Charlie, my boss, poked his head in the door. "You about done in here?"

"Can you give us about five minutes?" I asked.

"You got two," he said. "Wrap it up."

Cheyenne gave Charlie a little wave and a wink as he shut the door.

I kicked her chair. "Cheyenne, over here. Remember, you're getting married—to another guy."

"I'm just being polite. He's cute. You should hook up with that," she said.

"Oh, yeah. Sure. I'll get right on that."

Charlie Ricci wasn't just cute; he was movie-star fine. Tall. Dark. And he had these powerful arms, with biceps that gave his T-shirts a run for their money. They were arms I had imagined around me more often than I liked to admit. Unfortunately, Charlie was also the owner of Ricci Construction—and about two light-years out of my league.

"Let's get you married first," I told Cheyenne.

She flashed me another smile full of those blinding-white teeth. "So, you can do it this Saturday?" she pleaded. "Please say you're doing it."

I paused for a second. It wasn't much money, even for a Benston wedding. Normally, I'd have to ask for at least five hundred for a rush job with a dress included. But looking into Cheyenne's eyes, I could see she was in love. And who can say "no" to love? That's what we wedding planners do—give couples in love their perfect day.

"I'll do it," I said, taking the two bills off the table.

"Thank you!" she squealed.

"I've got your cell number," I said. "I'll call you when I've got something put together."

"I can hardly wait to tell Tony," she squealed again. Then she stood, ran around the desk, and gave me a hug without actually touching me. That was understandable, since I'd been out flagging construction workers all morning in the sun, and I smelled like the inside of a shoe.

We stepped out of Charlie's office and onto the worksite. The heat and dust engulfed us, but none of the grit seemed to stick to Cheyenne. The guys watched her butt sway as she walked away in her tiny shorts and spiked heels.

I shrugged on my safety vest, stuck on my yellow hard hat, and grabbed my sign, invisible in a sea of girders and construction trucks. I didn't mind. I had a monkey wedding to plan.

Chapter 2

The great thing about flagging is that it uses about two and a half brain cells. I could spend almost the entire day visualizing weddings and jotting notes in my little red book, which I kept in the pocket of my orange safety vest. Some people come up with great ideas in the shower. Mine come while I'm holding a Stop sign and directing cement trucks.

Ricci Construction was working on a new Benston sewage plant, located in a grimy industrial area. Two weeks before, it was just dirt and rocks and a few abandoned cars, but after some prep work, we were adding tons of concrete. That meant dozens of cement trucks were coming in and out all day long. Well, I assumed they were cement trucks. I barely noticed, because I was focused on creating a classy monkey-themed wedding for Cheyenne. With only five days, I had to make use of every spare second I had, even if most of those seconds were spent playing traffic cop to a stream of loud, grubby trucks.

My walkie-talkie beeped. It was Denise, my best friend since second grade—and the world's best wedding planner assistant. We were also flagging buddies. I could see her on the other side of the site. You couldn't miss her, even though she was barely five feet tall. She always wore pink, and work was no exception—she was decked out in her favorite color from her hard hat down to her steel-toed boots.

I flipped on my walkie-talkie to reach her. "How're you doing? Hanging in there?"

I could hear her sniffing back tears. "I can't stop thinking about him."

I sighed. Her boyfriend Kenny had dumped her at IHOP the night before. She was heartbroken, but secretly I was thinking it was time to celebrate. The guy was a total loser.

"Denise, we got a wedding," I said, trying to get her mind off Kenny. "Cheyenne's going for it a third time."

"I heard." She stopped and blew her nose. "To that guy you dated back in high school."

"*That's* the Tony?" I said, the connection slowly dawning on me. "Holy shit. I should have guessed." On our one and only date, he broke us into the zoo, then pulled out a six-pack of Rainier Beer. We got buzzed watching monkeys sleep in trees for what seemed like an eternity. I finally left him there and walked home.

Tony's obsession apparently began with an uncle who had a pet shop. During our night at the zoo, Tony told me his uncle had given him a little monkey named Cornwall Jackson, which Tony kept in his bedroom. I didn't date Tony long enough to find out if that was a true story. But why would you lie about something like that?

A grubby cement truck roared up, interrupting my monkey-filled trip down Memory Lane. I could tell it was Kenny's rig. I held up my Stop sign. The truck geared down and the dust cloud piled up behind it and rolled my way. I held my breath for a couple seconds to avoid inhaling the worst of it.

Kenny leaned out. "I don't got time to stop. Move your ass." He spit a brown wad of chewing tobacco onto the hot asphalt in front of me.

"Guess who just pulled up?" I asked Denise over the walkie-talkie without waiting for an answer. "Think I'll let him sit a while and think about what he did."

"You can steer him off a cliff for all I care," came back a voice with a few less tears and a little more venom. Where were cliffs when you needed them?

Kenny leaned on his horn. I raised my Stop sign higher.

Kenny leaned on the horn even longer as another cement truck pulled up behind his. I coolly motioned the other truck around. After it was past him, Kenny jumped out his cab and onto the asphalt.

"You bitch!" he yelled. "This is about Denise, isn't it?"

My fists clenched around the handle of my sign, trying to keep myself together. Kenny and I had loathed each other since the moment he and Denise started dating last year. It was chemistry plain and simple—some people fall in love at first sight, we wanted to see each other hit by a bus. For my part, I just found him flat-out disgusting. His lip was always full of chew, and he got real mean when he drank. Not to mention he was always checking out other women, even in front of Denise.

Denise told me he could be charming and sweet. I never saw that side. I figured the only reason she was dating him was because he was a step up from the guy she'd been seeing before him—some idiot who robbed gas stations. Baby steps, I had told myself then. For his part,

Kenny probably hated me because I knew Denise could do better.

"Of course it's about Denise, you dumb shit. Who dumps someone in the middle of an IHOP?"

Kenny spat another huge gob of wet tobacco at my feet. "I ain't staying with some dumb bitch who wants to keep the baby."

The words hung there as I tried to process them. Did he say baby? As in a little person with diapers? Denise was pregnant? He must be talking about someone else. She would have told me something like that.

"What did you just say?" I said, pointing my sign at him for emphasis.

"You heard me, Sheila. Now I'm getting back in the cab, and I'm driving through."

I don't know if it was the smug look on Kenny's face as he turned back to the truck, or finding out from him that my best friend was pregnant with his baby—probably more of the latter—but suddenly my Stop sign was coming down on the back of his head.

There was a thud, and he wobbled a bit, but he didn't fall. He grabbed the spot where I'd hit him, and his hand came back bloody.

He spun around. "Now you done it!" he shouted. His eyes narrowed, and he looked like the mean little weasel he was. His right fist balled up, ready to land one on me.

"Don't you even think about it," I said. But before the words were out of my mouth, he was taking a step toward me. Reacting, I swung my sign like I was going to hit one out of the park. I don't know why he didn't cover his head—maybe because he wasn't thinking too straight after the first smack. The sign connected this time with the side of his head. The reverberation ran up my arms and into my neck, leaving my ears ringing.

Kenny crumpled to the dusty ground, blood oozing from a couple of places on his head and seeping into the dirt.

Charlie ran up. "Jesus, Sheila! What the hell are you doing?"

"He came at me. I had to."

Charlie looked at me, no longer the friendly boss. He pointed toward the parking lot. "You're outta here. Now!"

"Why?"

"Because you're fired," he said. "This is an assault. Pack your shit and get outta here."

"But—" I started to protest.

He lowered his voice, looking me in the eye. "I'm doing this for your own good. If you're not out of here in five minutes, cops will be here to escort you out. Trust me on this."

Crewmen were gathering around. I smacked my Stop sign against Kenny's truck tire. "I can't believe this!" I yelled. "It was self-defense."

But Charlie didn't hear me. He was too busy listening to Kenny moan something about killing me with his bare hands.

All eyes were on me as I stalked away. I could feel them staring into my back. Some guys were chuckling.

I spun around and pointed my Stop sign at them. Two dozen steel-toed boots took a step back. "Yeah. That's right. You should be scared." I jabbed my Stop sign at them to make my point. "You don't mess with a gal who knows how to use one of these things." I threw my sign at them and marched off.

"Hey, what's happening?" I heard Denise's voice crackle over my walkie-talkie.

I took a deep, jagged breath. I couldn't tell if I was madder at Kenny for being an asshole, at Charlie for not defending me, or my best friend for not confiding in me that she was pregnant.

"We need to talk," I finally replied.

Chapter 3

I walked the three and a half miles back home to the Wheel In RV Park, thinking I could burn off my anger in the hot sun. Denise had called me twice while I trudged along the highway, and I told her to meet me a couple of hours later at the Brew and Suds Sports Bar (or "the BS" to us regulars). I needed to get my head in the right place before talking to her.

On my way, I stopped by the post office to pick up my mail—a credit card late notice and junk mail, but no new issue of *Best Bride magazine*. *Best Bride* was my bible when it comes to wedding planning. I hadn't missed an issue since I was nine years old, when the only weddings I could plan were for my stuffed animals and the neighbors' pets.

My mood darkened as I stood in line to talk to a postmaster. When I finally reached the front of the line, I stood face to face with a fat little man, with a surely attitude.

"Can you search your stuff back there and see if there for an issue of Best Bride. It's late. It's never late."

"Sometimes things get lost."

"Yeah, well, maybe you could go look."

"Maybe your subscription lapsed. Take it up with the magazine."

"It did NOT lapse,"

"Take it up with the magazine. You're holding up the line." He looked past me. "Next."

"You shouldn't test me. I almost killed a man today," I said trying to sound menacing.

He shook his head, unphased, and motioned the next person up.

Fifteen minutes later, I got to the Wheel In drenched in sweat, wondering if maybe hitting Kenny upside the head with the Stop sign wasn't my best move. But how are you supposed to respond to something like your best friend being pregnant? I mean, holy crap, there was going to be a baby in our lives. And babies scared me. I had never babysat growing up. Ever. Babies were too small and fragile. Not to mention they cried and pooped and couldn't talk. There were so many ways to make mistakes. I'd spent my whole life avoiding them, and now there was going to be one in my life. What was I going to do if Denise or her scary little baby needed me? I tried to push my fears away, but they just hung there like a wet diaper.

I walked through the RV park, deep in thought. To the average person, the Wheel In looks run down—because it is. There are 237 units circled around a forty-year-old laundromat and a swimming pool that hadn't been operational, except as a bird sanctuary, for almost as long. The pool was also growing something so dense and green on top that the residents were worried someone's dog might try to walk across it, sink in, and die.

Each lot had sewer and water hookups, and the price was right—$200 a month. We had no view to speak of, except of the laundromat, or in my case, the Benston Highway, because I'd turned my 1973 Airstream around to face it instead. Across the highway was a shitty little strip mall that housed the Brew and Suds, which was flanked by a nail place and a Mexican restaurant, which were in turn flanked by a check-cashing outfit and a pet-grooming place.

When I was in high school nearby, the joke was that the Wheel In RV Park was where people went to park and die. Now I knew that was kind of true. Every year, a couple of RVs got towed away because someone finally cashed it in. But in my case, I vowed to leave there some day as a professional wedding planner. I'd be trading my Airstream in for an apartment with a bathtub.

I had a vision of my future—planning weddings with receptions under big white tents. Tables would be set with real china and glass flutes—no paper plates and Solo cups. I'd carry an iPad instead of my red book, I would order food from caterers, instead of the deli mart, and I book real bands and throw away the boom box. Most of all, I would get paid real money. I would have enough to stop flagging at construction sites. I could get a two-bedroom apartment with an extra bedroom for my wedding supplies. And I'd have enough cash left each month to get my hair and nails done. I could see it as clearly as I could see the scuffs on my steel-toed boots.

Maybe getting fired was just a sign from the universe that I needed to focus on me. This monkey wedding had potential. As I made my way down my row, I could see my Airstream up ahead, with a sign out front that said "Weddings Here." There wasn't a lot of traffic at the Wheel In, but you never knew.

My neighbor on the left was Jim Meyer, a well-worn 67-year-old divorcée. His paunch hung over his busted-out shorts as he mowed his two square feet of grass—beer in one hand and cigarette in his mouth.

"You're home early," he said.

"Fired."

"Shit. That sucks. If you want a beer, there are some cold ones in the back."

"Thanks," I said, helping myself to a tallboy to take back home. I'd usually stick around and enjoy it with him—I just didn't feel like it at that moment. Over many a brew, Jim had told me stories about his beautiful, funny, and sexy ex-wife, Betty. I'd seen pictures of Betty. She looked like a fat T-Rex—with teeth that were too big, eyes too buggy, and little pudgy arms. I always thought maybe Jim was lucky to escape before she ate him. You can't argue with love, though. My goal was to get him on eHarmony and hooked up with someone normal. I mean, he's only sixty-seven, not ninety-seven. I figured if Betty is what got him going, his bar was clearly so low, he was bound to find someone.

My neighbor on the other side was Carla Beetle. She was old, but not as old as Jim. She had parked her rig, a 1981 Dodge Heritage Motorhome, at the Wheel In ten years before, and since then had pretty much stayed to herself. In fact, months at a time went by when I never even saw her. Sometimes the only reason I knew she was still alive was the big bag of Purina cat food I saw delivered each week for her four cats. She rarely had any human food delivered, and I never saw her come home with groceries. I suspected she and the cats all liked to eat Purina, but I never had the guts to ask.

I'd already decided that Jim and Carla would never be a love connection, mostly because they hated each other. I wasn't really sure why. Something happened between them one day years ago when I was at work. I suspected it had something to do with a cat that went missing. Whatever it was, it was best for all of us that my place stood between theirs, or they might kill each other.

As I walked up my steps, I waved at Carla, who for once was actually leaning out her window, watering the dead fern in her window box. She waved and slipped back inside.

Inside my Airstream, it was roasting hot. I kicked off my boots, pulled off my vest and T-shirt, peeling down to my sports bra, then slipped on a pair of short shorts and cranked up the fan. I popped open Jim's beer and sat back in my threadbare captain's chair. I opened the past issue of Best Bride.

I took a deep breath, inhaling the scent of the pages, which still had the faint aroma of the perfume samples they always included inside. I flipped through the section on backless dresses, then browsed honeymoon ideas, and finally checked out the new summer shoe collection, which featured some bad-ass silver stilettos. Then I stopped dead. The eighth annual Best Bride Budget Wedding Contest was underway. I had forgotten all about it. I applied every year and hadn't once even gotten an honorable mention. But that was before I had a monkey wedding in the works. Before I was fired and had time to focus on putting my submission together. I could hear the sounds of wedding bells. Was the universe telling me I was meant to win this year? Yes. I was sure of it.

The wedding bells turned out to be the muffled ringtone of my phone tucked in my back pocket. It was Denise texting, "I'm on my way to the BS."

Chapter 4

Denise was late. I was already three shots of tequila and one basket of peanuts into the afternoon when she walked in to the BS. She slipped into my booth, sitting across from me.

We sat there, a silence hanging between us. Not that it was all that quiet. A TV over the bar blared a sports recap show, and near one of the pool tables behind us, two obnoxious guys were trying to impress inebriated girlfriends with their dartboard skills. Neither of them had even hit the board yet. Some people wondered why Denise and I met here to plan our wedding gigs. The biggest reason was because I could walk home after three tequilas.

Denise finally spoke up. "What the hell were you thinking?"

"Let me see," I began, "I guess I was thinking . . . My best friend's pregnant. Why am I hearing it from a scummy little twerp instead of from her?"

"Oh," she said quietly, looking at her stomach. It was covered by an oversized T-shirt. I tried to see if there was a bump, but it was impossible. And even harder was imagining her months from now, waddling around. Denise, with her big blue eyes and blonde hair, had always been so small and slim. It would be like hanging out with a fat, pregnant elf.

"So, how pregnant are you?" I asked.

Denise grabbed a peanut and examined it, trying not to make eye contact. When she spoke, I could barely hear her. "Three and half, maybe four months."

"You've known for FOUR MONTHS, and you never TOLD me?"

The guys playing pool stopped and looked over at us. I gave them the finger, and they went back to their game.

"I'm sorry. I just thought I should let the dad . . . Kenny, know first, and I kept putting that off and . . . I'm sorry. I was going to tell you. Really."

Denise motioned for a waitress. I grabbed a peanut and cracked it open, trying to keep from saying the wrong thing. I hated Kenny, but I loved Denise. She was a true romantic like me. But unlike me, she imagined that jackasses like Kenny would hear the word "baby" and become father of the year. You've got to give someone with that much optimism a little credit . . . or a lobotomy. Since Denise in all other ways was amazing, I decided to cut her some slack.

"Are you going to ask how he's doing?" Denise asked.

"Oh my god, you're having a boy?"

"Not the baby. Kenny."

I motioned for the waitress to hurry. "I hope that jerk's in intensive care."

"He's got a concussion and has to stay in the hospital for twenty-four hours. But they think he'll be back to work next week."

"Great. Let's throw a party!"

Denise looked at the table, tears welling up in her eyes. The tequila turned in my stomach. I was being a shitty friend. Her day wasn't going much better than mine.

"I'm sorry. I didn't mean it about the intensive care. Well, I meant it a little bit, but . . ."

"Charlie laid me off," she said.

"But you didn't do anything." My voice must have gotten louder because people were looking again.

"He doesn't want any pregnant flaggers. Their insurance doesn't cover it or something."

Our waitress, Sally, who coincidentally used to babysit us when we were little, came with our drinks. Back then it was orange juice; today it was tequila and a daiquiri. Funny how some things don't change all that much.

As Sally set the drinks on our table, she gave Denise's shoulder a little squeeze.

"Thanks," Denise said, looking up and smiling.

My stomach lurched again, but this time not because of the tequila or because I felt like a bad friend. Something wasn't right. I couldn't quite put my finger on it. On a hunch, I reached for Denise's glass and took a sip. It was a *virgin* daiquiri. Denise glanced nervously at Sally.

I was trying to put it together, which would have been easier without three shots of tequila messing with my mind. Then it dawned on me. Denise had switched up from Coors Light to daiquiris months ago.

"Oh my god, Denise, you told Sally before me. SALLY, the babysitter!"

15

Sally said something under her breath and huffed off.

Denise grabbed my hand. "I'm so sorry, Sheila. I couldn't drink alcohol with the baby, and that near beer tastes like shit. Sally guessed as soon as I switched."

"Who else knows?"

Denise mentally tried to add up all the people. "Let's see. The doctor, my mom, Kenny, of course. Sally, and Charlie. Oh, the mailman knows because—"

"OK. I get it," I said, feeling like a jilted lover. "I just thought we promised we weren't going to get knocked up until we had our wedding planner business up and going."

There was an awkward angry silence as we sipped our drinks, trying to figure out what to say next.

"Want to help me name the baby?" she asked behind a frothy, pink daiquiri mustache. "She's a girl."

The anger evaporated as I imagined a little girl sitting here with us some day, one who looked like Denise, planning weddings with us. "Yes!" I said quickly. "We'll find something perfect. Nothing too weird, but something people will remember. Something with style."

"Just as long as it isn't Estelle."

I nodded. Estelle was her grandma's name, and Denise was still under the impression that her grandma had stolen her dog Sweetie, an ancient Pomeranian, and took it out to a farm while she was at school. Everyone knew Sweetie was run over by my Uncle Clarence. But sometimes you have to let sleeping dogs lie, or in this case let dead ones stay on the farm.

We ordered burgers and extra-large garlic fries and started work on Cheyenne's wedding. This one had to be ultra-romantic, I explained to Denise. Women with bad luck like Cheyenne needed a fresh start.

And maybe it was the tequila talking, but I told myself this wedding was bigger than Cheyenne. The incident with Kenny at the construction site was a sign—and not the Stop sign, although that did play a role—but a real sign. A sign that I was ready to become a full-time wedding planner. Putting together a killer monkey wedding for *Best Bride* would show people what I could do. It was our ticket to weddings that paid more than $200.

Denise glanced at my notes. "I guess we should be happy they want a monkey theme. It could be worse. Like spiders." She shuddered.

I nodded and moved on to logistics. "Doesn't Bobby Haynes still work at the zoo?" I asked.

"Yeah," she said, "but he doesn't work with the monkeys. He handles the visitor services. He hands out passes and cleans bathrooms. Stuff like that."

"That's perfect. What's his number?"

She grabbed her purse, a huge thing that within five months would probably serve as a diaper bag as well. She dug through it, hunting. "Dang, I must have left my phone in the car." She looked up and caught me grinning, then asked, "What are you smiling about?"

I held up the old issue of *Best Bride*. "They're doing the budget wedding contest again."

I opened the contest and handed it to her. Denise was also a *Best Bride* fan from way back. She had helped me check sofas for change and steal from our moms' purses to get enough cash for the steep $10 cover price. But it was worth it. No other magazine compared to *Best Bride*, with its glossy pages and gorgeous photo spreads. You could almost taste the wedding cakes and champagne.

Denise downed the rest of her daiquiri as she mulled over the contest. "We do it every year and haven't even got honorable mention."

"But look," I pointed out, "this year the prize isn't just $10,000 and a trip for two to Los Angeles to meet the editor. The winner will also appear on the first episode of *Best Bride*'s new reality show *Small Budget, Big Wedding*."

She wasn't convinced. "You think we can do it with a monkey wedding?"

"Hell yeah! We've got a *$200* monkey wedding. We're going to crush it this year. It's why the universe had me fired."

"You got fired because you hit Kenny with that sign."

"That was just a bonus. Now stop being so sensible," I said. "I'm trying to build some excitement here."

Denise contemplated. "Do you really think *Best Bride* would be blown away by a chimpanzee wedding? It doesn't seem quite their style."

"Sure," I admitted, "it would have been easier if Cheyenne was going to marry a pool cleaner. Something easier to work with. But we can do this."

Denise looked down at her hidden bump. "We only have five days."

"That's perfect. Because the contest ends in six days."

She looked up at me. She was almost convinced. I gave it all I had. "Think about the clothes. When we win, we'll have to buy some fabulous maternity outfits for L.A."

Denise patted her tummy and smiled. "Did you hear that Helga? We're going to L.A."

I sighed. We'd talk about baby names later.

By the time we had polished off the last of our burgers and garlic fries, we had an outline of a wedding. I had two pages full of ideas in my little red book. We both agreed that this would not be an average wedding. And it wasn't because of the *Best Bride* contest (although that didn't hurt). We both knew that women who have bad luck like Cheyenne can get cynical and start thinking marriage is just a piece of paper and a ring. They believe romance is for others. Cheyenne wasn't at that point yet, but I could tell during our consultation that she was on the edge.

"When do you think we should buy the bananas?" I asked.

Chapter 5

After Sheila smacked Kenny with the Stop sign, Charlie's day had turned into an endless stream of calls from attorneys and insurance adjusters. He filled out a mountain of forms and squeezed in two trips to the hospital to wish Kenny a quick recovery—and to find out if he planned to sue the company. Charlie need not have worried; Kenny was more upset with the hospital for not serving beer than any legal suit against Ricci Construction. And he had no intention of telling anyone that he had been beat up by a gal.

Charlie just hoped his dad didn't hear about all this. His father was CEO of the family company, RIC, and Charlie's baby, Ricci Construction, was one of the company's many subsidiaries. Any family member who wanted to move up in the parent company had to complete business school and run one of the subsidiaries for five years, while showing a significant improvement. Charlie had been at Ricci Construction for six years, and until the incident with Sheila and Kenny, he had run it profitably and without major incident.

Finally, at nine o'clock that night, Charlie found himself sitting in his blissfully quiet office, signing the last insurance form. He set down the pen, leaned back, and stretched. His busted-up chair creaked, threatening to collapse. Charlie couldn't care less.

As he worked the kinks out of his neck, he looked around the office, littered with all manner of empty coffee cups, receipts, and sandwich wrappers. He knew he would have to get organized when this blew over, but right then he was only interested in going home, cracking open a cold beer, and renting some mindless movie filled with car chases and loose women. He held onto that thought for almost three happy seconds when there was a knock at his door.

His first instinct was to slip out the back door, but unfortunately he didn't have one.

"It's me, Sheila," he heard. "Are you in there? I need to talk to you."

"Come back tomorrow. I'm busy."

The truth was he didn't have the stamina for a conversation with her right at that moment. Talking to Sheila wasn't like talking to normal people. She had a way of derailing him. He would say no to her on one thing, like letting her use his office for her wedding business, and in the next breath, he would somehow be agreeing to just half an hour. Or when she got him to order a pink hard hat for Denise, or the women's honey bucket. After a conversation with Sheila, he always felt like he had been on a journey, but wasn't entirely sure where he had gone.

"It'll only take a minute. Swear."

"Sorry, I'm—"

She opened the door and barged in. Damn it, Charlie scolded himself. He was going to have to remember to lock that door.

"OK, make it quick," he said.

"I will." She walked up to his desk.

Charlie hadn't seen her without her flagger vest on since the day she came in to interview for the job two years ago. Seeing her rock a pair of short shorts, heels, and a form-fitting tank top caught him a off guard. Not to mention the highlighted brunette hair stacked high on her head, glitter-painted nails, glossy lips, and thick eyelashes that made her big brown eyes look even bigger. She kind of reminded him of a stripper. But in a good way.

Charlie took a deep breath. "I mean it. It's been a long day."

"I need a favor."

"A favor? I just spent most of the day convincing our attorney not to press charges against you."

She leaned in. "Charges for what? Hitting Kenny? That was self-defense."

The way she was leaning toward him over the desk, Charlie could see down her shirt. He quickly looked away, but not before he noticed a red-and-white polka dot bra and a better-than-average rack.

"You assaulted an employee. It's a felony," he said.

"Bullshit. That asshole deserved it. They should pay *me* for a public service."

"If you hit every guy who deserved it, I wouldn't have a crew," he said, knowing she was right. He moved on. He was going to stay in control of this conversation. "What is this favor?"

She leaned in again. "You have to hire Denise back."

There was fire in her eyes, but it was her perfume that did a number on Charlie. It was something flowery and soft, likely purchased from the local drugstore. He liked it—a lot. His girlfriend, Julie, told him once that he was a sucker for cheap perfume, and not in a good way. In fact, the previous Christmas she threw a bottle he had gotten her straight into the trash, telling him, "I don't intend to smell like a cheap hooker."

Charlie had never smelled any hookers, and he certainly didn't realize he had purchased their perfume. He apologized, a little hurt, promising to ask Julie before he purchased "a fragrance" for her again. But that didn't stop him from liking whatever Sheila was wearing. He took another whiff before he pointed to a chair.

"Why don't you sit down?"

"No," she said, leaning even further over his desk. "I'm not moving until you tell me you're hiring her back."

"I will, right after she has the baby. She's almost seven months pregnant. I can't keep her on the road crew. It's too dangerous."

Sheila took a step back on her platform heels. "Did you say seven months?"

"I think that's what she said." This was weird, he thought. Didn't girls talk about that kind of thing? And was Sheila wearing polka dot panties that matched her bra? He shook his head. That perfume was really doing a number on him.

"Since she's pregnant, she's going to have expenses. It's all the more reason to keep her on."

"Doing what?" he asked.

"Look at this pigsty. You need an assistant."

They both looked around his office. To the untrained eye, it looked like a storage shed filled with a sea of paper clutter, tools, and other junk, with a desk and two chairs in the middle.

"It's not that bad," he lied

"Trust me. You need Denise. She can get this place back in shape. She's every organized. Her place never looks like this." To make her point Sheila picked up a handful of bills, reports, memos, and miscellaneous mail.

She stopped. Dangling from her hand was a pair of lacy, hot pink panties. The panties hung there between the two of them for a second before Charlie reached for them. She pulled them back and smiled.

"Dude, you bring women back here? Seriously? You can do better."

"I don't bring women . . . I mean, I found those in one of the trucks and . . ."

How did she do it? He could take control of an entire crew of barbarians, but after two minutes with Sheila, he was back on his heels, defending himself.

"We're grown-ups. You don't need to explain." She gave him a sly little wink.

He felt his face redden. Even his ears burned. "Just give them to me. Denise can start on Wednesday."

"Here you go." She held out the panties, and he snatched them, shoving them into a desk drawer.

"Now, get out of here before I change my mind."

"You're the best," she said, giving him a warm, thankful smile. He found himself almost smiling back.

A moment later she was out the door, her heels crunching in the gravel, with only her perfume lingering. Charlie suddenly realized he was going to miss her.

Chapter 6

There aren't many days you can say you knocked out a guy at work, found out your best friend is knocked up, and committed yourself to a monkey wedding. And it was only ten p.m.

The Uber driver dropped me off outside the Wheel In RV Park. One look at the place and the 20-something driver told me he wasn't driving in. He'd heard some stories about how they steal cars there. I couldn't disagree. That's why I didn't have a car and was using Uber.

I walked back toward my place, not only exhausted, but depressed too. The panties on Charlie's desk were a blast of reality I didn't need. It's one thing to know someone like Charlie is out of your league, but it's another to hold the panties in your hand.

The tequila from earlier in the day still churned uncomfortably in my stomach. What I needed was a relaxing evening watching *Dirty Dancing* and going through *Best Bride* magazine again to firm up more details for Cheyenne's monkey wedding.

I walked up to the Airstream. There was a yellow notice attached to the door.

"Shit!"

Just then, Swayze and Axel, two six-year-old trailer-park twins, dressed in hoodies, pulled up at my drive on their beat-to-hell Big Wheels. They rode around the park endlessly. I had a theory that they were like feral cats, roaming the streets of the Wheel In RV Park, and everyone just left food out for them so they didn't starve. I had yet to meet their parents, who I mentally cursed for not watching their young children, though I gave them points for coming up with excellent names.

"She's getting evicted," said Swayze to Axel.

"Remember when that lady in Lot 27 got one?" said Axel.

"Yeah, the police came and pulled her out, and they put all her stuff out on the street. Sheila's going to be a homeless lady now," said Swayze.

"With a shopping cart," said Axel with an unhealthy sense of glee.

"For your information, this is a late notice, not an eviction notice," I said, trying not to let it show that they were kind of freaking me out. "No one is throwing me out on the street. Now, go home. It's late."

Swayze looked at me, stuck out his tongue and gave me a raspberry. "We go home when we want to." They pedaled off in unison, and the sound of plastic hitting pavement receded around the next corner.

I shoved the late notice in my purse and let myself in. I threw on a light, grabbed a beer from the fridge, and dropped onto the sofa, which would later transform into my bed.

The reality of being jobless began settling in. With a week to catch up on rent, and just $200 from Cheyenne in my purse, money would have to show up soon. I had used up the last of my cash the week before, when I needed to replace the propane stove. I would have to add job hunting to my to-do list for the next day.

I popped the cap off the beer and took a long swallow. The brew met the tequila, and it took a minute before they decided to make friends. I kicked off my heels and leaned back. My place may not be a mansion, I thought, and all 152 square feet may be showing some wear, but it was home.

My mom left me the 1973 Airstream—along with three months back rent and a clogged toilet—when she married some guy from Idaho with a hardware store four years before. I learned all this one night when she called me from Vegas. I should have been upset that she left me with a 45-year-old piece of crap and a pile of bills, but what really hurt was that they'd eloped.

She and Ernest—that was the hardware guy's name—met when she was buying some duct tape and Bondo to fix her car. He volunteered to come over and help her with the repairs, and she said it was love at first sight. The next week they flew out to Las Vegas and found a little chapel off the strip. She sent me a picture. It looked like a cool wedding. They were standing on a patch of AstroTurf under a canopy of white plastic flowers. My mom wore a brushed denim miniskirt and white lace top, and Ernest wore his Ace Hardware button-down. Beside them stood an ordained Elvis, dressed in a lime-green spandex jumpsuit and cape. He was winking at the camera and not a hair on his head was out of place. It's true, Mom and I have had a rocky relationship for years, and I couldn't have put a wedding like that together in Benston, but it killed me that she never even asked.

I set down my beer and threw a bag of popcorn into the microwave. It was time to focus on the monkey wedding—specifically wedding dress ideas. If I wanted to get out of this place, and make a real living as a wedding planner, I had to step up my game.

I looked at my *Dirty Dancing* poster—the only thing of value I owned. It was signed by Patrick Swayze, and it was my inspiration. It's the poster where Baby's arm is wrapped around Johnny's neck, his hand around her waist, and they're touching head to head. *Dirty Dancing* was the foundation of every one of my weddings. Every bride was Baby, and every groom was Johnny, and every wedding should be a perfect mix of passion and romance, just like in the movie.

As I finished off the beer, I thought Cheyenne and I both needed an incredible wedding.

I pulled my little red book out and checked the list that Denise and I had put together back at the BS. There was a lot to accomplish in five days. In the morning I'd try to knock off the first couple of items, including figuring out how to break into the zoo. This wedding was going to require a great location.

Chapter 7

By seven a.m. the sun poured in through the main window of the Airstream, bouncing off the chrome fixtures, and lighting the place up like a five-thousand-watt bulb. It was better than an alarm clock, and it was also the reason I kept sunglasses by the bed.

I was making coffee when my cell phone buzzed. Mom. That was never good sign, so I ignored the call. I'd deal with whatever she wanted later. I had a wedding location to check out.

I heard Denise pull up, grabbed my purse, and headed out the door, making sure to give Patrick Swayze an air kiss for good luck.

Denise was already jumping out of her beat-to-shit pink Chevy Beretta, wearing a bright pink Hello Kitty T-shirt and pink leggings. Before I could get to the car, she ran up and hugged me tight.

"You did it! I go back to work tomorrow."

"That's great," I said, not hugging her back because now I could *feel* the baby bump. A really big bump. And I was upset with her.

"What's wrong?" she asked.

"Let's see. Oh yeah, Charlie said you're SEVEN MONTHS pregnant!"

"Oh, yeah." She looked sheepishly down at her bump.

I walked the rest of the way to her car, feeling hurt all over again. "Why aren't you telling me the truth? I'm your best friend. Or am I not?"

"Of course you're my best friend. I just needed some denial time."

"How much time do you need?! You wait any longer and she's going to be in school."

"I know, I know." Denise slid behind the wheel. I got in the passenger's seat and was assaulted by even more pink. Not that I could complain. It beat walking or Ubering everywhere.

She spoke to her bump. "She's right, Pocahontas. We have to get ready."

"Pocahontas?"

Denise tried to start the pink monster. It coughed a couple of times, belched a black cloud, then finally caught.

"What's wrong with Pocahontas? I like it. It's exotic."

"What about Gidget?" I suggested.

"Isn't that like a cell phone or something?"

"No, that's a *gadget*."

She considered it as we drove out of the RV park. "I think it would be confusing," she finally said.

"You're probably right. Let's keep thinking."

\#

We parked outside the Point Defiance Zoo & Aquarium. As soon as I saw it, I knew it would be the perfect venue for Cheyenne's wedding—with a stunning view of Puget Sound, sailboats sliding across its blue surface, and snow-covered Mount Rainier looming in the background. Best of all, there were monkeys inside. Lots of monkeys.

The zoo was part of the Tacoma park system, and I had seen lots of beautiful weddings held on the grounds there over the years. Brides and grooms stood on grassy knolls, or in the rose garden and under towering fir trees. Ours would probably be the first to be held next to the monkey cages.

My plan would be to sneak the wedding party in after hours and have everyone look like we belonged. It's not like I'd ever seen any wedding police at the zoo.

We checked out the parking lot as we made our way up to the main entrance. Even though it was early in the day, families were already unloading kids, strollers, snacks, and god knows whatever else kids need. If this was going to be Denise soon, I thought, she was going to need a bigger car.

"Are you sure about this place?" Denise pointed to the security cameras on the light poles. "It looks hard to get into. Maybe we should check out the Rec Center. We could find someone with a monkey and—"

I held up my hand, cutting her off, taking the place in. "This is the place. Nothing less for Cheyenne. And if we're going to win *Best Bride's* contest, we need something better than the Rec Center." I said. "This is definitely the place."

Denise looked out over the stunning view of Puget Sound. "It would be fun to win."

"We'll win," I said confidently. "I can feel it. This is our year. The year of the monkey wedding."

"If you say so." Denise smiled and pulled out her cell phone. How long had it been since I'd seen her just smile? It had been a while. Geez, I thought, I was going to have to up my game as a friend when this was over.

"Who are you calling?" I asked.

"With all this security, I think I know a better way in than Bobby Haynes. You remember Reese?"

I shook my head.

"Sure you do. His sister was the fat bikini barista at Benston Beans. Anyway, her brother shovels shit here. Bet he could get us in the back entrance."

We drove around to the back of the zoo. We smelled the service entrance before we reached it—the stench was like a cross between a landfill and wet dog.

"Ooo, wee, that reeks," Denise said, holding her nose. "It smells like my little brother's room, only worse."

"It smells more like when your folks raised rabbits in the house that summer."

"I forgot about that. You're right. It *does* smell just like that, only if they had about ten thousand rabbits." Denise smiled again. "I should get a bunny for the baby when she's older. Children need pets."

We pulled up, got out of the car, and tried to breathe through our mouths. Though if I thought about it, that seemed almost worse, like eating shit instead of just smelling it. I shook it off. No one said wedding planning wasn't brutal.

Standing at the back entrance was Reese, waving with one hand, an enormous shovel in the other. He was wearing zoo overalls covered in various stains I didn't want to know about. He was tall and had an easy smile—as well as a mop of red hair tucked under a zoo baseball cap.

"Denise!"

"Hi, Reese. This is my friend Sheila."

"Hey there," he said, raising his shovel. "I'm right in the middle of cleaning out the elephant cage. So I don't have a lot of time."

"We're planning a surprise wedding here this weekend," said Denise. "Wondered how hard it would be to sneak in here."

"Not too hard. You sure you want to use this entrance though?"

"Security is pretty tight up front," she said. "And we don't have the money for a regular permit."

Reese nodded knowingly, like he dealt with wedding planners every day.

"Does it always smell this bad?" I asked, wondering if the stink was going to cling to my clothes. I was wearing my favorite halter top.

"It never smells great back here," he said. "But normally it's not this bad. We're just cleaning out a couple big pens today."

"I think we can work with that," I said.

"We can?" Denise's eyes were starting to water. "The Rec Center's sounding pretty good."

I ignored her and pushed ahead, needing to wrap up this interview before I passed out from the stench. "What about security guys here? Do they watch pretty close? Hang out at the weddings?"

I looked around for cameras, but from what I could see there were none.

"I'm not too involved in the weddings," Reese said. "I handle more of the dung. But the security guys I know are pretty cool."

"Do you think you can get us in this Saturday night? Around seven?" I asked. "I can throw in a six-pack."

"Sure thing."

"Do you ever get to pet the elephants?" asked Denise.

Denise had a serious thing for elephants. She'd been trying to figure a way to incorporate elephants into a wedding for years, but to-date, no luck.

"Nah, above my pay grade," Reese said. "But I can get you a good deal on elephant shit," he said. "It's great for the garden."

"We'll keep that in mind," I said. "We'll be in touch. OK?"

He nodded and ambled back to his piles of poop. We ran from the fumes for the car.

"It really smells bad. There is no way it'll work," said Denise as we scrambled to get inside.

"You heard him. It doesn't smell this bad every day."

"But he said it never smells good."

"We'll find a way to make it work," I said.

Chapter 8

Charlie got to the worksite Tuesday morning feeling good, with the morning sun warming his shoulders. Kenny was being released from the hospital and wasn't going to sue the company or Sheila. The treatment plant construction was on time and under budget. And it was his birthday. He decided he was going to do something relaxing for himself, maybe see if any guys wanted to grab a beer after work. When he reached his office, he knew his day was going to take a different turn.

His girlfriend, Julie, stood at the door. She smiled at him, looking beautiful and completely out of place, as if someone had cut a picture out of a fashion magazine and glued it to a photo of a construction site. She was slender, with blonde, short-cropped hair, blue eyes, and thin lips that always sported a coat of dark red lipstick. Although she was obviously trying to dress casually—jeans, boots, and a sleeveless sweater—Charlie guessed her outfit cost more than most of his guys' rigs.

She walked up to him and kissed him on the cheek. "Happy birthday," she cooed.

"Thank you."

"Surprised to see me?"

"I am. You've never been to one of my construction sites."

She glanced around. "Can you blame me? These places are filthy." She playfully took his hand and squeezed it. "But it's your birthday, and I've got a big surprise for you."

"Let me guess. A new truck?" Charlie said, knowing full well she despised riding in them. She had told him once that it wasn't normal to climb up into a vehicle.

"Better than a truck."

"Wow. . . really?" What was better than a truck, he wondered.

"I've arranged a birthday lunch at Palisade. And your mom and dad are coming. They're flying in from New York as we speak. Surprised?"

"I couldn't be more surprised if you ran me over with a new truck."

\#

When Charlie and Julie walked into Palisade, Charlie immediately spotted his mom and dad at a far window table. Palisade was his mom's favorite place to eat in Seattle—it was a big, open restaurant with a sweeping view of Elliott Bay. There was a pond in the center of the restaurant where starfish hung out, just waiting, Charlie thought, to make their escape. His mom said Palisade reminded her of her childhood, which Charlie found interesting, since she grew up in Ohio.

Julie took his hand and led him toward the table. "Isn't this great? All of us together."

Charlie's mom spotted him first. She stood and came around the table to give him a hug. She was 65, almost as tall as Charlie, and kept herself in great shape. She looked 40, in part because of the extreme workouts she did with her trainer, Guy, but mostly because she also had an extremely talented plastic surgeon, Dr. Nelson.

His mom rolled her eyes at Charlie's dad, Rodney, who barely looked up and was deep in conversation on his cell. "Ignore him. It's some acquisition. You know how he gets. Let me look at my little boy. Are you eating enough? You look slim."

"I'm eating fine, Mom. Look at you, though. You're in better shape than I am."

She gave him another hug and a smile, which meant a lot to Charlie. Ever since she started getting "the work done," she was under the impression that if she smiled too big her face would spring back into its more natural, aged version. So she rarely smiled.

"You guys didn't need to come all the way out here," said Charlie.

His dad slipped his cell phone into his breast pocket. "We took the jet. Made great time. Didn't we, Mary?"

"Is Camella with you?" Charlie asked. His sister was three years older and despised birthday parties. "They waste time and cake," she was fond of saying. Still, he thought it might be nice to see her.

"Did you hear?" asked his mom.

"Hear what?"

Julie jumped in. "She's getting married. Douglas proposed."

"No shit. Really." Douglas and his sister had been dating since college, so it made some sense. But both were so obsessed with work and traveled so extensively, they rarely saw each other except over Skype.

After they ordered from the extensive seafood menu, they enjoyed a little small talk. Charlie wondered how long it would take his dad to ask the question. It turned out to be 6.2 minutes, a personal record.

"Have you set a date for when you're coming back to run the company?"

"Rod, the food hasn't even come," Charlie's mom scolded. "Give him a break. It's his birthday."

"All the more reason to address the issue. He's thirty-two years old, and it's time. I was running the company by the time I was twenty-five."

Charlie knew it was time and then some. The Ricci family was strict about their family succession plan—getting an education and then running a piece of the company successfully before moving up the ranks—but it turned out Charlie liked the construction business. He liked the process of building things, working with the guys, and the pride of seeing completed projects. And he liked the more relaxed pace of the West Coast. He had tried to tell his dad that maybe it was a better fit where he was, but his father wouldn't hear of it. Rod was determined to see his own son in the company's driver's seat before Charlie's idiot cousin Aaron got there first.

"Soon, Dad. I'm doing some interesting stuff at the site, I think you—"

"It's a construction company, for Christ's sake. A monkey could run one. It's time."

"Let me think about it," Charlie said, trying to stall yet again.

"No more thinking, son. It's time to cut the play time here and get your ass to Manhattan."

Thankfully the food came before Charlie had to give an answer. He changed the subject, telling them about the new treatment plant he was working on, but Julie stopped him mid-sentence with a quick kiss.

"Enough with the boring stuff. It's your birthday." She handed him a box.

He gave her a little kiss back and lifted the lid. There were two tickets inside.

"Box seats," she said, beaming. She really was gorgeous, thought Charlie, in a flawless, high-maintenance way.

"Cool. Box seats to a Knicks game?" he asked, taking them out.

"The Westminster dog show! We're going to have such a great time."

"No doubt. A blast." He did his best to smile and was pretty sure he pulled it off. "Thanks, honey."

Julie had been obsessively into dogs the past six months, after purchasing her pedigreed miniature Schnauzer, Angelica. Charlie sensed the dog hated him. It had peed in his shoe the last two times he'd flown out to visit Julie for the weekend. His mind wandered and he wondered if Sheila had a dog. He couldn't imagine it. Maybe a cat—a mean cat that could take on that little shit Schnauzer. He smiled at the thought.

"What are you thinking about?" his mom asked.

"Just work stuff," he lied, taking a deep breath. Shit, had he been thinking of Sheila just now? He had. Thank god no one could read minds.

His mom pulled out a little box from her purse. This box was small, old, and worn around the edges. She pressed it into Charlie's hand. "Thought you might like this."

Charlie lifted the lid. The dog show tickets had been an odd surprise, but this was just weird. A woman's wedding ring.

"It was your grandmother's. You were so close to your grandfather, I thought you would want it."

His grandfather's ring was a plain band of gold, and he could remember it catching the light when they were out fishing—his grandpa telling him youthful tales of stolen cars and fast women. His grandmother's ring, on the other hand, was a monstrous, glistening diamond. Everyone in the family knew that it eclipsed a smaller diamond set on the side because grandpa upgraded the ring after he made his money. Charlie's grandmother had passed away over a year ago, and Charlie suddenly wondered how his mom had come into ownership of the ring, as grandpa was still alive and kicking.

"It's beautiful," Julie said. "May I?"

Before Charlie could answer, Julie had already slipped his grandmother's diamond on her own finger.

"I talked Charlie's grandfather out of it," said his mom. "It was just sitting there, and I thought Charlie might find a use for it some day." That's when Charlie saw it—the conspiratorial smile between his mom and Julie. It had all been planned. He tried to draw a breath, but couldn't. This was a full-on ambush, and he wasn't prepared.

"Is it OK if I wear it for a little while?" Julie asked, giving Charlie an innocent smile.

"Of course," said his mom. "It looks like it belongs on your hand. Don't you think so, Charlie?"

Charlie could feel the perspiration building on his lip. He wiped it away. Looking at his mom smiling at him, Julie ogling the ridiculously large diamond ring, and his dad nodding at him, he felt trapped. Like a rat, with three hungry cats eyeing him. All he wanted to do was sprint back to his construction site.

"Son, your mother asked you a question," said his dad. "What do you think?"

"It looks nice," Charlie said, feeling a headache take root.

How could he complain? A beautiful woman wanted to marry him, and his dad wanted him to run a multi-billion-dollar conglomerate and live the good life in New York. Most people would die for that, but Charlie was wondering how hard it would be to fake his own death.

Julie gave him another kiss, this one longer, sweeter—and promising more. "I love you," she whispered.

"I love you too," he said out of habit and, at the moment, shock.

Dad lifted his glass. "To our new CEO and his beautiful fiancé."

"Fiancé?" gasped Charlie, probably a little louder than he meant to.

"You don't want to marry this beautiful woman?" asked his father.

Charlie stammered, "That's not what I meant. I meant . . ."

"What *do* you mean?" asked Julie, looking ready to burst into tears.

"I meant . . ." Everyone was waiting for his answer. He could feel his heart pounding in his ears. He wanted to say, "Screw you guys for ganging up and manipulating me on my birthday. I'm out of here!" But instead he quietly said, "Dad, I just thought maybe you would have let me do the honors of proposing."

A relieved round of laughter erupted around the table, and Rod ordered Champagne. He clapped his son on the shoulder and gripped hard—something Charlie knew he did when he meant business.

"I've already talked to the board," said Rod. "We'd like you to be on Saturday morning to sign papers. You'll be in the captain's chair on Monday."

Charlie tried to smile, thinking this must be what people felt like when they were drowning.

Chapter 9

After lunch, Denise and I went out shopping for a wedding gown. We were halfway to Value Village when my cell buzzed again. Without thinking, I answered it. As soon as I heard her voice, I considered pitching the phone out the car window.

"Finally! I know you've been ignoring me." Mom's voice was shrill and intense. It always reminded me of a feral cat.

"Mom, I've been busy. I've got this—"

"I'm out of money. Ernest is gone. He moved out two nights ago."

"Bummer. But not much I can do about that." I would have liked to feel bad for her, but I knew she deserved it. Ernest, a sweet guy with bad teeth, had hung in there longer than most. Two years was probably a record.

"I'm coming up there to sell the Airstream. I need the cash."

I slammed my fist in the car's dashboard. Denise jumped. "You stay the hell away from my home!" I yelled into the phone.

Denise's eyes narrowed. "Hang up on her. Now."

Denise hated my mom. In fact, my mom might be the only person she despised. Denise was there when things got bad, when I was 13 and Mom went to jail for armed robbery. I didn't find out about Mom's Walmart heist, though, until she didn't come home to the Airstream for a week, and there was a call from child protective services looking for me.

I hid from the agency people who showed up at the door, but by week three the food had run out, and by week four I was asking to sleep over at Denise's. Her parents never said a word when the sleepover lasted a year and three months. For that I will always be in their debt. My mom, however, I may never forgive.

"I'll take my Airstream if I damn well please," Mom said.

"I swear. If you come close to my place, I'll shoot you."

Mom grunted a laugh. "You don't even own a gun."

"I didn't say I was going to shoot you with bullets."

"Just move your shit and be out tomorrow. You're lucky I've let you stay in it this long."

"Lucky? You left owing three months of back rent, and the—"

Denise took the phone out of my hand and turned it off. "We don't need her energy today. It's bad for Baby Portland."

"The bitch wants to take my house. My HOUSE!" I wanted to hit something, but my fist already hurt from smacking the dash. "Hey, wait. Did you just say Portland? That's not a baby name."

"People name kids after cities all the time. Look at Cheyenne. And Portland's where she was conceived."

My stomach lurched at the thought of conceiving anything with that creep Kenny. If only I could hook him up with my mom. Those two deserved each other.

"Think about it," I said. "What are you going to say when she asks about her name? 'Oh that's where your loser dad and I hooked up.' And she's going to say, 'Mommy, what does hooked up mean?' What are you going to do then?"

"Good point. But I still like Portland," she said, pulling into the Value Village parking lot. Denise sighed. "I didn't think naming a baby would be this hard."

#

Value Village was my first stop for all my brides' wedding dresses. They seemed to get higher-end dresses than our local Goodwill and St. Vincent de Paul. But you pay for the quality. I sometimes forked over as much as fifty bucks for a wedding dress at Value Village, versus ten or twenty at Goodwill.

We hunted for bridal gowns, came up with nothing, and moved on to a rack of prom dresses, hoping to find something white I could work with. Just then Dakota stepped up to us. She was a pierced freak show who had worked there since she was 13. She was in the same class as Denise and me in high school and had the dubious honor of having the most kids at graduation—two little snot brats who screamed the whole way through the ceremony. But I always thought Dakota could be kind of cute—if she lost half the metal in her face and dropped about 70 pounds.

"Hey, Dakota. You got any dresses in the back?" I asked.

"We're all out of wedding dresses. Guess Cheyenne's fuck out of luck, huh?"

"How'd you hear about the wedding?" Denise asked.

"Hear about it? I'm invited," Dakota clicked her tongue piercing

36

against her teeth for emphasis. "So, where's it going to be? Cheyenne says it's going to be romantic as fuck."

"She's right. We were scoping out venues this morning."

Denise held up a little girl's white princess costume. I shook my head. The dress was too small, even for Cheyenne.

"Dakota, I'm curious. How'd you get your name?" asked Denise.

"My mom screwed some guy in Dakota. Why?"

"No reason. Just wondered." Denise gave me a don't-even-say-it look.

Dakota looked down at Denise's bump and smiled, showing off a new pierced ring under her lip. "You gonna name her Dakota? Fuck yeah."

"She's still working on it," I said. Denise nodded and gravitated toward a rack of pink T-shirts.

"You at least got a veil back there?" I asked. "Anything?"

"Like I said, nothin'. It's fucking wedding season. *You* should know that."

"Yeah, I know. Just doing my job," I said, "See you at the wedding."

In the end, Cheyenne wasn't "fuck out of luck." We found a dress at Goodwill. It was a beautiful creamy satin number with a plunging neckline, and it only cost twelve dollars. There was one small problem. It was a size 23. A dozen Cheyennes could fit into the dress, along with the maid of honor and a couple of groomsmen. It had so much material, they had to find a garbage bag for me to carry it out in.

Turning the giant gown into a size 2 was going to take some thinking, which I would do later, because we still needed to find a DJ.

Chapter 10

By late Tuesday afternoon we were ravenous. You can only do so much wedding planning without food, and we needed some before we could search for a DJ. And I kept forgetting that Denise was eating for two. We stopped at the Brew and Suds to refuel our bodies and rejuvenate our souls.

The place was mostly empty, just a couple of older guys playing pool in the back and Sally, our old babysitter, tending bar. Sally nodded at us as we slid into our regular booth.

Denise sniffed the air. "Must have been nacho night last night; the place smells like old cheese."

"We can go somewhere else, if it makes you feel sick or something."

"Are you kidding me? It's making me hungrier. I'm starved." Denise called out to Sally, "Can I have a double order of chili fries and a virgin daiquiri? And can you bring us some nuts while we're waiting? A lot of them!"

Since we were yelling out orders, I added one order of chili fries and a shot of tequila.

Denise looked at me. There was a scary desperation in her eyes. "When they say you're eating for two, they don't tell you you're eating for two truck drivers. I've never been so hungry."

"What about those protein bars you always have in the glove compartment?"

"Hell, I ate them before I got to your place."

Sally came over with a bowl of peanuts, and Denise tore into them before they hit the table. She was shelling peanuts like little kids open presents on Christmas morning.

My stomach rumbled, but it could wait. I could lose a finger trying to snag a peanut just then. Instead, I pulled out my little red book and turned to Cheyenne's wedding. I put a question mark by venue. We would have to figure out how to handle that smell. I checked off the dress and sighed at the list of items left to do—music, flowers, minister, cake, and more.

"I thought we'd be a little further along by now," I said.

Denise spit out a peanut shell. "We seriously need to consider another venue. The zoo, it's pretty and all, but it smells like the wrong end of everything. And what if there are diseases. Anything that smells like that can't be good."

"Reese said it wouldn't smell *as* bad. I think we should trust him," I said trying to convince myself more than her. "And the zoo would look so awesome in shots for *Best Bride*. I mean it's not like you can smell the place in a magazine."

Denise motioned for more peanuts. "Did you already forget what that place smelled like? Half as bad would be terrible."

I had to agree. And on a hot summer night, it was likely to be toxic. But there had to be a work around. This was *Best Bride*.

A fly buzzed off the peanuts, and Denise deftly swatted it away. "I know that look," she said. "You think you can make it work. But think about the flies on the cake. I don't know that Cheyenne's family would notice. But *Best Bride* would freak when they saw those photos."

"I know, but it's so perfect. And it's got monkeys."

"Can we just keep our options open? I get kind of pukey now with the baby, and I don't think I can handle it."

"Fine," I agreed, trying to grab a peanut, but Denise swatted my hand away as deftly as the fly. "But Cheyenne does need a great wedding."

Sally came with our chili fries and drinks. Good thing. Denise was close to gnawing on the peanut dish. I dug into my fries and washed them down with the tequila. Things instantly felt better with some food and tequila.

Denise looked up, a bit of chili sauce on her chin. "If you don't eat all your fries, can I have the rest?"

"You're not even done with yours."

"I will be, though."

"God, relax. You can have them." I took out the latest issue of *Best Bride*. I turned to an article on Twelve Romantic Centerpieces and pointed out the fourth option to Denise. It was a sweet little floral arrangement—tiny yellow flowers and greenery wrapped around a base of a single white candle.

"Beautiful," she said slurping her daiquiri.

"I thought we could replace the candle with a banana. Give it that monkey feel."

Denise stopped eating. "Dang! That's good. If you want, I could add a little monkey hanging off it."

"You have little monkeys?"

"My little brother had that Barrel of Monkeys game. I'm sure it's around somewhere."

"Yes!" My wedding mojo juices were flowing again. "And I could add some of those monkeys around the cake, too. That would look so great—those little guys holding hands around the base." I sketched it in the margins of my red book.

Something about the sketch of the cake made Denise giggle.

"What? You don't like the cake?"

She was giggling harder, trying not to spill her drink. "No. It's this wedding theme. It's just so . . . stupid."

Her giggling got me chuckling. "I know. It might be the stupidest wedding we've ever done."

"And we have done some stupid ones," she said, finishing off her last fry. "Remember that Corgi wedding? That was bad."

We were both laughing now. Sally was giving us the stink eye—like 2 p.m. was too early to get drunk. "I forgot about the Corgi one," I said. "I was thinking about that one we had at the KFC."

"Everyone stunk like fried chicken," laughed Denise. "I couldn't eat KFC for a month."

My cell phone rang. I stopped laughing when I saw it was my mom again. I shoved the phone deep into my purse. Leave it to her to ruin a good mood.

"Your mom sucks," said Denise, now sobered too.

I nodded.

Denise took one of my fries. "Fast Food Fast Gas is hiring," she said. "You already worked for them before, so you'd probably get hired right away."

Fast Food Fast Gas, locally referred to as The Shits, was a little gas station about three blocks away. They'd never had an employee of the month, because no one ever stayed there that long.

Denise grabbed another of my fries. "You need the money. Just take the job, get paid, and give some to your mom to get her off your back."

"I'm not giving her any money."

"Don't give her any. Use the money to pay rent."

I changed the subject. I wanted to get back on track with our planning and forget about rent and my mom for at least one more day. "Let's look for a DJ next. I was thinking of my cousin Kevin, but he's in jail."

"Not any more. Your Aunt Trish told me he's out on work release."

"Awesome. Let's go find him."

"Maybe we can get some fries to go."

"You're still hungry?"

"Not now, but what if Petunia gets hungry later?"

I groaned. "Not Petunia. No way. That's like a name for an old lady, or a cat."

"Why do you hate all my names?"

"It's not me. Everyone will hate this one." I yelled over at Sally. "What do you think of Petunia for a baby name?"

"It's terrible," said a voice from behind the bar.

"Well, aren't you all just the expert baby-namers," Denise said, standing, pissed off, peanut shells falling from her lap. She turned and stalked out, leaving me with the bill.

Twenty minutes later, we were in the car on our way to Kevin's mom's house to see if she knew where he was working. Or so I thought. A still-sulking Denise pulled her car into the Fast Food Fast Gas parking lot.

"I'll wait here while you apply," she said with a smug little smile.

I wanted to tell her this was stupid and that I'd probably be fired in two days. But she was right. I needed a job. Maybe hitting Kenny hadn't been the best move.

Walking through the door, I was hit by the smell of week-old pizza on the warmers, just waiting to give some desperate soul a crippling case of food poisoning. The place hadn't changed since it went up in the '80s. The aisles were still crammed with chips, snacks, and odds and ends. On the store's back wall, hung the same New Kids on the Block black light poster for sale that had been there when I worked there almost three years ago.

The owner, Monte, stepped out of the bathroom with a dripping mop. He was an older Asian man, maybe sixty, with little patience for mistakes. He also had a thing for gangster movies. He said it helped him learn English and played them night and day on a tiny TV behind the counter.

"You hired," he said, before I could even get a word out. "Be here at

8 a.m. Don't be late and don't eat the pizza."

"How do you know I'm applying for a job?"

"I know." He started mopping.

When I got back in the car, Denise smiled. "You got it didn't you? Yay. Now we both have new jobs tomorrow."

"Sure. You're happy. You're seeing Charlie every day. I'm going to be at The Shits working with Monte."

"Don't be like that," she said. "I've got good news. Our DJ Kevin is three miles from here."

Chapter 11

We found my cousin, along with six other guys, picking up trash along the side of Pacific Highway—an ugly stretch of road between a weigh station and a county rest stop. Each was wearing the same orange reflective vest, shoving litter into bags using hand-held trash grabbers. It looked like miserable work in the hot, afternoon sun.

At six foot three, Kevin was easy to spot with a mess of blonde hair and perpetual grin. I would say his grin was from too much weed, but he'd had that same goofy look since we were kids. Whenever I saw him, the first person I thought of was Scooby-Doo's friend, Shaggy.

Kevin was a born DJ. He loved music and loved get a crowd going, but unfortunately, he also loved breaking and entering. He never stole anything; he just liked seeing if he could break into a place. They call people who like to play with fire pyromaniacs, but what do you call a guy who likes to get into houses? The safety vest he wore was the real evidence that he was a much better DJ than he was a breaking in

Sheila parked the car off the side of the road near the weigh station, about a hundred feet down from the guys. I got out and walked toward Kevin. I saw a cop in a car watching the workers and thought I probably had five minutes.

Kevin spotted me before I got to him. His grin widened. "Hey, Sheila, what's up?"

"Not much. See you got busted again."

"Doing a solid for a friend and got caught." He shrugged, grabbed a beer can with his trash picker, and shoved it into his bag. "So what're you doing out here?"

Off to the side, I saw the police officer had spotted me and was getting out of his car. He was short and squat, with dark glasses that hid his eyes. I talked fast.

"I have a wedding Saturday. I need a DJ."

"Paying gig?"

"Beer."

"Sweet. I'm in."

The cop yelled out, "Ma'am you can't talk to the men."

"It's at Point Defiance Park. Saturday. Be there at 7 p.m."

Kevin's grin faded to a half-grin. "Shoot, can't."

"Ma'am, step away." The officer was thirty feet away.

"Why not?"

Kevin pointed to his ankle. "Too far away. Can only go a few miles with this ankle bracelet on."

The cop was by my side, gently grabbing my arm. "Ma'am, I'm serious. These men are working."

"What? Kevin's my cousin."

"Sure he is. But you need to move on."

"OK, I'm going." I turned to Kevin. "I'll handle everything."

The cop's brows furrowed. Never a good sign. "Handle what?"

The officer turned to Kevin. "You wouldn't be stupid enough to buy drugs out here, would you?"

"I'm not a drug dealer! I'm a wedding planner." I could hear my voice sounding angrier than I wanted.

The cop held out his hand. "Ma'am. I need to see your purse."

I begrudgingly handed it over. "I was talking to him about a wedding."

The other men had stopped and were staring as the officer rummaged through my things, checking out my mascara, lipsticks, perfumes, nail polish, and my little red book. The sun was beating on my neck, and perspiration was starting to trickle down my back.

Kevin sighed. "Officer, you don't have to do that. She's not a drug dealer. She's a hooker."

The officer and I both stopped and turned to him.

"Ask the guys here," he motioned to the other convicts. "Hookers kind of have a thing for me."

Kevin gave me a nod, like he was helping me out, as the officer looked around. The other guys were nodding in agreement.

"Oh my god. I am NOT a prostitute!" I said. "Look at me. Do I look like a prostitute?" I was wearing my favorite white miniskirt and a magenta crisscross crop top with matching heels. This was hardly the wardrobe of a hooker.

The officer gave me another look, then handed my purse back. "Here you go. Take it somewhere else."

I grabbed my purse, gave Kevin a blistering glare, and stalked off. I could feel every man's eyes on my ass as my heels clicked across the hot asphalt to the car. I got inside and slammed the door.

"How'd it go?" asked Denise.

I jerked down the visor to check myself in the mirror. My cheeks were red and perspiration was beading up on my forehead—but my makeup looked perfect. Eyeliner wasn't running and lipstick still looked fresh. "Do I look like a prostitute?"

"No. Why?"

"That cop thought so."

"Maybe he thought you were a really expensive one."

"Is that supposed to make me feel better?"

"Some of those really high-priced ones look like supermodels," Denise said, starting the car. "But just to be on the safe side, maybe we should make sure you aren't in any of the *Best Bride* pictures. We don't want them getting the wrong idea."

"That I'm a hooker?! What would make them think I'm a hooker?"

"I don't think so. But if the police officer thought . . . never mind. You look great."

I put the visor back up and took a deep breath. I'd rethink my makeup later. I had a wedding to plan. And I needed some space between myself and the cop to focus.

Chapter 12

Our last stop of the day was 8175 South Monroe—our florist. This woman had the best flowers in the business—multi-colored roses, enormous dahlias, and loads of baby's breath. They came in every color, and the stems were long, so they held up well in vases, which you find out is important as soon as you try putting an arrangement together. The only downside was that the woman had no idea she was in the wedding flower business.

The homeowner's name was Alice, but Denise and I just called her Flower Bitch. She was probably in her sixties, with thick grey hair that she kept back in a ponytail or tucked up in a floppy hat. She wore the same khaki pants around the small front yard every day, her pockets filled with clippers, and she carried a big watering can.

Last year, we asked her once if she would share some of the flowers for a wedding. She just stared at us like we were crazy—I think her exact words were, "Go away."

Later in the summer, when we were desperate for a bridal bouquet, I went one more time.

"We really need some roses. Our bride loves them, and I can't find any anywhere."

"They have flower shops filled with roses," she said coolly.

"But they cost money. And we're out of money. The bride had to have this hat for her dog, and it broke the bank," I pleaded.

"That's not my fault."

"But they grow back. And all I need is about 20 of those white and red ones. That red is exactly the color of the dog's hat."

"The answer is no. And if you step into my yard one more time, I'm going to call the police," she said.

Which just meant we were left with sneaking into her yard at night to cut a few. There were no other roses like hers in town. It's not like we had a choice.

It didn't take her long to figure out that some of her rose bushes were being thinned. By late August, she was staying out in her front yard until 10 p.m., waiting and watching. It was a nightmare waiting to cut until she went to bed, because the lighting is so bad at night. With only the streetlight, most of the flowers looked black and white. We sniffed out the sweet peas, roses, and carnations. But sometimes we'd come back with oranges when we thought we had pinks, or reds when we thought we'd cut purples. Which was really a bigger pain because we'd have to go back the next night for more.

This year we had a better plan. We would drive past her place and take some pictures. Then when we came back later, we would be able to make the right choices.

Denise gasped when we turned the corner onto South Monroe. A sea of roses assaulted us. Flower Bitch's bushes were at least six feet tall—bigger than the previous year. The red, yellow, and cream buds were just opening, and the heady scent was wafting into the car through our open window. I could already see the banana centerpieces and yellow bridal bouquet in Cheyenne's hands.

Unfortunately, Flower Bitch had also built a substantial five-foot picket fence around her yard with an ornate wrought iron gate.

"Wow, that's some fence," said Denise. "You're going to have to climb over it. I'm sure pregnant women aren't supposed to do things like that."

"No problem," I said. "I'll climb over and let you in."

I pulled out my phone to take some pictures of the roses that peeked over the top of the fence. "Look at these things. They're monsters!" I said, leaning out the window to get some shots on my phone.

Denise inhaled the scent and smiled. "And they smell as good as they look."

"Oh, no. We've got a big problem," I said as we drove past the gate.

"What? What is it?" Denise asked, craning to see, but we had already passed the house.

"Something's on her porch. I think it might be a bear."

"A bear?! How much tequila have you had?"

Denise put the car in reverse and backed up until we got to the gate and could see the porch.

"Oh, shit," said Denise. "Oh, shit. Oh, shit. Oh, SHIT!"

We couldn't take our eyes off Flower Bitch's two enormous dogs. They each had short black hair like a Doberman, the muscles of a Rottweiler, and the teeth of a shark. They were sprawled out on the wraparound porch, gnawing on bones the size of my leg. God, for all I knew the bones had at one time been someone's leg.

Denise, who is deadly scared of big dogs, was drawing deep, ragged breaths. "They're even bigger than Puddles," she managed to squeak out.

Puddles was a miscalculation made by Denise's parents when she was six. They wanted to surprise her with a puppy on her birthday. They couldn't find a puppy in time, but they did get a great deal on Puddles, a two-hundred-pound Newfoundland with a heart of gold. They snuck Puddles into Denise's room while she was asleep, so she would be surprised in the morning. It worked. People say her scream was heard around the block when she woke to a Saint Bernard-sized dog licking her face.

"I think they're about the same size as Puddles—just less hair and more muscle," I said as we listened to the crunching sounds of the dogs grinding their bones into sawdust. The hair on the back of my neck stood up.

"That is so much worse," Denise said trying to keep her breathing steady.

"We don't know," I said. "Maybe she's just babysitting them. Or they're super friendly."

"Are you kidding me? Look at them! They look like they tear people apart for fun."

"They do kind of remind me of those gargoyles that come to life in *Ghostbusters*," I said.

As if on cue, they turned toward the car, staring at us with their beady eyes, then in unison they jumped up and ran to the fence, snarling.

Denise shrieked so loud I nearly peed my pants. The dogs stopped at the gate, almost frothing with excitement to get through and eat the car, with us inside it.

Denise hit the gas, drove a couple of blocks down the street, and parked.

"Do you think Flower Bitch got the dogs because of us?" she asked.

"We did disconnect that camera she put up . . . and shot out her motion sensor lights."

"I told you we shouldn't have done that. You never listen."

I had to admit, Flower Bitch might be completely unromantic and stingy with her flowers, but you had to give her points for dedication in protecting her goods.

"So now where are we going to get flowers?" Denise asked.

"We can still cut these," I said. "I just have to think of a way around the dogs."

"Are you crazy? I love a good floral arrangement as much as anyone, but I also love my arms and legs and everything else too."

"I'll do the cutting. You're pregnant. We don't want to put baby Tammie-Lynn in danger."

Denise gave me a long, hard look, not saying anything for about ten seconds. I got worried. Maybe the scare messed her up.

Finally, she reached into her glove compartment.

"Tammie-Lynn? That name sucks," she said, pulling out a small can of mace. She handed it to me. "You need to be armed if you're going in there."

I put the mace back in her purse. "Relax, will you?"

"Relax? Those things are huge—pony huge," she said. "I think we should find flowers somewhere else."

"I don't know of any other places as good as Flower Bitch's," I said, "and we only have a few days."

"Let's at least look," Denise suggested, pulling away fast enough to leave a little rubber on the road.

We drove home deep in thought, both of us in gloomy moods. It was Tuesday night; we had no flowers, a size 23 dress, a stinky venue, a convicted DJ, and a wedding on Saturday. We needed something to go our way.

But bad days sometimes have a way of getting worse. When we pulled into my place, we saw my mom's '78 baby blue Camaro parked out front.

Mom was out of the car and circling the Airstream, checking things out. She hadn't changed much in the last few years—still tiny and mean looking. She had the same ever-present cigarette dangling from her lips, the same leather biker's vest, and the same teased hair and bad dye job framing her pinched little face. She always reminded me of a rabid ferret with lipstick.

"Get out of here before I call the cops," I said, stepping out of Denise's car.

"That's one hell of a way to talk to your mother," my mom snapped back.

"Most moms don't come over to steal their daughter's home."

I couldn't see Jim or Carla, but I knew my neighbors were inside listening. I pulled out my phone and pointed it at Mom. "I'm serious. I'll call the police."

"Oh, please," she said, stamping out her cigarette with the toe of her black leather boot. "You're such a drama queen. Just pack your shit and be out of here in twenty-four hours."

"And if I don't?"

"I'll have someone with me to kick you out."

"You don't scare me," I said. That was a lie. She totally scared me. After she came back from prison she had changed. It's not like she was a warm, fuzzy person to start with, but afterward she had "mean bitch" down cold.

Mom took a step toward me, not blinking. "You just be out."

It was suddenly hard to swallow, and I was glad there were witnesses eavesdropping, because I wouldn't put it past her to test out her shanking skills on me—just a little.

Mom pulled a cigarette from her vest pocket and lit it.

"And that goes for you kids too!" she yelled out into the street. I turned around, but no one was there. She slowly walked toward her car, opened the door, and glanced back at me. "Twenty-four hours. And lose some weight, you're getting fat."

Mom slid in and started the old Camaro, which desperately needed a new muffler. She hit the gas and sprayed us with gravel on her way out.

Denise let out a deep sigh of relief. "I'm sorry, Sheila, but your mom is scarier than both of those dogs."

"She's scarier than the boogie man," said a voice behind us.

We jumped and spun around.

There in the driveway were Swayze and Axel, wheeling out of the shadows on their Big Wheels, wearing their hoodies on the seventy-five-degree night.

Axel yelled from his Big Wheel, "We caught that lady trying to break in earlier."

Swayze jumped in. "We scared her off good!"

"What did you do?"

Axel smiled; his little teeth glowed in the moonlight. "We shot at her with the dart gun I got on my last birthday."

"We only got her once," said Swayze. They looked at each other and smiled.

"Oh. Thanks," I said, thinking as if these kids weren't scary enough, they were armed too? Who were their parents?

"We take cash," suggested Swayze.

"Oh. OK." I pulled two fives and a ten out of my wallet—all the cash I had left—wondering if there was something illegal about it, although I couldn't put my finger on what.

Swayze pedaled up to retrieve the bills.

"Be careful," Axle warned me. "That lady is really not nice."

I nodded as the two pedaled back off into the night. It seemed like Axel, Swayze, and I could all use decent parents. Not anyone fancy, just decent. Parents like Denise's mom and dad. Her mother, Cammie, was a waitress at Denny's, and her Dad, Mitch, was a diesel mechanic. They fought sometimes, but they were always sane, never in jail, and would never break into Denise's apartment, or let her take her Big Wheel out at midnight.

"Where do those kids live?" asked Denise.

"No idea. And I've been afraid to ask," I said. "You don't think I'm getting fat, do you?"

"No way! I'm the one getting fat!" said Denise.

"What am I going to do when Mom comes back?"

"I have no idea." Denise gave me a little hug. "But we'll think of something. Right now, I need to get little Destiny to bed."

"You know that's kind of a stripper name."

She smiled. "Don't be late for work."

Chapter 13

Charlie spent Wednesday morning on the worksite in a state of shock. How could the course of his life be altered during one lunch? Was he really engaged? He must be. Julie had called him twice that morning—once to ask if he preferred an outdoor or indoor wedding, and then again to find out what he thought of a destination wedding. He wasn't even sure he knew what a destination wedding was.

He tried to focus on the day's equipment deliveries, and the building inspector that was due, but everything felt off balance—like he was on a ship at sea and couldn't get his footing. Could he really be headed to the East Coast to work with his dad? In an office in Manhattan? He could still feel his dad's bearlike hug when he left the day before, and his words, "I'm proud of you son. It's time."

Charlie walked past his crew, busy laying cement. A couple of the men waved. But most were too involved in what they were doing to notice him—just the way he liked it. He was proud of this project. Although it wasn't sexy, the treatment plant was going to have one of the most advanced systems in the state. He liked it out in the Pacific Northwest too. It was so much more relaxed than New York. Mostly though, he liked working with his own team—building things, not just making decisions behind a desk. And damn it, he was good at it. Didn't that count for something?

"Dude, you look terrible."

Charlie jumped. Art, his second in command—who always reminded Charlie of a round, balding Kevin Bacon—stood in front him. Art looked like he had a little paunch. But Charlie knew there was no fat. Art was just a ball of muscle, with very little neck. When Charlie interviewed him years back, he asked Art, a father of three, how he stayed in shape. When he answered "barehanded catfishing and chess boxing," Charlie knew Art was his guy.

"I mean it," Art said assessing Charlie. "You look messed up. You didn't eat any of Martin's homemade beef jerky, did you?"

"Huh? What about jerky?"

Art gave Charlie another serious look over. "Something's wrong. You missed the safety meeting this morning. You never miss those."

"Shit. I'm sorry. I just forgot."

"And why is Denise in your office? She's been in there for hours."

"Oh, yeah," said Charlie. "I hired her as an assistant. Did I forget to tell you she starts today?"

"When'd you hire her?"

"Monday. I think." God, that seemed a lifetime ago.

Art contemplated his feet, something Charlie knew he did when he was worried. Art finally looked back up at Charlie and smiled. "Why don't you go grab us some lunch? Take a break."

"Is it lunch time already?"

Art nodded, even more concerned. Charlie wondered why he didn't just tell Art what was going on. He needed to know—Art would be running the crew in three days if all went to his dad's plan. He just didn't want it to be true. And if he told Art, that meant it was the real thing. If he could just think of a way out.

"All right," Charlie said. "I'll get us some fast food. Sound OK?"

Art nodded, and Charlie walked past the guys now smoothing cement between the forms. They were all laughing over something, and Charlie would have done about anything to just walk over and join in. Instead, Charlie walked off the site and down the road toward a cluster of fast-food joints that his guys called fast-food row. His phone buzzed, and he saw it was Julie. His chest tightened, and he let it go to voicemail, something he knew he would later regret. But he was already tired of the questions. Hell, it was only 11:30 a.m. This was moving too fast.

When Charlie caught the smell of donuts and fried chicken, he suddenly realized he was hungry. Had he even eaten breakfast? No matter, a hot dog, smothered in ketchup, relish, and mustard sounded perfect, with a Coke to wash it down.

He walked up to the first joint he came to, opened the door, and stopped cold. There was Sheila behind the counter selling some guy a pack of cigarettes. Sheila was wearing a "Fast Food Fast Gas" apron over a tank top and jeans. Her large brown eyes were framed in Cleopatra-style eyeliner, her hair was teased, and her lipstick, Charlie noticed, was a deep cherry red—the same color as his first car. She stood just like she did when she was flagging for him—strong and sure and ready to take on anyone who tried to pass. Could he be missing her already? He slipped behind a rack of potato chips, so she wouldn't spot him—he wasn't sure why.

He peeked between the fun-size Doritos and Cheetos to eavesdrop. He already didn't like the situation. The loser at the counter was in his mid-twenties, the type of guy who thinks he's cool because he drives a four-wheel-drive truck. Charlie knew the type. He'd hired more than a few. But from what Charlie could tell, if this guy had a truck, it was all he had going for him, what with his greasy man bun, dirty T-shirt, and mouth in desperate need of dental work.

The loser set down a lime green Slurpee on the counter in front of Sheila. "And I'll have another pack of Winstons." Charlie felt himself bristling when he saw the way the guy gave Sheila a knowing smile, showing off his darkened dentures.

Sheila set the pack on the counter, probably trying to stay downwind of the guy. "Nine-fifty," she said flatly.

"That's highway robbery, sweetheart," he said, still smiling.

"I don't price it. I just sell it."

"You remember me? Mick? From high school?"

"Yeah. And it's still nine-fifty."

"You know my apartment's just down the block," Mick said. "The Cedar Grove complex. You should stop by after your shift. We can play a little Wii, drink some beer—"

"Thanks. But I'd rather have a screaming case of herpes," she said, cutting him off. "Nine-fifty."

Charlie was experiencing feelings he hadn't had since he was six years old and two older boys were pushing his sister around during recess. One moment he was watching, and the next he was throwing his body between the older boys and his sister, swinging haymakers. It had all ended badly, with Charlie sporting two black eyes, but it had been worth the fight.

"It doesn't have to be tonight, babe. How about tomorrow?"

Charlie watched her staring at Mick, taking in his nicotine-stained teeth and a body that looked like Wii was probably the only the exercise he'd gotten in years. She glanced at the tattoo on his arm—a half-naked woman with gravity-defying boobs sitting astride a motorcycle. Charlie couldn't breathe. Was she going to say yes?

Mick must have been thinking the same thing. "Like what you see?" he said, with confidence born of testosterone and the belief that he was trolling in friendly waters.

"I don't date anyone who can't spell angel?" As she spoke Charlie could feel his entire body exhale. Why the heck did he care who she dated, he wondered. But he did care. A lot.

"What do you mean?" Mick asked. "I don't get it."

"Your tattoo says Living Angle about the topless angle."

Mick looked down of a tattoo and snorted, amused. "Come on," he said. "You're not even giving me a chance."

"Are you going to pay for the cigs or not?"

"Come on, babe, let's just—"

"Don't babe me. Just hand over the money," she said, working hard to keep it together.

"Or what?" His smile turned into a dirty little grin.

Charlie smiled as Sheila's eyes narrowed. That loser had challenged the wrong gal and he could only guess what was going to happen next.

Sheila crawled over the counter toward Mick who was grinning ear to ear. "I knew you'd come around," he said.

Charlie watched transfixed as Sheila grabbed the waistband of Mick's pants. The guy's mouth dropped open a bit, imagining god knows what. Then she picked up his lime Slurpee, poured it into the front of his pants, and kicked him in the balls.

Mick yelled out, backing up and almost hitting the fun-size chip stand that Charlie stood behind. Mick, in pain, tried to quickly gather himself together.

"You, bitch!"

"Like I give a shit what you think. Get out!"

Charlie watched Monte scamper out from the stock room. "You fired!" he shouted.

Sheila spun around to face him. "It was his fault!"

"Like I kicked *myself* in the balls," Mick said.

Before Charlie knew what he was doing, he was stepping out from behind the chip display and approaching Monte.

"Sir, you can't fire her."

Sheila turned, startled to see him. Then she smiled. Charlie felt a warm rush from head to toe. If this is what it felt like to save damsels in distress, he was going to do it more often.

Monte pointed to the green Slurpee dribbling out the cuff of Mick's pants and onto the floor.

"The dame played this goon. She's gotta go," Monte said in an accent that was a unique blend of Jackie Chan and James Cagney.

Charlie, who had a passing friendship with Monte, knew it was easier just to go with it. "This goon was putting the moves on her," he explained. "He's lucky he didn't leave in a meat wagon."

"I'm not a goon," said Mick.

"Shut up," said Charlie. He turned back to Monte and pulled out his wallet. "What kind of scratch do you need to keep this broad on?"

"Did you just call me a broad?" asked Sheila.

He thought she was almost smiling.

Monte suddenly recognized Charlie. "You the big boss, Mr. Ricci, right?"

Charlie nodded.

"Keep your money. If you tell your boys to come eat at Fast Food, Fast Gas, the broad stays."

"It's a deal," Charlie said and shook Monte's hand.

"She kicked me in the balls!" moaned Mick, still trying to catch his breath.

"I apologize. It was an accident," said Sheila, smiling. "Let me refill your cup."

In one move, Mick grabbed the cup out of Sheila's hand, threw it on the floor, and flipped her off. He turned and limped out. Charlie followed him out. In the parking lot, Charlie grabbed Mick by the arm and tightened his grip until he saw the guy wince.

"What did I do to you man? Let go."

Charlie didn't let go. He got up close to Mick; close enough to know the guy had only a passing relationship with soap. "You ever say so much as 'hi' to that woman again, even if you see her in the street, I'll come looking for you. Understand?"

Mick reluctantly nodded. Charlie let go and watched him slowly ease himself into his truck. Mick started up the vehicle and hit the gas, squealing out of the tiny parking lot while giving Charlie the bird.

Charlie felt a tap on his shoulder and spun around. Sheila stood there holding a hot dog smothered with ketchup, mustard, and relish.

"Kind of weird," she said. "Two days ago you were firing me. Now you're saving my neck."

"It was either that or hand you a Stop sign."

She laughed and handed him the hot dog. "Just a little something I give the guys who jump out of no where and rescue me."

"How'd you know I wanted a hot dog?"

"Lucky guess," she said. "You have a hot dog practically every day for lunch."

"I do?"

She planted a quick kiss on his cheek with those cherry red lips. "Thank you."

She turned and jogged back to the store in her heels. Charlie took the moment to enjoy the view. He even noticed a tattoo on her shoulder blade. A bird? No, it was a wedding veil. What other tattoos did she have? For a brief moment, he wondered if he had been too hard on Mick—who wouldn't want to be with Sheila?

Chapter 14

I stood behind the counter at The Shits all afternoon, replaying in my head the scene of Charlie stepping out from behind the Doritos display and telling Monte he couldn't fire me. Me! This was a full-on KFC day—finger lickin' good.

The door dinged, and a girl, probably age fourteen, stepped in. She walked straight up to the counter. She was all purple hair, attitude, and ripped jeans. She kind of reminded me of myself at that age.

"I'll have a pack of Lucky Strikes," she said with complete confidence.

"Really? How old are you?"

"Old enough."

"I need to see some I.D."

As she reached into her back pocket, my cell phone buzzed. It was Denise. "Hey, what's up?" I asked.

"Are you sitting down?"

"No, I'm standing at the counter waiting for I.D.," I said. "What's wrong? You sound weird." I suddenly had images of her going into labor in a back alley somewhere needing hot water and towels Not that I knew of any back alleys, or what women in labor needed, but a person's mind is a strange thing.

"I'm fine. This is about you."

The purple-haired girl handed me the lamest fake I.D. I'd ever seen—an Alaska driver's license with a photo of a large, middle-aged Samoan woman. The teenage girl in front of me had skin so pale she looked like she might burst into flames if she stepped in front of a glow stick.

"Denise, can you hold on?" I looked at the driver's license again and then at the girl.

"Seriously? Your name is Rongomaiwhenua Safotu, and you're thirty-seven years old?"

"The cigs are for my mom. I'm adopted." The girl's eyes narrowed, daring me to call her a liar. I smiled back. I'd used that same look when I was fourteen.

"Nice try. I can't sell cigarettes to minors."

"Fine. Have it your way. Can I have my I.D. back?"

"Spell your mom's name, and it's yours."

"Keep it," the purple-haired girl said, trying to shrug it off. She eyed the cigs behind me.

"Don't even think about stealing them," I said. "My mom spent a year in jail for stealing cigarettes."

"No one gets a year for stealing cigarettes."

"You do if you bring a gun and empty the cash register while you're at it."

The girl rolled her eyes and walked down the candy aisle. I got back on the phone with Denise. "Did you hear that? Were we that bad back then?"

"Sheila, I found out some things!" Denise's voice was almost frantic now. "Charlie's rich. Really rich. Not like 'We've got a hot tub' rich but like 'We've got a yacht' rich."

"How do you know?"

"This guy called for Charlie today, and when I asked who it was, he said he was Douglas Ricci. The name sounded super familiar, so I Googled him."

Denise's voice was getting faster and higher. "He's a billionaire." Her voice was nothing more than a squeak now. "Do you hear me? Like with a B!"

"Yeah, a billionaire buys hot dogs at The Shits." Through the mirror mounted over the aisle, I watched the teenager move back toward the wine coolers. "I've got one better. You know that shit-for-brains Mick Schneider?"

I kept my eye on the girl. She was making her move, taking a Mike's Hard Lemonade from the cooler and slipping it under her shirt. "He was in here hitting on me so I kicked him in the nuts and dumped a Slurpee down his pants. And I got fired."

"Oh my god!" Denise cried. "You lost your job? It's your first day!"

"I'm not done. Here's the good part. Charlie stepped out of thin air, all Johnny Castle and got my job back for me!"

I walked around the counter, ready to intercept the shoplifting teenager. "He stood up for me in front of Monte. I've never had a guy do something like that. It was knight-in-shining-armor shit."

There was silence on the other end.

"Denise, did you hear me?" I came around the Hostess snack display to cut off the purple-haired girl.

"Maybe I shouldn't tell you," Denise said.

"Hold on one more second."

Blocking the girl path to the door, I held out my hand. "The Mike's please."

The girl reached under her shirt and pulled it out. I snatched it. "Don't be an idiot. Just find a friend who's old enough to buy it for you." God, I was starting to sound like a parent or something. She flipped me off and marched out of the store.

"If you're going insult me, you're going to have to do better than that," I yelled to her back. "OK, Denise, I'm here."

"Charlie's getting married"

I stared at the bottle of Mike's in my hand, the cold condensation dripping off my fingertips, trying to process the information.

"Married?"

"Married."

"Married?!"

"Yes. *Married!*"

The same guy who just hours ago stood up for me? The man who I had always imagined as the Jake Ryan in my *Sixteen Candles* life? The two of us sitting over my birthday cake, or at least a piece of cake. My brain wasn't having it.

"When I Googled Douglas Ricci, there was an announcement that his son had just gotten engaged," said Denise. "I saw the ring. It's like the size of a Jolly Rancher. It's huge."

My world shifted. I looked down the candy and beef jerky aisle, but my mind saw a wedding aisle with Charlie at the end, standing next to a long-legged woman in white. I saw him smile at her and slip a Jolly Rancher on her finger.

I felt something in my chest like heartburn, but I was pretty sure it was heartbreak.

I twisted open the Mike's Hard Lemonade and drank it down.

Chapter 15

After my shift at The Shits ended, I decided I had to get Charlie out of my head and focus on my monkey wedding. Real wedding planners don't let things like crushes stand in their way. They are single-minded professionals. I went straight home and got to work on the banana centerpieces.

I started by copying a candle centerpiece design from *Best Bride*—then I added my own flair. I replaced the candle with a banana. I wrapped the base of the banana with ivy I'd pulled from the alley behind the hairdresser's on Third Avenue, and topped it all with a circus peanut. It worked. It had a certain monkey flair.

As the place filled with bananas and circus peanuts, I kept seeing the image of Charlie standing in a church next to a beautiful woman, who I assumed was the same woman in the pictures I saw in his desk. She was blonde and supermodel gorgeous. I could never compete. I slipped in my *Dirty Dancing* DVD and broke out the tequila. Everything was better with *Dirty Dancing* and tequila.

I was on my seventh and last centerpiece—and Johnny was showing Baby how to do the lift in the water—when the Airstream started to shake. A short tremor shifted everything to the left, and then a more violent tremor shifted things to the right. I grabbed centerpieces as they started to topple off the table and chairs.

What was the earthquake protocol in an Airstream? There wasn't really space under the table to crawl in and hide. And anyway, what if something fell on the trailer, like a light pole or a tree? When the next tremor hit, I decided to take my chances outside. I grabbed my little red book and made a run for it.

As I threw open the door, the Airstream shook again, sending me flying off the front step. It felt like everything was in slow motion as the ground came toward me. I put out my hands to protect myself and was thankful to see I not only had the red book in one hand, I had a banana in the other. I hit the ground hard, and the book and the banana saved me from some seriously scraped hands, but I could feel the knees tearing out of my jeans as I slid across the pavement.

I jumped up, ready to run for cover.

"Holy crap! You scared the shit out of me," said a deep voice to my left. I swung around and instinctively threw the smashed banana in the direction of the voice. The mutilated fruit bounced off the chest of a huge, hairy man, maybe 350 pounds, wearing a Lenny's Towing T-shirt.

As Sheila and the tow-truck operator were having a stare-down, Charlie was walking into the Brew and Suds. Denise had mentioned that she and Sheila liked to go there, and he thought he might check up on her. Make sure everything was OK. Maybe she needed a little more rescuing?

He had gone down to the gym to hit the bag, clear his head, and try to get some perspective on his life. But all he'd done was get more frustrated with its new direction. Why couldn't he just tell his dad, "I'm not interested in being a CEO?" Maybe Sheila could give him some pointers with dealing with his dad.

He looked around the dimly lit place and didn't see any sign of Sheila. He tried to ignore the fact that he was more disappointed than he should be.

As he approached the bar, a guy at the pool table yelled, "Hey, Charlie!"

Charlie looked over. It was Joe, a young guy on his crew who handled the rigging. "Join us. No one is shootin' worth shit tonight."

Charlie joined them and, within twenty minutes, was eating nachos and being slaughtered by Joe, who was a much better pool player than he let on. Charlie was already into him for twenty bucks.

"So, how's Kenny doing?" asked Joe.

"Fine. He'll be back to work next week."

"Too bad you had to fire Sheila. That idiot has been asking for it for years."

"You know Sheila well?" Charlie asked, trying his best to sound casual.

"We went out once. She's nice but weird. She's into '80s movies. I mean *really* into them." Joe leaned over and dropped a ball into the corner pocket with ease. "I think she spent a lot of time home alone as a kid, just watching them or something." Joe banked another shot.

Charlie wasn't up on his '80s movies. He remembered seeing *Flashdance* with his sister once. It was set in a dingy place like the

Brew and Suds. In fact, it didn't take much to imagine Sheila in a teddy, dancing on the bar, then dropping into a chair, grabbing a chain overhead . . . water cascading over her—

"Charlie. Your turn," said Joe.

Charlie blinked out of his fantasy and nodded to Joe. He grabbed his cue stick and walked around the table eyeing a shot. Damn, was he just imagining Sheila dancing "Flashdance style" in a bar? This wasn't like him. It must be the stress of facing the city, the wedding . . . and well, Sheila certainly wasn't ugly.

Charlie aimed, shot, and dropped the ball in the corner pocket.

#

The big dude outside my Airstream scratched his scruffy chin. "Where'd you come from?" he asked, still trying to put two and two together.

"I *live* here," I said, wishing I had another banana to throw at him. "What the hell are *you* doing here?"

He pointed to a tow truck with "Lenny's Towing" printed across the cab door—the cause of my earthquake. He was in the process of hooking up my home to his rig and driving off with it. How could I not have heard a tow truck drive up? How loud was I playing *Dirty Dancing?*

"I'm Lenny. I got hired to tow this rig into town," he said. "The owner said she was taking it on a trip. She's been storing it here."

"She lied to you. She doesn't own it. I do."

He scratched his scruffy chin again, looking from me to the Airstream. "Can I look inside?"

"Be my guest."

He ambled over, opened the door, and peeked inside. "Well, shit. You do live here."

"Of course I live here," I said, inspecting my stinging knees, which were starting to ooze blood. "That woman is my mom, and she's trying to steal my place."

"Come to think of it, she did look a bit like you. Damn. How do I know you're not a squatter?"

I went inside, grabbed the eviction notice from my purse, and took it outside to show him. "See. Shows I'm late on my rent. Squatters don't pay rent. And my mom is asking you to steal my home."

"Well, that really throws a wrench in things," he said sadly, hiking up his enormous pants. "Tonight's date night. I was going to use the money from this tow to take my gal Reba out."

As if on cue, Reba's head popped out of the cab of Lenny's tow truck. "Honey, what's taking so long? Something wrong?" Reba was in her 30s, petite, with loads of dark hair and freckles. If she weren't missing a couple teeth, she'd be downright cute.

"There's a gal living here," said Lenny.

"My name's Sheila."

Reba waved to me. "Hi, honey." She looked back at Lenny. "What about date night?"

"I'm torn baby. I don't want to tow her, but—"

"But, nothing!" I said, sensing the conversation was taking a dangerous turn toward my homelessness. "You two are coming inside. I've got a movie, popcorn, tequila, and a few beers. You'll have date night right here."

And that is how, at 11 p.m., I was sitting on the floor, cutting down a gigantic wedding dress while Lenny and Reba snuggled on my couch watching the end of *Dirty Dancing*. Lenny had drunk about half a bottle of my tequila and eaten all my popcorn, as well as two of the centerpieces.

We were watching the final dance number—the part when Johnny motions to Baby to run into his arms so they can do their lift. As Baby ran and Johnny caught her, lifting her high overhead, Reba sighed. "That's so romantic."

"Be more exciting if he dropped her," said Lenny. Reba punched him in the shoulder, then kissed him long and hard on the mouth.

"Hey, guys," I said, trying to break it up. "Maybe it's time to take the date home."

The kiss broke, and they looked at each other sadly. "Can't," said Lenny. "Reba's married, and I don't want to bust that up."

"Lenny's got a missus too," said Reba. "We just have these stolen moments."

It was kind of romantic—in a cheat-y kind of way. "Well, if you two ever decide to divorce and get married, keep me in mind. I'm a hell of a wedding planner."

"Sure will," said Reba, giving Lenny a big smooch on the forehead as she stood up. "Come on, honey, we better get going."

Lenny stood, stooping to avoid bumping his head on the ceiling. "Thanks for the hospitality."

"Thanks for not towing my house."

I watched as they walked out to the tow truck. Lenny went to open the passenger door for Reba, but stopped. Reba looked up at him, confused.

In the dim glow of a street lamp, Lenny bent down and grabbed Reba by the waist, his huge hands almost encircling her. He lifted her slowly over his head. Reba smiled and held out her arms. He turned her around once, and then twice, before setting her down softly.

It was a beautiful moment. And a sad one too. It's depressing to know that your local tow-truck driver has a more romantic life than you do.

Chapter 16

It was 5:30 a.m. on Thursday morning. My shift at The Shits started at 7 a.m., where I would be selling coffee, donuts, and gas to the work crowd. There's nothing like watching the sunrise as yesterday's hotdogs rotate on the spit to remind you that you want a different life. That's why I was up early. Before work, I planned on taking a bus to the zoo to check out the wedding venue, this time from inside the zoo. This wedding was going to catapult my career, so help me god, I told myself as I waited at the bus stop.

I had two days and twelve-and-a-half hours until the wedding. I needed a pastor, a way to get rid of the stench at the back zoo entrance, an ankle bracelet removed off my cousin Kevin, tables and chairs, a cake, and a way past two man-eating dogs to get some decent flowers. Oh yeah, and I almost forgot, I needed to finish creating a spectacular wedding dress from a mountain of material.

I had already taken the first step earlier in the morning—protection for my home. I hadn't slept well, partly because I kept finding popcorn left over from Lenny and Reba's date night, but mostly because my mom was still on the loose, and when she gets mad, she's capable of just about anything. One time she drove her boyfriend's Nova into a lake because she saw him flirting with another gal at the bowling alley. Turns out the boyfriend was just catching up with his sister, who was visiting from out of town. Mom said it didn't matter. "It was still his fault for not introducing me to his family," she told me, feeling completely justified.

I had decided to hire Swayze and Axel to guard my place. If they had chased her off once, they could chase her off again. The problem, of course, was that it was five in the morning, and I wasn't sure they were up. As luck would have it, their Big Wheels were parked outside the laundromat.

I walked inside the warm, but run-down, building to find the two little six-year-olds in their signature hoodies. Axel was pulling a small box of Biz detergent from the vending machine while Swayze stood guard.

"What do you guys need detergent for?"

"What detergent?" asked Axel, slipping the box inside his hoody.

"Never mind," I said. "I've got a real job for you two, and it pays."

Both perked up.

"Just as long as it's not babysitting," said Swayze.

"We hate babysitting," Axel agreed.

I wanted to say "Babysitting? Where are your parents? You're only six year old! And worse, who would hire these two terrors?" Instead I said, "I need someone to watch my place while I'm gone. My mom might come back, and I thought maybe you could scare her off again."

They turned to each other and smiled. Axel raised an eyebrow, communicating some kind of silent twin language.

"What does it pay?" asked Axel.

"What do you want?"

"Two packs of cigarettes and a case of BBs," said Swayze without hesitation.

"How about three bags of Cheetos and a box of laundry soap," I counter-offered. "And not this little stuff you just ripped off. I'm talking about the big boxes you get at Walmart."

They shared another look. One frowned, the other shrugged, and they turned back to me.

"Get us some Twinkies too, and we'll take care of her," said Axel.

"By *take care of her*, what do you mean?"

"We'll get rid of her for you," said Swayze, turning to fist bump Axel.

"Yeah, but how?"

Axel and Swayze grew serious. The laundromat was so eerily quiet, you could have heard a fabric softener sheet falling.

"Do you really want know?" asked Axel.

I was sure I didn't, but I was having visions of standing in a courtroom as a judge asked if I'd paid two six-year-olds Twinkies and laundry soap to take out my mom.

"Just tell me you're not going to kill her."

"We might," said Swayze. A little shiver ran up my spine.

"If you can die of dog poop," said Axel, and they both broke into little-kid giggles.

A weight instantly lifted off my chest, and I could breathe again. I tried not to smile, imagining my mom being pelted with poop. "Great. You can dog doo her all you want."

"Oh, we will," said Axel.

"Let's go get some," said Swayze.

The two ran for the door. Then Axel stopped short of the entry and turned back to me, deadly serious. "We expect payment tonight."

"Sure thing," I said, wondering for the second time that morning, just who were their parents?

Feeling confident that my home was fairly well protected, I hopped on the bus. I had looked at the zoo's layout on Google Maps, but the image wasn't good enough. I thought I'd seen the monkey cages, and where I might be able to set up some chairs and tables nearby, but I didn't want to be surprised on the day of the wedding and find out I'd been looking at the penguin exhibit. I needed to see the monkey exhibit in person.

My stomach growled. I tried to remember the last time I ate and realized it had been popcorn and tequila last night. Lucky for me, Monte was nice enough to give away anything past its pull date to employees. That meant when I got to work, I could probably grab a toxic four-day-old hot dog, which in all honesty, weren't half bad. For the moment though, I ignored my stomach and checked the time. I had an hour and a half before work—more than enough time to sneak into the zoo, check the site, get back on the bus, and be to work to clock in on time.

We were two miles from the zoo when the bus stopped. I looked out the window and sighed. A white-haired old lady was inching her way to the bus on her walker. She was moving so slowly, for a moment I thought she had died standing up. Seeing that she was going to take forever, I jumped from my seat to help her in.

As I ran to the door, I *barely* bumped some dude in his 40s, wearing a ratty suit and sitting in the front seat. "Watch it, will you," he said, giving me the stink eye.

"Maybe you could help me get this lady on the bus." I said.

"Why? You've got two arms," he said.

I noticed he didn't have a wedding ring. Big shock.

The bus driver let me out, and I stepped up to the old woman, who was exactly what I imagined my grandma would look like if I'd ever met her—lots of white hair, thick red lipstick, and wearing a Red Wind Casino T-shirt.

"Can I help you?" I asked.

"Oh, yes. Thank you." I gave her one arm to hold and grabbed her walker with the other hand. We slowly hobbled to the bus, which was at least faster than if she'd done it on her own. I got on the bus ahead of her and asked the douche in the front seat to please give the old lady his spot.

"There's a seat behind me," he said.

"Give her a break. It's six seats back. It'll take her forever to get there."

He shrugged. I could feel my patience evaporating as I lifted the walker over his head to get it on the bus. It was then I, maybe, accidentally—but probably not—whacked him in the head with one of the legs. "Dick," I muttered instead of apologizing.

"Bitch," he hissed.

I whacked him again, much less accidentally. This time he jumped to his feet. "That was on purpose!" He turned to the bus driver, "Did you see that!? She hit me."

"Just take the seat back there and let the lady have yours," said the driver, who had stood to help the old lady up the stairs.

The man finally took the seat farther back, rubbing his head, shooting me the finger. We arrived at the zoo at 6:08 a.m.

It took seven minutes to get to the back of the zoo, where Reese was supposed to let me in. The sun was coming up. It was going to be a hot day; I could feel the rays already warming my shoulders. It was also warming up a bunch of animal doo as the stench wafted out the back entrance. It stunk almost as bad as it had two days before.

The gate to the back entrance was locked, and Reese was nowhere to be seen. I looked around for other ways in—maybe someone left something open. Maybe a window? Nothing. My heart rate kicked up a notch as I felt the minutes ticking away. I didn't want to be late for work on my second day. I had already been fired once already.

I glanced around and didn't see any people or vehicles, so I decided to scale the gate. It was your basic seven-foot-high utility gate they used on the construction sites I had flagged at, with a single strand of barbed wire across the top. I knew could do it. But I wish I'd known the situation ahead of time, because I would have worn something other than my denim miniskirt. I made a mental note to jot that down in my little red book later—wear pants when checking out venues. I needed to scale it quickly, because I was starting to get lightheaded from the manure fumes and a severe lack of solid food.

I grabbed hold of the gate where it met the brick zoo wall, and I used the hinges as footholds. Luck turned out to be on my side. I was halfway up when the gate started to open for an outgoing truck. I jumped down and slipped through. It was 6:13, and I was back on schedule. But where were the monkey cages?

It was hard to get my bearings, having previously come to the zoo through the front entrance. I headed down the main asphalt road, trying not to look suspicious—just your average zoo-goer walking around before hours.

As I walked, I jotted notes in my little red book. The smooth, tree-lined road would be a perfect path for the wedding guests on Saturday, but I would have to add signs pointing toward the actual ceremony site. Maybe I could hang some colorful flowers from the trees. That would definitely give it a jungle feel.

The foul smell from the back gate was fading the farther I walked, and the grounds became more manicured and lush. Sprinklers were watering the grass before people arrived, creating little rainbows, and birds chirped in the trees. With every step, I knew this was the absolute perfect venue for Cheyenne and the *Best Bride* contest.

I spotted the monkey cages up on a knoll. The chimps were swinging around, enjoying the morning sun. I sketched furiously, noting the public bathroom nearby (bonus!), the spot in the shadow of the monkey cages where Cheyenne and Tony could take their vows, and a grassy spot where tables could—

"Ma'am what are you doing here?"

I spun around. Two security guards stared back at me. The older one was about sixty, with a protruding paunch that stretched his button-down shirt to the point of bursting. I expected to see the buttons flying like bullets any moment. The younger guy, about twenty-five, was so skinny his pants hung precariously off his hips, almost defying gravity. Together the two guys completed each other.

"I'm just enjoying the zoo," I said.

"It doesn't open for two hours," said Fat Guard.

"Really? Because the gate was open, and I walked right in."

The skinny one squinted at me. "What gate?"

"I don't know. The one that was standing open."

The fat one turned to his partner, "It's probably those damn concessions people. They're always leaving things open."

The skinny one wasn't having it. He glared at me and nudged his partner, pointing to my little red book.

The fat one nodded to his partner. He held out his hand for my book. "Can I see what you're writing?"

For a moment I panicked. My little red book was sacred. I wasn't handing it over to a doofus in a security uniform. I told myself What's he going to see? Some dress sketches, notes on wedding favors. He's just going to hand it back. Somewhat calmed, I handed him my book.

The chubby one opened it and scowled, worried. He showed it to his skinny partner. "Looks like some kind of plans."

"Yes, that's exactly what it is," I said, trying to sound confident. "I'm a wedding planner. I'm planning a spectacular wedding right here."

The skinny guard looked back at his partner, nervous. "Think we should call the police?"

"Why would you call the police?" I asked a little too loudly. "You must have other wedding planners in here."

"Because I think you broke in. And it looks like you've got a plan here . . . " he tapped the page with a sausage-like finger, "to steal some monkeys."

I looked to see what he was looking at. There was my sketch of the path, stick people walking down it and walking toward the monkey cages.

"Those are guests. Why would I want to steal your monkeys?!" My heart rate was speeding upward, and my pits had started to sweat. I would make another note later in my red book—carry deodorant on recon missions!

"Check the gate," I said. "You'll see. It's still open!"

Neither of them was about the check the gate; instead they turned back to my book.

Fatty flipped through the pages. It was all I could do not to snatch it out of those chubby paws. He stopped on a drawing of a cake. "Looks like a bomb," he said.

"A bomb!?" Skinny almost screamed.

"A cake. A WEDDING cake, you idiots." It wasn't my best sketch.

"Did you call us idiots?" Fatty shouted, his chest puffing out.

"Yes! That's exactly what I called you. IDIOTS! Anyone with three brain cells could tell that I'm a wedding planner."

Fatty gaped at me, using his three brain cells to come up with a response. Skinny grabbed his radio and reached behind him for his cuffs.

In that moment, I saw an image of myself once more unemployed, sitting in a dank jail cell, and Cheyenne's monkey wedding taking place at the Rec Center. I snatched my book and ran for the exit. I heard Skinny call the police.

I felt like I was in *The Terminator*, when Sara Connor was being chased down by cyborg Arnold Schwarzenegger. Only in this version, I was dreadfully out of shape. Within about ten yards my side started to burn, and I heard this weird rushing of wind, only to realize in horror that it was my heavy breathing. How long had it been since I'd run anywhere? Ninth grade gym class? Even then, I don't know if you'd call it running.

I reached the gate, gasping for breath. It was closed, so I started to climb. Maybe it was the lack of oxygen from panting so hard, or visions of being hauled off in a police car, that made me decide to jump from the top of the gate to the ground outside.

I only fell about a foot and half before I was jerked back violently and something bit into my waist. I looked behind me to see my miniskirt hung up on the barbed wire strand. I was dangling there with my skirt hiked up to my waist, flashing anyone nearby with a spectacular view of my magenta bikini panties—an issue neither Sara Connor nor the Terminator ever had to deal with.

I tried everything to pull free, but I couldn't get my skirt loose. I pulled my phone from my purse and was texting Denise for help when the police arrived.

Chapter 17

The police station looked fairly modern, but it smelled like a combination of disinfectant, old socks, and coffee. I sat at a desk across from an officer, a gal around age thirty with hair pulled back in a ponytail. She quickly flipped through my red book.

"You said you're planning a wedding?" she asked.

"Yes, that's my planning book." I looked at the clock on the wall. It read 7:30. "Can I give my boss a quick call? My shift started a half hour ago."

She nodded, and I quickly dialed before she could change her mind. Monte answered. "Fast Food Fast Gas."

"Monte, it's me. I know I'm late but—"

"You fired."

"No, wait." I jumped into old-timey gangster mode. "It ain't my fault. It was the coppers, see? They busted me and took me to the big house. They got me mixed up with some other doll."

The woman cop looked up at me, confused. I shrugged.

"I'm going to blow this popsicle stand here real soon."

"You got one hour, doll," Monte said, then hung up.

The officer smiled. "You must work at Fast Food Fast Gas."

I nodded.

She handed me back my book. "Some nice work in there."

"Really?"

"Yeah." She stretched out her hand to show off a beautiful half-carat diamond engagement ring. "My fiancé proposed last month. The planning, though! What a pain in the ass."

"You got my number. Call me if you need help."

"Might do that. In the meantime, buy a ticket next time you go to the zoo."

"Yes, absolutely." I put my red notebook safely back in my purse. "Can you tell me if there's a bus stop close to here?"

"You already have a ride."

"What?"

She pointed behind me. Standing outside the glass door of the police station lobby stood Charlie. He gave me a little wave. What was he doing here? Not that I was complaining. He was the best thing I had seen all day. And it wasn't even noon. I desperately wanted to check my makeup and pull up my bra, but he'd already seen me.

I walked out into the lobby, tugging at the hem of my miniskirt (which after spending part of the morning hiked to my waist, kept creeping its way back up).

"Denise told me you needed a ride to work. I volunteered." He gave me a knowing grin.

"What are you smiling at?" I thought I knew, but I hoped I was wrong.

"How the hell did you end up hanging off a gate at the Point Defiance Zoo?" He opened the lobby door for me, and as I walked past him and into the hall, I caught a whiff of him. He smelled like morning coffee and Irish Spring soap. The thought of him, naked, probably just an hour or so ago, in the shower, lathering up, would have to be a daydream for later.

"How do you know about the zoo?"

He handed me his phone. There was a picture of me hanging from the gate in all my underwear-displaying glory, giving the guy taking the picture the finger.

"Some guy at the zoo took it and sent it to Denise," Charlie said.

"Shit!" I felt my cheeks burning.

"It's not that bad," he said.

"Not bad? I've been trying to get a wedding planning business off the ground for years. And now I'm trying to get into *Best Bride*. I can't have a picture like that show up. It . . . doesn't inspire confidence."

"You do look fierce though," Charlie said, still smiling as he opened the front door for me. I brushed past him, closer this time. Did he smell this good every day? God, I was acting like I was in junior high. What was I going to do next, slug him in the arm?

As we walked down the police station steps, he pointed to a lot, a block away. "My truck is over there. By the way, what were you doing exactly?"

"Checking out a wedding site." My stomach growled loudly.

"Have you eaten?"

I shook my head.

"We need to get you some food."

"I need to be at The Shits by eight," I said.

"We've got time," he said as we reached his ride, a black 250 Ford Ranger. He opened the passenger door, and I noticed the floor of the cab was littered with fast-food wrappers. He pushed them under the seat, then took my hand and helped me in.

"Sorry about the mess."

"No problem." I tried to remember if a guy had ever helped me into a car before. I thought it was a first, and I kind of liked it.

In minutes, we were sitting at the drive-thru at McDonald's picking up a bag of egg McMuffins—two for me, three for Charlie. I was already ripping into the sack as he pulled into a parking spot to eat.

"We never had fast food when I was a kid," he said. "Now, I always feel like I'm getting away with something when I order it."

I bit into my McMuffin. My stomach screamed thank you. "Wow, this is the best McMuffin I've EVER had," I said between bites. It really was, but then again, I was so hungry I had been craving toxic, week-old hot dogs.

Charlie scarfed down his first McMuffin in two bites and washed it down with a giant slurp of Coke. He smiled as he tore into the next one. "You know what's even better? French toast at IHOP. Have you eaten there?"

"Denise and I are avoiding the IHOP for a while until she gets over Kenny."

He looked at me confused, then shrugged it off and dug back into his breakfast. It was like watching a little kid eat. I could watch him all day.

"So, I hear you're getting married," I said.

He choked on his mouthful of McMuffin and grabbed his Coke to wash it down. "How'd you hear that?"

"I'm a wedding planner. We have a secret website."

"Really?"

"No, Denise told me. But she did read it online."

His gleeful fast food mood had vanished. It was replaced by what I call "dude dread." Some people call it cold feet or nerves. But dude dread is worse. It's a combination of trapped and defeated. I wished I felt worse for him, but something, I think it was hope, was blossoming. I felt a nervous little flutter in my chest. Could Charlie want out?

"If you need a wedding planner, I'm a pretty good one."

"I'll let Julie know. She's making all the decisions," he said. "How is the wedding planner business going—not counting the arrest this morning?"

"I wasn't arrested. Just taken in for questioning. But thanks for asking. Right now things are a little slow—well, not slow. I just need clients who want to pay me more than $200 for a wedding."

"Solid business plan," he said.

"This weekend I've got a monkey wedding at the zoo. I'm going to send the photos to *Best Bride* for their budget wedding contest. It's important to get your name out there. I don't want to work at The Shits and flag for you the rest of my life. Sorry, no offense."

God Sheila, shut up! I told myself.

"None taken," he said. He was smiling again. "You do know I didn't want to fire you, right? I just wanted to get you out of there before the police and insurance guys came. In fact, I admire you."

"Yeah, I'm sure. You took one look at that picture on your phone of an insane chick hanging from a gate by her miniskirt and thought, now there's a person I can look up to."

He laughed as he finished off the last of his breakfast and tossed the wrapper on the floor of the cab. "That's what I mean," he said, wiping his hands on his pants. "You know what you want, and you go get it. You don't let anyone stop you or tell you can't."

"It also gets me fired a lot."

Charlie started the truck and put it in drive. "See what I mean? Most people are scared of the fallout. Unemployment. But not you."

"Thanks, I think."

"You're welcome," he said, studying me with this look of real respect and maybe a little surprise. And he was really looking. It sent a warm wave through my entire body. I could have lived on that look for the rest of the week.

In twenty minutes, we were pulling up to The Shits. What I would have done to just stay in that truck and keep driving. But slushies and lotto ticket sales awaited me.

"Thank you. For everything, picking me up, breakfast—"

"It's nothing. You made my day."

"Maybe tomorrow I can fall into a ravine or get stuck on a Ferris wheel and really rock your world," I said, trying to unlatch my seatbelt.

But it was stuck. My miniskirt had gotten caught in it. I tugged. Then pulled. Then yanked. Nothing.

"I'm going to burn this skirt when I got home," I said.

"Here, let me."

He reached across me and took hold of the seatbelt. His chest was pressed against mine, and his hair tickled my nose. "You really got it stuck."

Change of plans, I told myself. Not burning this skirt. Keeping it forever!

Then I felt a *RIP!*

"Oh, no," he said.

The skirt hadn't just torn—one entire side had ripped apart. Charlie held the two sides together in his hand.

He looked helplessly at me. "Shit. I'm sorry. I didn't mean to do that."

Our faces were inches away. For a few seconds we didn't move. We just looked at each other. It was just like that movie *Top Gun*, when Kelly McGillis and Tom Cruise are in the elevator at the flight academy, and they are so close, and they just want to jump on each other, but they can't let it show. Only Charlie and I were in a truck outside The Shits, and he was holding my skirt together.

I don't know what came over me. Maybe I was inspired by Maverick's moxie in *Top Gun*, but I took the moment. Go big or go home, I thought, and I kissed Charlie on the mouth. Not some dumb little peck, but a full-on kiss that says, "I've seriously got a thing for you."

I don't know what I expected, but it wasn't his free hand in my hair, pulling me closer. Nerve endings I didn't even know I had started tingling and my heart began beating so hard I felt dizzy. I wanted to tell him, "Take me to bed or lose me forever!" But there was a loud rap at the window.

The kiss broke and I turned to see Monte's face peering at us through the glass. "You late, doll. Get to work."

I turned back to Charlie. "Don't worry about the skirt. I'll duct tape it at work or something." Did I just say duct tape? That should leave him with a wonderful image.

"OK. Sure," Charlie said, a little dazed.

I jumped out of the truck, making sure to hold my skirt together.

There was no way I was going to let him see my underwear twice in one day.

Monte gave me one look. "Duct tape in the back."

Chapter 18

I sipped my tequila at the Brew and Suds, waiting for Denise. The cool booth on a warm day, the sounds of pool balls being racked, and the whir of a dilapidated fan overhead let me think. I needed to focus. With each hour that ticked away, the monkey wedding was that much closer.

Denise slipped in across from me with an order of curly fries. She shoved a couple in her mouth as she reached for the ketchup. "God, I am SO hungry. Seriously. On the way here, I ate the pack of gum in my purse."

My cell phone rang. I looked at it and groaned.

"Who is it?" asked Denise.

"Cheyenne." I was kind of surprised she hadn't called me yet that day. Brides are notoriously a pain in the ass. And having done two weddings for Cheyenne, I knew she was about a four on the scale of 1 to 10. But I'd never done someone's third wedding. Maybe brides get more intense with each wedding. Only one way to tell. I picked up the phone.

"Hey, what's up?" I asked.

"Is the dress done? Can I try it on? I'd really like to see how it fits." Cheyenne's voice was tense, and her words were coming a little too fast. Not a good sign.

"The dress is almost done. Relax. You're going to look like a runway model."

"What if it doesn't fit?"

"You can come by tomorrow and try it on if you want." I tried to sound cool and in control. Truth was, the dress was only about half done and in pieces on the floor of my Airstream. I changed the subject. "Did I tell you I found a great location for the wedding? You're going to love it."

Denise held her fingers to her nose.

"The real reason I called was because you've got a problem. A BIG one," Cheyenne's words were rushing out even faster.

"Calm down. What is it?"

"My family's not coming unless there's alcohol."

"You only gave me $200. That wouldn't even cover your cousin Mikey's tab."

"I know. But they aren't coming unless they can drink. This is a nightmare!" Her voice cracked. The next step was tears. I don't do well with tears. Screaming, throwing things—even kicking—I can deal with. Tears are another story. I get panicky to find a solution.

I know I should be calm like other wedding planners and hand out tissues and say, "It's OK. It will be all right." But during the last wedding when the bride broke down, I freaked, handed her my lip gloss and said, "Just put some of this on. You'll feel better," and walked away. Luckily, it worked. It was great lip gloss.

I could tell Cheyenne's tears were ready to spill. I took a deep mental breath to gather my thoughts. There was no way I had money for booze. And Cheyenne's family didn't just drink, they *drank*. They went through whiskey like most people go through bottled water.

"How about this?" I suggested "We tell them it's a BYOB wedding."

"My mom says that's not classy."

"Yes, but—"

"They WON'T come. Did you hear me?"

"I heard you. They want alcohol. Give me a couple minutes to think."

"It's already started," she wailed. I swear I could hear a tear falling down her cheek. "My bad luck. It's started."

"No crying. Just stop it. This is your wedding, goddamn it. Get happy."

"You don't understand."

"This is my third wedding for you, Cheyenne. If anyone understands, it's me. Now listen. Your bad luck isn't starting. Your wedding is going to be amazing. And I'll think of something."

"Really?"

"Really," I lied.

"Thanks," she said, sniffing back the tears. "I'll be by tomorrow afternoon to try on the dress."

She hung up, and I tossed back the rest of my tequila.

As a wedding planner, you learn to lie—and lie well. Early on I learned you have to tell brides what they want to hear, like, 'You can barely see those tattoos' or 'You're totally cuter than the bridesmaids.' You lie because you have to. Every wedding would fall apart without a truckload of lies—big, small, and everything in between.

"We're screwed," said Denise, using her finger to lick the rest of the ketchup from her plate. "There is no way we can get enough booze for that mob of alcoholics."

"She says they won't come without it."

"Even if you could get that much booze into the zoo, what are you buying it with?"

"You're not being very supportive."

"I'm just trying to keep it real. You want this to be a killer wedding for *Best Bride*, but we've only got a day and a half. This might not be the one."

"It HAS to be this wedding," I said, grabbing a peanut that Denise had managed to overlook. "I'm not making Fast Food Fast Gas my career. I am *going* to be a wedding planner!"

"OK. God, you're starting to sound like one of the brides."

"Sorry. So, how was your day?"

Denise patted her stomach. "Moon Beam Star Catcher and I had a good time, didn't we?"

"Moon bean?"

"*Beam*. Like rays of light."

"Sounds like a fairy princess."

"I know," said Denise, smiling as her second plate of curly fries arrived. I grabbed one as she tried to swat my hand away.

"Remember junior high?" I said.

"Yeah. It sucked."

"Well, imagine what it would it would have been like if your name was Moon Beam Star Catcher."

She took a moment to mentally run through all the terrible highlights of junior high. "Good point. You got something better?"

"I do. I thought of it while I was dangling off that fence this morning." I paused for effect. "Mona Lisa."

"Keep thinking." She washed down a mouthful of fries with a Diet Coke. "So what's on the agenda this evening—besides finding a swimming pool full of alcohol?"

"I might have a way to cover up that smell at the zoo gate."

"I don't believe you."

"But first we need to find Pastor Bee. I tried to call him, but he wasn't answering."

"With only a day and a half, why don't you do it? You did her other two."

That was true. I got ordained over the Internet a couple years before. I even had a black robe I wore that I'd picked up for half price at the Halloween store. I'm still amazed at how many hats we wedding planners have to wear. But this wedding was different. I couldn't stretch myself too thin.

"This wedding needs to be classy," I said. "It's going to look cheesy if I'm the wedding planner *and* the pastor. This is *Best Bride*." And, I thought, maybe Cheyenne was right. Maybe we were dealing with a little bad luck. We needed to change things up.

"Agreed," said Denise grabbing the ketchup dispenser. "Let me just finish my fries."

Chapter 19

Denise pulled her car into Bee Wrecking Co., just outside Benston. The place was a wreck—a 3D advertisement for the business. A beat-up singlewide was surrounded by a couple of big trucks, piles of twisted metal, and junk that Pastor Bee had collected at various demo sites.

The pastor's daughter, Sheena Bee, was a year ahead of Denise and me in school. She told us that he'd started out as a pastor, but when he got drunk, he was always smashing things up with an excavator he'd pieced together. Sheena's mom, Mindy, told him to leave after he destroyed the church shed. She was afraid the next building he leveled might be their house—or the church.

"Busting shit up is the only thing you've ever been good at," Mindy said. Pastor Bee agreed and Bee Wrecking was born.

Luckily for me, Pastor Bee kept his credentials, even after he became a demolition dude. When I needed the real thing, for the price of a six-pack, I could get him to come out and do a wedding. He said he still liked keeping his foot in the door, just in case.

We got out of the car. Bee Wrecking always looked the same. Battered. Dirty. And really weird. Pastor Bee collected things from sites that he thought he might be able to sell someday. It gave the place a freaky junkyard carnival feel. His two best pieces were on either side of his office door. On the left was a six-foot-tall carved troll with googly marble eyes, and on the other side was a bright pink VW Bug, standing on its nose.

I knocked on the door to the office. "Pastor Bee? It's Sheila Johnson."

"This place just gets weirder and weirder," said Denise, checking out a birdbath that looked like an ape's hand reaching out of the earth.

I knocked again. "Pastor Bee. You in there?" I opened the door. Empty. Shit, when would I get a break?

Denise went to move the birdbath and it fell over. "It's plastic!" she yelled. "I thought it was going to weigh a hundred pounds. We should try to get this. We could use it at the wedding to hold beer. It's so . . . monkey."

I inspected the birdbath—a hairy ape arm that looked like it was coming straight out of the ground, and the hand held a large banana leaf. I could already picture the leaf filled with monkey-themed hors d'oeuvres. "You're right. It's perfect," I said. "Stick it in the car. I'll leave Pastor Bee a note that we borrowed it."

I ripped a page out of my little red notebook and started writing a message to Pastor Bee.

"I forgot to tell you," said Denise. "You aren't going to believe this."

"What?"

"Kate Michaels is going to be Charlie and Julie's wedding planner."

I stopped mid-scribble. "Kate? Editor of *Best Bride* Kate? Why would she be doing Charlie's wedding?"

"Because she's the wedding planner of the rich and famous. And I've been *trying* to tell you, he's really rich."

"If he's so rich, how come he's working putting in a treatment facility in Benston? Benston is the anus of America."

"It's not that bad," said Denise. "More like the armpit."

"OK, armpit of America. No one who is rich and famous lives in Benston."

"Well, he's rich enough that they're considering that Chateaux place in France for their wedding."

I tried to speak, but nothing came out of my mouth. By "that Chateaux place," she meant the Chateaux de Vaux-le-Vicomte, in Maincy, France—*Best Bride's* wedding destination of the year in 2015 and 2016. A reception alone at the Chateaux was $60,000.

"What did I tell you," said Denise. "Rich."

I'd seen dozens of photos of the place. It was more palace than castle. It had grounds the size of Disneyland and ballrooms bigger than the Wheel In RV Park. It was the kind of place you expected Cinderella to waltz into at any moment and drop a slipper. Now I had a picture of Charlie and Julie waltzing around in it, and it made my heart hurt. It also made me want to hit something.

"Ouch," Denise said rubbing her tummy.

"What's wrong?"

"Nothing. She's stretching. Come over here."

I stepped over an incredibly lifelike plastic tortoise and around a mini fridge to Denise. She took my hand and laid it on her tummy. It was tight, like someone had hooked Denise up to a tire pump and inflated her.

"What am I supposed to feel?"

"Just wait."

Two seconds later, it happened. A little foot—or what I assumed was a foot—slid across her stomach and under my hand."

I jerked back. "Oh my god! There's someone in there."

"Of course there's someone in there. I'm pregnant."

"I know you're pregnant. I just . . . I didn't picture something living in there."

"Not something. A little girl." Denise patted her tummy. "Betty, don't listen to your Aunt Sheila. She's still processing."

"No. No. No. Betty is an old lady name," I said. "Can I do that again?"

"Sure. Put your hand right here," Denise said.

I did, and again the little foot slid across my hand. I couldn't help it, but all of a sudden there were tears standing in my eyes making the world all fuzzy. There was going to be another person soon, a tiny little person.

"Kind of cool, huh?" said Denise.

"It's amazing."

"And Betty is not an only lady name."

"What about Betty White?" I said taking my hand from her bump.

"Just because Betty White's old and her name is Betty doesn't make it an old lady's name," said Denise. "Someday Beyoncé will be an old lady, and that's not an old lady name."

"When Beyoncé is old, Beyoncé will be an old lady name."

Denise threw up her arms. "Then every baby name is an old lady name."

"Eventually. When they—"

The roar of one of Pastor Bee's demolition trucks pulling in cut off my words. A cloud of dust turned up by the truck rolled in and engulfed us. Pastor Bee stuck his head out the window.

"You two must have a wedding this weekend. If you've got a six-pack of Heineken, I'm in."

"Sheila, don't forget to ask him if we can use his ape-hand birdbath too," said Denise.

Chapter 20

We left Bee Wrecking with a pastor lined up and the ape-arm birdbath filling the back seat. The next stop was Walmart. We needed to get our hands on the solution to that reeking zoo entrance.

The parking lot of Benston Walmart was fairly empty. I felt it might be a bad sign, but I wasn't going to tell Denise. She, as usual, was a little nervous about my plan.

"There's got to be a better way," she said. "You've already been to the police department once today."

"That's why you're stealing it," I said.

"Me? You didn't tell me that part."

"Because you worry so much. And in this case, you don't have to worry because they don't throw pregnant gals in jail."

"They throw them in all the time!"

"OK. Will it make you feel better if I tell you, *if* we get caught, I'll say it was all my idea and I'll go to jail."

"A little," she said.

I'd had this flash of inspiration while I was selling cigs to a guy at The Shits. He told me he didn't like smoking, but he was doing it to try to cover up the smell in his car. Something had died in the back seat, and every time he drove somewhere the smell clung to his clothes, and his girlfriend was complaining. His girlfriend was right. He smelled like he'd rolled in blue cheese.

"Wait here," I had told him, running down aisle two. I came back with a can of Febreze.

"Let's try this. It's way cheaper than cigarettes."

He nodded. A minute later we were standing outside the front door as I sprayed him down. I started with his head and moved down to his feet, circling his body as I went.

"OK, OK. Enough!" He coughed.

I stood up. "Let's see what you smell like."

We both took a big whiff of his arm. "I smell like a gal's bathroom," he said.

I held out the can for him to read. "No. You smell like Fresh Twist Cranberry. And that's way better than a dead animal."

"Maybe," he said, not at all convinced.

But it had convinced me. Febreze might just be able overcome the stench at the zoo back entrance.

"How many cans of this stuff do you need?" asked Denise.

"I don't know. Seven?"

"Where am I going to hide seven cans?"

"You're pregnant. You'll just look more pregnant."

"Why don't I just steal one bottle of perfume?" she asked. "That's a lot smaller."

"We went over this. Because it won't smell like a monkey wedding. Febreze comes in Bamboo, Orchid, and Bora Bora."

"OK," she sighed. "Let's just get this over with."

I had hoped more people would be shopping, but when we walked into the place it was, as I suspected, almost empty. Not good. When stealing wedding supplies, I like to have a lot of people in the store to distract the staff. If Mom taught me anything, it was how to shoplift.

"I'm going to create a distraction. You get the Febreze," I said.

Denise nodded and walked toward the cleaning supplies. I headed toward the fresh produce. When I got there, I played the part of a casual shopper, checking out the different fruits. I stopped at a cardboard display filled with apples, out of sight of any shoppers. I reached for an apple toward the back and at the same time gave the display a hefty kick. The plan was to spill apples everywhere and cause a distraction for Denise. But the display was sturdier than I anticipated. It didn't even wobble after the second kick. Or the third.

Next I tried to rip the side of the display. I tugged and pulled. Nothing. I hated to do it, but finally I had to resort to my pocketknife. I made a tiny incision down the side. Finally, success.

"Oh, no!" I screamed as apples poured onto the floor, rolling in every direction. I waited. No one came. What was with Walmart today? "Apple problem in produce!" I yelled. Still no one came!

Shit. What if they hadn't heard me because they were all arresting Denise for putting cans of Febreze up her pink Baby on Board T-shirt?

I moved over to the oranges. This stand was a little less sturdy. As I grabbed for one of the fruits, I ripped the side of the display and oranges toppled around me, smacking the floor and rolling around with the apples that I'd already spilled.

"Oh my god!" I yelled. "Did you see that? There's something wrong with your displays! Seriously wrong!"

I waited. Looked around. Crickets. Jesus, was everyone on break? Discouraged, I walked out of the produce department and looked for Denise by the door. There were no alarms. I didn't see employees running to the cleaning supply aisle. In fact, I didn't see any employees at all.

I left the store to wait for Denise at the car, but when I got there she was already waiting for me in the driver's seat.

"Good god, we should go back in and steal the rest of the supplies. It's like everyone's on break," she said pointing to a pile of air freshener cans in the back seat, next to the ape hand.

"Did they have the right scents?"

"They were out of Bora Bora, but they had plenty of Bamboo and Orchid," Denise smiled.

"Sweet."

Chapter 21

Wedding planning is a roller coaster. One moment you're on top of the world—scoring a dozen cans of Febreze and an ape-inspired birdbath. The next moment you're staring at two little kids with Super Soakers standing in front of your home looking like they had just come from a war zone.

I jumped out of Denise's car and ran up to Swayze and Axel. "What happened? Are you OK?"

The two looked exhausted. Their little shoulders were slumped and their hoodies filthy, but both sported tiny smiles, their white little teeth gleaming behind the dirt. Just for a second I wanted to give them a hug and tell them it would be all right. But self-preservation stopped me.

I looked around. Something was off. I couldn't quite place it. Then I saw it. The Airstream had moved. When I had left that morning, the door faced the road, but now the entire vehicle was off at an angle, and the door faced the Brew and Suds.

Axel, who was particularly dusty stepped up. "Your mom already had your house hooked to some kind of big truck when we got here."

Swayze chimed in. "But she was having problems getting the truck started up."

"That's when we got these." Axel held up a Super Soaker.

"She ran away from squirt guns?" I had a hard time picturing these two little guys chasing my mom off with water on a hot summer day.

"They're filled with ammonia," said Swayze proudly.

"And we got her good," said Axel.

"Oh my god!" said Denise, taking a step back.

"Your mom was yelling really bad words, but she kept trying to start the truck," said Swayze.

"So we used one of these," said Axel, pulling out a can of mace.

"Where did you get that?" I asked. "No, don't tell me."

"You should have heard her scream THEN," said Axel smiling, his eyes lighting up as he replayed the scene in his mind.

"She was grabbing her eyes. You would think she was dying," said Swayze. "She said she was going to call the police."

"Did she?" said Denise, her hands pressed on either side of her baby bump, like she was going to keep her from hearing the story.

Swayze nodded. "We told your mom, 'Go ahead, we'll just tell the police you're stealing Sheila's home.'"

"And while she was rubbing her eyes, we unhooked your home from the truck," said Axel.

I couldn't help myself. I reached down and hugged Swayze with one arm and Axel in the other.

"Hey, what are you doing?" asked Axel.

"I'm thanking you." I gave them each a little extra squeeze.

Swayze stiffened. The smiles were gone. "I thought we were getting paid."

"Oh, I almost forgot." Denise and I went to the back of her car and pulled out a box of industrial detergent, some chocolate, and two packs of Twinkies. I also threw in a couple of cans of Diet Coke.

"Where do you want us to put these?" I asked.

"Just put 'em on the back of our Big Wheels," said Swayze.

I didn't there was a back to a Big Wheel, but the two had somehow attached women's belts to hold, I assumed, loot they stole from around the RV Park. As they pedaled away with their reward, Denise turned and stared at the Airstream. "Your mom is terrible."

"You're telling me."

"But those kids may be worse. Promise me they are never coming near the baby."

I put my hand on her tummy. "I swear."

As the Big Wheels rounded the corner and out of sight, my neighbor Jim threw open his trailer door. "Are they gone?"

"The kids? Yes, they just left," I said.

"If I see your mom or those kids again, I'm calling management."

"How come you didn't call management when my mom was stealing my place?"

"And get your mom pissed at me? Forget it."

I couldn't blame him. My mom was mean. "Hopefully, the kids put a scare into her," I said.

Carla joined the conversation from inside her motorhome. "Those kids used mace! My cats and I are very sensitive. That mace could have killed us."

"Sorry about that," I said to her open window.

"Are you eating OK?" asked Denise. "We see a lot of cat food deliveries."

"Of course, I'm eating OK. What kind of question is that? It's your kids that are the issue."

"They aren't my kids," I said.

"I don't care. Keep them under control."

"We will." I said. "Have a good day."

"Cut the crap," she said, and I saw a hand close the window.

Chapter 22

Charlie spent the rest of Thursday wrapping up projects, feeling like he did back when he left home for college. Only when he left for college, he was excited about the life ahead of him. Today he felt nothing but dread. His life was changing drastically, and he felt out of control.

The crew had left for the day, and he was alone on the site, packing up some things in his office. The only thing that had kept him sane was replaying in his mind that morning with Sheila at Fast Food Fast Gas. Sheila leaning in, her eyes staring into his, and then that kiss. He had never been kissed like that before—his scalp tingled, and a rush of emotion hit him so hard, he forgot to breathe. Her hair was so soft, and she smelled liked a carnival. He just wanted to—

Art, his right-hand man, threw open the door to Charlie's office.

"When were you going to tell me you are leaving?"

"I'm still not sure I am," Charlie said.

"Your dad called me just now. Said 'Congratulations, you're the new foreman.'"

Charlie's chest tightened. His dad was serious this time. This was happening.

"I'm sorry about that. I told him not to call."

"Jesus, you really are leaving."

"I don't want to, but I can't figure out how to stall any longer," said Charlie. "It's all part of the Ricci plan."

"I know you, Charlie. You hate the corporate life. The meetings. The ties. You really want that?"

"Hell no!" he said. "But I don't really have a choice."

"Nothing personal, but with all that money, aren't you supposed to be free to do what you want?"

"That's what they tell you, but with money comes a lot of responsibilities."

"Dude, it's your dad, not the money, that's got you by the balls."

Charlie wanted to argue, but Art was right. He wasn't built to confront his dad. He wasn't even sure what it was his dad had over him.

Charlie changed the subject. "Before I leave, though, I wanted to ask you. Will you be my best man?"

"What?! You're getting married too?"

"I guess so," Charlie said. "So, is that a yes?"

Charlie noticed a vein in Art's forehead bulging as he studied his feet. Art looked back up at Charlie. "Do you love her?"

"Um . . . yeah. Sure."

Art threw his hands in the air. "Um . . . yeah? That's your answer? Dude, you need to get your shit together and nut up before it's too late." He turned and left the office, the door slamming loudly behind him.

Charlie looked around at his orderly office—not the dirty mess it had been before Denise got to work on it the last two days. She had even taken the photo of Julie out of the drawer and placed it on his desk.

Even Denise saw what Art saw—a man who couldn't stand up for what he wanted. That afternoon, when he had gotten off the phone with his dad, Denise approached him, very serious, sensing the tension.

"You know, if you want, you could have Sheila talk to your father. She's really good at talking to parents"

"Thanks. But this is a pretty big deal."

"I had a big deal once. A really big one. I backed the car into a Frosty Freeze sign. You know that one that's kind of crooked on Eighth Street?"

Charlie knew exactly what sign it was. It listed wildly to the left. No one parked under it because it was ready to go at any moment.

"That was me. I backed into it when I was sixteen."

"It's been like that since you were sixteen?!"

"That's not the point. The point is, I was so scared to tell my dad, I was thinking of running away from home. I even started packing my bags. But Sheila said, 'Let me tell him. I'll handle it.' And she did. I don't know what she told him, but it worked out. My dad made me pay him back for the repairs to the car, which took about three years, but everything was OK."

"I appreciate the offer, but I need to handle this on my own."

"Think about it," Denise said. "She's good at being brave."

Charlie let the words echo from earlier that day—she's good at being brave. Was he a coward? Was that his problem?

He needed some air. He walked out of his office. The heat of the day still lingered in the evening air as he walked to his truck.

An hour later, Charlie was in Arnold's, a gym for boxers just outside Benston. He had visited the place occasionally. It looked pretty sketchy on the outside and was even sketchier inside, but the guys who worked out there seemed decent.

He slipped his hands into the pair of well-worn gloves his grandpa had given him many years before, and he pounded his fists together, flexing the leather. His grandpa would love this place. Beat-up ring mats worn in the middle from countless matches, busted-up lockers with doors that hung askew, and the lingering scent of old sweat that permeated everything.

Charlie's grandpa had taught him to box when he was twelve. Charlie was a skinny kid for his age and his grandpa was a bull of man, standing almost twice as tall as his own son, Charlie's dad.

His grandpa never said it out loud, but he was worried Charlie got picked on in school, which he did. He wanted to make sure Charlie knew how to throw a hook or a jab if necessary.

As Charlie got older, and the bullies became less of an issue, his grandpa still regularly met Charlie down at the gym for a little sparring.

"I got a little life wisdom for you," he'd say. "If you got a problem, just beat on a bag for a while, and everything will become clear."

Charlie had never really taken the advice, but now he desperately needed some clarity. May there was some way out he hadn't thought of.

He walked up to an ancient four-foot bag hanging from the ceiling. It had been taking hits since at least the 1930s—and it looked it. The brown leather was worn, and the seams had been re-sewn with thick new strips. How long would it take for things to become clear, Charlie wondered. An hour? A day? He was about to find out.

Charlie jabbed, and his glove connected with the bag. He could feel the impact in his wrist, arm, and shoulder. It felt good. He hit the bag again. *Bam. Bam.* He could feel a little of the tension in his back start to release. He saw his dad, then his mom, and then that damn ring. *Bam. Bam. Bam. Bam.*

Within minutes, sweat trickled into his eyes. He didn't see the bag or the dusty light that hung overhead, he saw his future. He saw himself putting on a tie. Men and women in suits at conference tables. He saw dinners at restaurants, all the same people.

Bam. Bam. Bam.

Charlie saw his dad smiling. His mom nodding. Julie in a white dress face hidden behind a veil.

BamBamBam. Charlie's arms were burning.

Charlie saw an apartment with gleaming appliances and a longhaired cat. Then he was at a golf game. He hated golf. But he was there. He had a golf cart that matched three other carts. All the men looked eerily alike—like Stepford husbands—with suntans, white shorts, and polo shirts. They were talking about work, checking their phones. He wanted to just throw his clubs and run.

BAMBAMBAM. His breath was coming out in hot bursts.

He saw a woman step out from behind one of the golf carts. He saw the miniskirt first, then the platform shoes. This woman didn't belong here, he thought. The men were turning. Stunned. Charlie didn't know who the woman was, but she was a welcome sight in this stuffy golf game.

The woman turned. It was Sheila, and she pushed the men aside to get to Charlie. One guy gave her a disgusted, you-don't-belong-here look. She smiled and flipped him off. Then she walked up to Charlie and ruffled his hair. She pulled a fifth of tequila from her purse. "You want to cut out of here?"

At a loss for words, he nodded.

"You OK?" she asked, worried.

Charlie blinked as Sheila morphed into an eighteen-year-old with bad teeth standing beside Charlie in the dilapidated gym. "You OK, Mister? You better lay up or you're going to have a heart attack."

Charlie's arms dropped to his sides. His heart was beating way too fast. He could see tiny spots in front of his eyes.

"I'm good," Charlie said, now back to reality. He saw relief in the kid's eyes. "And you know what? Grandpa was right. You can get clarity."

"Whatever you say, man." The kid handed Charlie his cell phone. "Your phone keeps ringing and some of the guys were complaining.

Charlie looked at this phone and saw four missed calls from Camella. He called her back and go her on the first ring "Hey, what's up?"

"Where the hell have you been?.."

"I'm at the gym. Is something wrong?"

"I wanted to give you a heads up," she said. "In case you were thinking of jumping ship, dad scheduled a big meeting for Saturday morning. All board members are to be in his office at 9 am to elect you CEO, and meet you personally. It's a command performance, press releases, the whole thing."

The sweat on Charlie's back and arms turned cold. He thought he might puke right there on his gym bag.

"Hello?"

"I'm here," he said. "I don't think I'm ready."

"Get ready," said Camella. "You knew this day was coming."

"What about cousin Aaron?"

"He's still an idiot," Her voice softened. "Just get your ass over here. Take the helm. I'll be here to help you out. Don't worry. You got this."

"But the construction company —

"They'll live without you. My assistant has the company jet scheduled to pick you up at 6 am at Seatac."

Charlie looked at his gloves, and thought of Sheila and her ripped skirt . . . and that kiss. She probably knew a thing or two about runaway brides. Maybe she could give him pointers on becoming a runaway CEO.

"Hello? Are you there?"

"I'm still here," he said "By the way congratulations."

"What for?"

"Heard you and Douglas are finally getting married."

"Thanks. I hear you're walking down the aisle too. Sounds like it's going to be some production."

"So I've been told."

"Hey, I got a call coming in I have to take. Cheer up big brother. You're living the dream." And with that she was gone.

Charlie put his phone back in his bag and headed to the locker room to shower. He wondered what use clarity was when reality stood in the way.

Chapter 23

It felt like the wedding was hurtling toward me like a comet in a white veil. Knowing that Mom had been scared off for the moment, I spent most of Thursday night working on the dress. I hadn't realized how fast bananas went bad, so I was eating browning centerpieces as I sewed.

I watched *Sixteen Candles* on my TV while turning the size 23 dress into a form-fitting size 2. *Sixteen Candles* is no *Dirty Dancing*—no movie is—but it's still one of the best. Some say, what about *Pretty Woman*? It's a classic. True. Both are about poor girls who find rich guys. But *Sixteen Candles* seems more realistic to me than *Pretty Woman*. I mean, who hasn't traded their underwear for a favor and lived to regret it? And there is the sister's looming wedding throughout the flick. It's almost a documentary.

As I watched, I noticed that Jake Ryan, Molly Ringwald's dreamy crush, resembled Charlie. It wasn't like they were twins separated at birth, but they both had the same dark eyes, broad shoulders, and quiet smile . . . Oh my god, I thought. Did I have a crush on Charlie because he reminded me of Jake Ryan? Had I watched *Sixteen Candles* so many times I'd lost track of reality? I finished off a gooey banana, considering it, then shrugged it off. I had about an equal chance with either, so what did it matter? Focus on the damn dress.

My cell phone rang. It was Mom. It was 3 a.m.! God, couldn't she give it a rest? She was like the Terminator. My stomach turned, partly from dreading talking to her and partly because I'd eaten my body weight in brown bananas. My fingers throbbed from hemming and sewing on buttons. It was time for a break. I needed to get this over with.

"Hi," I said, trying to keep all emotion out of my voice, but it just sounded like I was stoned.

"I want my goddamn Airstream." Mom's high-pitched voice grated on my nerves even over the cell phone. "You're going to give it back to me, or I'm taking you to court for assault."

"Go ahead, Mom. But you don't have the money for an attorney.

And you don't OWN it now. I do. Just leave me the hell alone."

There was a pause. I knew Mom. She was building up a frothy head of crazy. I'd watched her do this a thousand times growing up. She would be confronted with facts and her indignant, righteous, insane side would take a moment to decide on its plan—usually something so outrageous it was hard to argue against her.

"It's mine. It's always been mine," she said. "I'm going to tell the court how you stole it from me."

"You left town."

"Did I? Or was I moving, and you wouldn't come with me. You stayed—to keep the trailer. You stole it."

"That's bullshit. I couldn't come because you didn't tell me *where you were going*."

"And then today—you sick those two little midgets on me."

"They're six-year-olds."

"Now who's bullshitting? If you pulled off one of those hoodies, you'd find a man. Trust me on this."

I felt my blood pressure rising, and my head was starting to pound. I needed sleep, not this conversation. I took a deep breath. "Mom, stop it! You are not getting my Airstream. The end. Good night."

I wish I could have slammed the phone down like Sam's grandparents do on Jake Ryan in *Sixteen Candles*, but it was still pretty satisfying to disconnect and drop the phone into my purse.

I picked up my little red notebook and added "need fresh bananas for centerpieces" to my growing list. There were still so many big items to check off—alcohol, chairs, tables, flowers, cake. Granted, I was leaving a few of these until last minute, like the flowers and cake. I'd learned a long time ago that anything that can go bad should be done at the end.

I picked up the dress again and got back to work. I was attaching a pearl button at the neckline when I nodded off in my chair. The last thing I remember was seeing Molly Ringwald slipping into Jake Ryan's Porsche.

Chapter 24

I woke up Friday morning, my back aching from sleeping in a chair. The place smelled of overripe bananas. I picked up the peels on the table next to the sewing machine and threw them in the sink. When I looked outside, what I saw made me want to cry.

The clouds were swollen and dark. Rain was coming in. I love the Northwest—its beautiful trees, green hillsides, and mountains. But the rain? It's the kiss of death for outdoor weddings. I imagined Cheyenne standing, drenching wet beside a cage of equally wet and smelly monkeys. My chances for *Best Bride* would dissolve as quickly as the cake.

I tried not to panic. Could I get tents this late? They were way out of my budget and extremely hard to steal. Maybe it would clear by tomorrow? But I still needed to be prepared. I grabbed my red notebook and scanned through the pages to see if I had any notes about rain. All I found was, "White umbrellas are cheaper than tents," and "If the wedding party is drunk enough they don't care."

I thought quickly. Where would I find 50 white umbrellas? And if they weren't white, does white spray paint run in the rain?

I constantly fantasize about planning desert weddings. Your only worries would be snakes, scorpions, and making sure the bride had on SPF 50.

My phone rang, and I dug around in my purse. It was Denise.

"Hi. What's up?"

"I saw your mom at the 7-Eleven this morning on my way to work. She looked terrible. I think she might have had a reaction to the mace. Her face was all swollen up. She looked like she had stuck her face in a beehive."

"Good. Serves her right." I couldn't help but smile.

"She was also with this big guy. He looked kind of like the actor John Cena, if he were Hispanic. And shorter. And not quite as strong."

"That doesn't sound too scary."

"He wasn't. He was kind of cute. He was wearing a T-shirt that said Big Time Auto Repair," she said. "Be careful. She's up to something."

"She's always up to something," I said. But now she was mad. Really mad. And when she gets pissed off, she *really* gets mean. And that's saying something.

Before I left for work, I came up with a plan. I would remove the tires on the Airstream. That way, if she came back, she couldn't wheel it away. It turned out to be harder than it looks to jack an Airstream up and take off the tires. I had to call on my neighbor, Jim, who was less than thrilled to be woken up before noon.

"I don't want to get in the middle of this thing between you and your mom," he said, standing on his front step, scratching one of his balls with one hand and drinking from a mug of coffee with the other.

"How would she even know you helped?"

"Because there is no one else dumb enough to help you."

"There are plenty of people as dumb as you," I said, trying to make a joke. He didn't smile.

I tried to recover. "I'm working at The Shits now. I can bring you home some day-old pizza."

"Pepperoni?"

"Sure."

"For a week?"

I paused. I wasn't sure anyone should actually eat that pizza for an entire week. I could already see an aid unit parked here and someone applying paddles to Jim's chest.

"You want those tires off, the price is a week of pizza."

"Done."

Once the tires were off, I rolled them over behind the laundromat. Feeling confident, I ran to catch the bus. Let her try to take my home now!

Chapter 25

I was ringing up two Slim Jims and a Mountain Dew for some old guy when Denise ran in—or what pregnant women would call running. It was more of a fast waddle.

"Can you get off for lunch?" she asked, a little out of breath. "I know where we can get booze for the wedding."

"If you're thinking about the Coors guys, I already talked to them. And the liquor store has a new alarm system."

"No. We can talk to Reuben." Her eyes sparkled.

"But—"

"I know you're going to say it's uncomfortable because you dated. But he makes his own whiskey. He may sell us some cheap—or invest."

Investing was a term I came up with a few years ago during a Seahawk tailgate wedding. I needed alcohol, but like this one, had no money. I got a guy, Martin, who makes his own brew, to set up a tailgate bar at the wedding and charge for shots. He could take home whatever he made. It kind of worked until Martin, who was selling the brew, started doing shots himself. In no time, he was buck-ass naked on top of his truck singing "Here Comes the Bride" and the police shut the whole wedding down.

I wasn't a complete loss as a wedding planner. It happened after the "I do's" and Martin was pretty well endowed, so there were no complaints in that department—I even got a few "thanks yous," including a couple from the bridesmaids and the bride herself. That said, though, the entire episode had added a level of chaos that wedding planners try to avoid.

Reuben, who I dated for a couple months after I graduated from high school, was a nice, quiet guy. He lived off the grid, in a small commune, in a patch of trees about twenty miles outside of town. I hadn't seen him in years, not since my "granola" phase, a phase that lasted about two months—the length of time it took me to realize you can't live without hair conditioner and nail polish. Those women looked like shit. Seriously, armpit hair was everywhere, and their legs looked like Brillo pads.

Reuben and I broke up when he caught me smuggling my makeup case and a curling iron into his yurt. We had a big fight. I called him a crazy bohemian butthead. I still felt bad. He really was a nice guy.

"I don't know, Denise," I said, "I'm not sure if Monte will let me off for lunch."

"Leave it to me and Baby Sweet Pea."

As if on cue, Monte came out. "You buying anything dollface, or are you just lollygagging?"

Denise thought Monte's old-timey gangster thing was hilarious and always played along. I tried to tell her he needed to assimilate better, but she never listened.

"This dollface needs to see a doctor," said Denise, patting her tummy. "Can you please let Sheila off for a couple hours to take me and Sweet Pea to the clinic?"

"Sweet Pea bad name."

"What do you mean? Sweet Pea is the bee's knees," said Denise.

He wrinkled his nose. "Pee not sweet. Belong in the powder room."

"Not that kind of pee! The kind you eat."

Monte gaped at her, horrified.

Sheila looked at me for support. I shrugged. What could I do? It was a terrible name.

Denise gave Monte her sweetest smile, "Monte, can you please let her off for a couple hours? Please?"

Monte looked at her, then me. He groaned softly and waved his hand. "Two hours and no pay."

"Thank you. You're jake!" Denise gave him a kiss on the cheek, and he reddened all the way to his hairline.

A half hour later we were pulling up to Reuben's yurt. It was just as I remembered, only now it was covered with an inch of moss and looked a little like a giant toadstool. We would have knocked on the door, but it was only a few pieces of burlap sewn together.

"This place just got more disgusting with time," whispered Denise.

"Tell me about it."

I yelled toward the burlap. "Reuben? Are you in there?"

A woman, about age thirty, stuck her head out. Her blond hair was combed, but looked greasy. And she wore no makeup, which she was desperately in need of. Her blue eyes were as pale as her skin, and her eyebrows needed serious attention. They were almost missing. God, these people were savages. I had dodged a bullet breaking up with Reuben.

"He's gone," she said.

"Like gone, gone? Or like gone-to-the-store gone?" I asked.

"We don't go to the store. We live off the land." She stepped out, topless, with a baby about a year old attached to one breast. Denise tried to hide a gasp, but did a poor job.

"I'm sorry. We didn't mean to intrude," I said.

"You're not intruding," she said, moving the child to the other boob. We tried to look away but Denise and I were both horrified, yet transfixed.

"So is this Reuben Junior?" I asked.

"No. Her name is Aster."

"Good name," I said. Denise nodded.

"Reuben's her love daddy though," the woman said, looking down at her little girl and running a finger across her cheek.

"So, where is Love Daddy?" asked Denise.

"He's down at the still."

"Thanks. I know where that is," I said. "You just keep on nursing." Why did I just say that? I turned and almost ran.

Denise and I made our way down the narrow dirt path. It was a full of weeds and tree roots just as I remembered, and almost impossible to walk without tripping, especially when you were wearing heels.

"Did you recognize who that was?" I asked Denise. "That was Jenny Spreadberry. We did a wedding for her a couple years ago to that freaky guy who cleaned carpets. She was the one who wanted to transform her porch into a chapel."

"Holy shit. You're right! That *was* her. She looked so normal then. Now she looks so . . . Ozark. Did you see the baby?"

"How could I miss it? Promise me, if I stop by your apartment, you won't come out bare chested with Baby Rapunzel attached."

"You don't have to worry. You know how self-conscious I am about my boobs. And I'm not naming my baby Rapunzel."

Reuben's still stood just around the clump of trees at the base of the hill. His yurt may have gone downhill, but his still had grown and gone high-tech. What once was a couple of old kegs in a woodshed was now four ten-foot-tall aluminum drums in a modern metal shed. Each drum was connected with pipes, and it was all being monitored by a computer.

Reuben stood to the side testing something in a glass beaker.

He turned, saw us, and dropped the beaker. It shattered on the cement floor.

"It can't be," he said, not taking his eyes off me.

He looked just the same, except maybe a little hairier. His dark beard was longer, almost to his chest, and his hair was pulled back in a ponytail. He had the same sleepy eyes that made him look dumber than he really was. The way he stared at me reminded me of the other reason why I broke up with him. Reuben was sweet, but he loved me too much. Like a golden retriever loves his owner. It was constant. Overpowering. And I just couldn't generate the same affection back. I still felt a little bad.

"Hi, remember us?" I asked.

He stepped over the mess at his feet and walked over.

"Wow, this place has really—"

He leaned in and kissed me on the lips. His breath smelled of whisky. "It's good to see you."

"Boundaries," I said, pushing him away.

"How did you find me?"

"You were standing right here when I left."

"And your Love Mama said you were here," added Denise.

"It's been a long time, Moon Rocket. I've missed you."

"It's Sheila. Just Sheila."

Reuben turned to Denise. "Have we met?"

"Yeah. A bunch of times. I used to come visit Sheila here."

He nodded, trying to remember, but he couldn't.

"I have a favor to ask," I said. "I know I left on bad terms, but—"

"Of course," he said, leaning in for another kiss.

"Stop it."

"Still the same Moon Rocket. All business. No time for love."

"We need some booze for a wedding," blurted Denise.

Reuben perked up. "You've come to the right place. I've got 100 proof, 85, 65. I've got Scotch. Bourbon. Blended."

"What do you have for twenty-five bucks that will serve fifty drunks?" I asked.

"I don't. My whiskey is a work of art. I'm selling it now to Seattle restaurants for a hundred a bottle."

"You'd think you'd have enough money for a blouse for Love

Momma up there," said Denise.

"She's just staying until she finds her next stop in life." Reuben turned to me. "There is always a place for you here. You know how much I loved you—still love you. Remember on the rocks at the beach? Then in the morning when you—"

"For the love of god, will you stop it! This is why I left. It's too much." A tension headache was forming above my eyes. I needed to get out. Too bad he didn't make tequila; I could have used a couple of shots.

I started to leave. "Sorry we couldn't do business."

"But Moon Rocket you just got here."

"We need to go," I said. "Nice seeing you, Reuben."

Denise nodded, and we turned and headed back up the path to the car.

"I'm sorry, Sheila," said Denise. "I thought he might have something."

"It's not your fault. I'm sure we'll find alcohol out there somewhere."

When we reached her car, a shout came from the woods. "Hey. Hold up!"

Reuben was clutching two bottles of clear liquid with no labels. "A batch went bad a few weeks ago. I got four cases you can have for free, as long as you don't tell anyone where you got it."

"How bad is it?"

"Straight out moonshine."

"Thank you, Reuben. This is really nice. Where are the cases?"

He smiled. "I'll tell you after you give me a kiss."

"Seriously?"

Denise elbowed me, hard. "Just kiss him already. I got a baby sitting on my bladder, and I gotta pee."

Chapter 26

I stepped outside after finishing my shift at The Shits. The clouds had cleared a little and the threat of rain had passed for now. I took a deep breath and centered myself. It was Friday, 5:30 p.m., just twenty-seven hours until the wedding—things had to come together. It was now or never. I just needed to focus and sprint to the finish line.

I was feeling good as I caught the bus for home. During work, I had figured out a way to disable my cousin Kevin's ankle bracelet, so he could DJ. It was amazing what information you could find on Google. Hopefully we would have him back in his apartment before the authorities figured it out.

As I was walking up to my place, a red Camaro with a blob of brown Bondo on the hood pulled in. It was Cheyenne arriving for her fitting. She stepped out of the driver's side, and her sister, Topeka, stepped out of the passenger side. Damn. Whenever Topeka showed up, it meant trouble.

Cheyenne could be a little emotional from time to time—that's to be expected from a bride. Brides get crazy. But Topeka was flat-out mean. She once told me that she superglued her nails on so they won't come off in a fight. She was also just butt-ugly, which I can't image helps her disposition. Topeka kind of looked like Cheyenne—if you ran a truck over her a couple times. Topeka was taller, wider, and thicker than Cheyenne, with a nose that had been broken way too many times. It just sat on her face like a glob of Play-Doh.

"Hey, Sheila," Topeka said, spitting her gum out at her feet.

"Hey, Topeka. Didn't know you were back in town. Heard you had moved to Eastern Washington."

"Couldn't miss my little sister's wedding," she said, giving Cheyenne a big smile. I noticed one of her teeth was missing—not one of the front ones, but definitely a major one.

"She got in last night," said Cheyenne. "They gave her time off."

"That's cool. What're you doing now?" I asked, trying to be polite and hoping I sounded nice. That's the one shit-sandwich part of being a wedding planner. You've got to be nice to everyone, especially the asshole family members.

"She teases hair at a salon in Spokane," Cheyenne said. "She's going to tease mine for the wedding."

"Let's see this dress," Topeka said, picking something out of a tooth.

I turned to Cheyenne. "It's hanging just inside the door. I still haven't hemmed the bottom. Wasn't sure what shoes you were going to wear."

"I'm wearing these," Cheyenne pointed to the spiked indigo-blue heels with rhinestones she was wearing. "You know. Something borrowed, something blue. These were my grandma's."

"Your grandma has good taste," I said.

"Go try on the dress. We don't have all day," Topeka barked.

Cheyenne trotted off toward the Airstream. As soon as the door closed, Topeka's face darkened. "I came back to make sure you aren't screwing this up."

"Relax, I've got it under control." I'd learned from Cheyenne's previous weddings to take control of any interaction with Topeka fast, or she would make life terrible. At the last wedding, she threatened to shave my head in my sleep if the wedding went south. Every time I walked by her, she'd flash these clippers in her pocket. I still jump when I see clippers now.

"That dress better be pretty damn fantastic. I heard she paid you good money for this wedding."

"She paid two hundred for a dress, a venue, a pastor, music, centerpieces, cake, and enough booze for your whole alcoholic family," I said correcting her.

"I'm just saying. This better be good."

I looked into Topeka's brown eyes, outlined with matching brown eyeliner and brown shadowing. It was like looking at two piles of dirt on her face. God, didn't anyone ever show her how to do her makeup? If there was a woman who could use it, it was Topeka.

"This wedding is going to be fabulous. Like I said, it's all under control. Trust me."

Topeka shoved a fresh piece of gum into her mouth. "I told Cheyenne not to hire you. The last two of your weddings were bad luck. She could hire me. I'd do a better job than your sorry-ass shit."

"You wouldn't know a good wedding if it walked up and took a shit on your shoes," I blurted, regretting it as soon as it was out of my mouth.

Topeka smiled, flashing the gaping hole where she was missing a tooth, which I could tell now was an eyetooth. "You little bitch."

It occurred to me then that she probably lost that tooth in a fight. God, if Topeka lost a tooth, what did the other person look like? I could feel nervous perspiration bead up on my forehead and under my arms. I'm great at weddings, but I'm shit in a fight. Ask anyone. I tend to just kick, scream, and throw things out of my purse at the other person.

As I contemplated what was in my purse, Cheyenne opened the Airstream door and stepped out. "So what do you think?"

Both Topeka and I stood speechless. The creamy silk fabric draped softly off Cheyenne's long, tanned frame, flowing to the ground dramatically. I had left a slit up the side to show off her long legs, and it hit about two-thirds up her thigh—high enough to be sexy, but not so high it was slutty. The neckline plunged, but not too deep, and tiny spaghetti straps seemed to magically keep it in place. I nailed it. When I was designing it, I was thinking: What would Penny in *Dirty Dancing* wear if she got married? This was it. And Cheyenne's long, leggy body had turned it into a spectacular wedding gown.

"You don't look half bad," said Topeka.

"You look spectacular," I said, walking toward her, and putting some much-needed distance between myself and Topeka.

Cheyenne spun around, and the early evening light caught the folds of fabric, making her shimmer. "It fits perfect. I love it."

How could it not fit? This was my third wedding for her. I practically had her measurements memorized. I looked back at Topeka, who was spitting out another wad of gum.

"You can wait there," I said. "I need to measure the hem."

"Whatever," Topeka grunted.

Cheyenne leaned in and whispered. "She's trying to quit smoking. She's a little cranky. But don't worry, she's fine."

I looked over and Topeka was pulling out another piece of gum and giving me the finger.

Chapter 27

Just as I finished the hem on the wedding dress, Denise drove up. I grabbed my purse and little red notebook, slipped on my comfortable heels, and ran out the door. It was Friday night, and we had a lot to do if we were going to have a wedding the next day.

I ran to the passenger side, threw open the door, and stopped cold. There was Charlie. For about two seconds my mouth hung open. I couldn't have been more surprised if Jake Ryan were sitting there on Johnny Castle's lap.

"Hi," he said. I nodded, still unable to form words. "Here, you take the passenger's seat. I'll get in the back."

"No you won't," said Denise, "Sheila get in the back."

I slipped in the back seat and closed the door, relieved I had something to do besides stand there with my mouth open.

The whole car smelled of Charlie. *Did* he use Irish Spring? Whatever it was, it was intoxicating. I stared at the back of his head; it was all I could do not to run my hands through his hair.

"I brought Charlie to help us get flowers," said Denise.

Charlie turned around to face me. "Denise said you have a big wedding to put on tomorrow." I nodded. My mouth still wasn't working. I just couldn't get my head around the fact that Charlie was right here, in the car, in 3D! Had I hit my head coming out the door? Was I walking right now in a coma? Well, if that was the case, I wasn't going to waste a good coma.

"It's going to be at the Point Defiance Zoo," I finally managed. "Should be really nice."

"I didn't know you grew your own wedding flowers," he said.

I looked in the rearview mirror for some direction from Denise. She gave me an, "I lied, so go with it," look.

"I don't exactly grow them," I said. "We have someone who grows them for us."

"I picked him up at Arnold's Gym," Denise said, changing the subject as she drove through the RV park. "Did you know that Charlie boxes?"

"I don't know if you'd call it boxing. It's more like pounding a bag," he said, smiling at me. I felt my heart thump hard in my chest. It was a real smile. Not a leering, "Can I get your clothes off?" smile, but a nice-guy smile. A Jake Ryan smile. "I like to do it when I get stressed. It's something my grandpa taught me."

"Does your grandpa live around here?" I asked, noticing a shopping bag on the seat next to me and two hefty bags on the floor. I peeked inside the shopping bag and saw two raw steaks. Jesus, Denise came prepared.

"My grandpa's got a place out in Montana. I don't get to see him much," said Charlie. "He's a great guy. Really into fishing and hunting—anything outdoors."

Denise put a hand up to stop him. "Tell her the good part. Sheila, you're not going to believe this. His grandpa hung out with Elvis."

"No way!"

"Well, they didn't hang out, exactly," he said.

"He went to his house!" Denise almost squealed. "Tell her."

"Grandpa owned a couple of casinos in Vegas back in the day. So he and Elvis got to know each other a little. Elvis had him over to dinner a couple times. Grandpa said he was a great host."

"In Vegas or at Graceland?" I asked.

"Both, I think."

"I *love* Graceland. If I could do a wedding there, I would die happy."

"Sheila loves everything Elvis," said Denise. "When we were in second grade, we snuck into these auditions for Elvis impersonators. Remember that, Sheila? You stole one of the capes and wore it to school for weeks."

I tried to shoot her my "You can stop now" look, but her eyes were on the road.

"Sheila, now you're only two degrees of separation from Elvis!" said Denise. "His grandpa, Charlie, and then you. Isn't that amazing?"

Yes, it was. And what the heck was that cologne Charlie was wearing? If the dogs didn't attack him, I was going to.

Denise slowed the car as we drove into Flower Bitch's neighborhood. It was getting dark. The streetlights gave the neighborhood a peaceful glow. Denise rolled down her window and let the warm air blow through the car. We could already pick up the scent of roses.

She parked across the street from the house. The place was dark and Flower Bitch's car was gone. That gave me some hope.

"I drove by earlier and saw her leave with some other ladies," said Denise, her voice low and serious. "That's why I got Charlie. I don't think we have much time. I heard them say they were having dinner in Tacoma."

Charlie looked from Denise to me. "She's not growing flowers for you, is she?"

I grabbed the black garbage bags and the shopping bag of steaks and jumped out of the car to avoid answering him I peeked inside the shopping bag again. Everything was there. Denise was on top of this.

Once outside, I could see the roses were gorgeous. Perfect. Giant red, yellow, and cream-colored buds, and blooms the size of cupcakes swayed in the evening breeze. There were no other roses like these in Benston. I knew. I had driven around every neighborhood, cul-de-sac, and community garden. Nothing compared. It's not like I *wanted* to steal her roses, but hers were the only ones worthy of a *Best Bride* wedding. We had no other choice. If only Flower Bitch knew where they were going and could see the look on the bride's face when she saw her bouquet, maybe she wouldn't put up such a fight. That was it! I'd take a picture of Cheyenne's wedding, and she'd see her roses were part of something beautiful. Then maybe she would chill. Maybe even get in the wedding spirit!

"Those are the biggest Rottweilers I've ever seen," Charlie said, eyes wide, fixed on the two massive beasts sitting on the porch, staring directly at the car—daring us to step inside the yard so they could rip out our spines and bury them in the backyard. I could feel a sharp shiver run up my spine.

"That's why we brought the steaks. To distract them." I held up the sack.

"You're not going to poison them, are you?" he asked

"No! We're not monsters," Denise said.

Semi-reassured, he looked over again at the dogs, now standing—on high alert.

"Here's the plan," I said to Charlie. "We walk up, open the gate, and when the dogs charge us, we throw the steaks as far as we can into the street. They chase and eat the steaks, and that should give us about two minutes to cut as many roses as we can."

"You're joking," said Charlie.

"You have a better plan?"

"Yes! We go to a store and buy flowers like a normal person."

"Have you paid for flowers? They're expensive," said Denise.

I opened up the garbage bag and pulled out my clippers and gloves, and then I pulled out Denise's pair of pink clippers and gloves and handed them to Charlie, along with a another garbage bag.

"Cut as many as you can. Drop them into your bag. And we run out before the dogs get back. Easy peasy."

"This is crazy," he said, glancing at the Rottweilers.

Denise patted his shoulder. "I'd do it, but I'm pregnant."

"No one should do this." Charlie looked back at me. "This is illegal. All illegal."

"Not when it's for love," I corrected him.

"Still illegal. Probably a felony." Charlie wasn't smiling. In fact, he looked downright scared, which was good. He would run faster if the dogs attacked.

"You're telling me," I said, "if I stood in front of a judge and said, 'I took these flowers for a wedding bouquet,' he would put me in jail?"

"Yes. Because it's a crime."

"Well, you don't have to worry. We have a much better chance of being mauled by the dogs than going to jail."

"You guys better get going," said Denise. "She could be back any minute."

I stepped out of the car, and Charlie reluctantly followed. I tried to act brave while walking toward the house, but my knees were a little weak, and it was hard to take anything but short breaths. Focus. Think about pictures of your wedding in the pages of *Best Bride* magazine.

We reached the front gate, and the dogs charged, snarling and growling. I thought I saw one salivating, like the dog in *Ferris Bueller's Day Off*. The enormous beasts came to a stop at the metal front gate, which now looked flimsy next to them. They could probably tear it off by the hinges if they wanted to.

Charlie, standing behind me, checked to make sure no one was watching. I opened the package of steaks and handed one to Charlie. He took it gingerly, wearing Denise's pink gloves.

He wrapped his free arm around my waist and pulled me close. I felt my legs get even weaker. Our faces were almost touching, and it felt like a scene straight out of *Dirty Dancing*—Johnny and Baby ready to take the floor—except for the steaks we were holding and the salivating dogs.

Charlie leaned in close, our cheeks touching, so he could be heard over the snarling dogs. "How about I take you to Posh's Flowers? I'll buy you some roses. I'll even take you out for a drink. Please?"

"Are you asking me out on a date?"

"If it means I won't be going to jail and/or be shredded by monster Rottweilers, then yes, I'm asking you on a date."

Oh, how I wished I could take him up on that. But I just couldn't. I tried to explain in a way he might understand.

"Posh's roses are flown in from somewhere. They are scentless imitations of these. Come on." The last couple of words only squeaked out. I hoped he didn't hear the fear. I wasn't as scared of the dog bites as I was of stitches. Needles and thread and skin—just the thought made me shudder.

"That's not it," he said. "There's something else you're not telling me."

"I'm supposed to do this on a budget. I'm trying to win the *Best Bride* Budget Wedding Contest. I can't have you stepping in and paying for it."

"They can't expect you to be eaten by dogs."

"I don't know what they want. I just want to win!"

He looked at me, reading my face. I couldn't tell what he was seeing there, but he finally let me go. "OK. Shit," he said. "Let's do this."

For courage, I breathed in the overwhelming scent of roses as their soft perfume wafted through the night air. This was going to work.

I got up close to the gate and waved my steak in front of the dogs "See it? Steak." The Rottweilers were a lathered up, hot mess. "Ready Charlie? On three. One. Two. Three!"

Chapter 28

Charlie stood frozen at the garden gate, wondering if he was still breathing. He was pretty sure he wasn't, and suddenly realized he forgot how.

He estimated that the dogs snarling at them weighed easily 150 pounds apiece. They were lean, and judging by the way they were showing their teeth, not happy to see two rose-cutting trespassers near their yard. Sheila was right, he thought, the jail time looked preferable to being mauled by these two, and then explaining to people the rest of his life about his useless arm or missing limb.

All he could hear was, "One. Two. Three!"

Sheila threw open the gate, and threw her steak behind her and to the right. He copied her, and threw his behind him to the left. He realized that he had screamed louder than the snarls of the dogs as they sprinted past him out of the yard and toward the steaks.

Sheila grabbed him by the arm. "Charlie, you take that bush," she said, pointing at a bank of roses easily six feet high. "I'll take this one."

She snipped wildly, letting buds and blossoms on long stems fall into her bag—yellow, red, bright orange, and maroon. Charlie was having problems just getting his snippers to work, and Denise's gloves were so small. The thorns were cutting into his wrist.

"Jesus. Faster! FASTER!" screamed Sheila, looking at her watch. "It's already been one minute. We've only got about 30 seconds left."

Charlie tried, but he was clipping maybe one flower to every six of hers. And it was impossible to concentrate, listening to the dogs devouring the steaks, the remaining bones breaking and snapping in their jaws. The sound made his mouth incredibly dry and his heart pound loudly in his ears.

"Holy shit! There it is!" shouted Sheila. Charlie looked over expecting to see a third dog, but she was staring at a magnificent white rose, deep in one of the bushes. It truly was incredible. "This is going to be the centerpiece of Cheyenne's bouquet."

Charlie stared at her, amazed, as she skillfully reached in for the rose, a smile on her face. Denise was right. She was truly brave—scared of nothing as she went after what she wanted. Or maybe she was truly deranged. It was a fine line.

"Time!" she yelled. They both turned and ran for the gate. But Sheila's timing had been off. The dogs were trotting back in and blocked their path to the gate.

"Don't move," she whispered.

"You think?" he whispered back, wondering how he was going to explain an emergency room visit to his dad. Yeah, dad, I helped this gal steal some flowers. It seemed like a good idea at the time.

"Oh no," she said.

The dogs were slowly walking toward them, snarling. Charlie, not for the first time, thought: Sheila is dangerous. Just being in her air space has consequences.

"Grab your bag and get ready," she whispered.

Charlie ever so slowly turned his head a half-inch toward her and craned his eyeballs to see what she was doing. She was gently reaching into her purse and pulling something out. Whatever it was, it fit in the palm of her hand.

"What is that?"

"See what I got, boys?" she said to the snarling dogs. "Treats." Then she threw whatever it was to her right inside the yard. Were those Skittles? I didn't matter. They went for the bait.

"RUN!" she screamed.

Charlie's legs unlocked and he sprinted after Sheila toward the gate. Charlie saw the dogs reject whatever she had thrown, then turn back to them. He pushed Sheila through the exit, and was almost sure he felt the dogs' hot breath on his back as he slammed the gate shut behind him. All 300 pounds of dog smashed against the metal, and Charlie's heart lurched as he saw the one of the hinges give.

"Denise, we got to go NOW!"

He turned and saw Sheila banging on Denise's car window. "Hang up! We need to get in! The doors are locked!"

Charlie heard a second hinge give as the dogs threw their weight at the gate.

Charlie saw Denise hold up her phone, tears in her eyes. What the hell was happening? The dogs were breaking through. Without even thinking, Charlie acted. He ran toward the car and grabbed Sheila by the hand.

Sheila turned and her eyes widened when she saw the dogs just feet away.

Charlie ran around the back of the car, up onto the trunk, and then up onto the roof, pulling Sheila and her garbage bag of roses along. They both stood on top as the dogs reached the car. Luckily, what the dogs had in speed and size, they lacked in vertical leaping.

God they were big, he thought. That thought was followed closely by, Sheila has her arms wrapped around me—tight. And I don't think she's wearing a bra. Maybe things are looking up.

Sheila gazed up at him, catching her breath and smiling. "I guess they don't like Skittles." She looked down at the garbage bag in her hand. "We got the roses, though."

She looked so incredibly happy, he had to smile back. "What are you grinning about?"

"I don't know. Just happy to live through my first felony, I guess."

"This is your first? I didn't know I was working with a virgin." She laughed along with him.

The thought of kissing her while standing on top of the car, under the streetlights, in front of two snarling and lathering dogs sounded nice. Charlie imagined running his hands through her hair and under that halter top. He had never felt so alive. Every nerve was buzzing. He could smell the roses, the dogs, and whatever perfume Sheila was wearing. It felt like a cloud of scents. He could hear a car alarm going off a block away and a TV playing from inside someone's house. It must have been a comedy, because he could make out the laugh track. It was perfect.

Before he could kiss her, Sheila stomped her foot on the roof of the car. "Denise!" she shouted. "Let's get out of here."

The car stayed still.

"DENISE!"

The car jerked forward, and Sheila would have toppled off and into the mouths of the dogs if Charlie hadn't caught her. They knelt together on the roof as the car slowly drove away.

The dogs followed for a block or two, until they were assured the intruders were leaving, then turned and trotted back to the house.

Once the coast was clear, Denise stopped the car at an empty four-way intersection. Charlie reluctantly let go of Sheila. It wasn't just that he realized he wanted to hold her all night long, but that letting go felt like the end. He was leaving early the next morning, and he worried this might be the last real excitement he'd ever have.

Once Denise stopped the car, I hopped off. Not that I wanted to. I could have stayed up there all night, with Charlie's arms wrapped around me, and smelling like roses and sweat—in a good way, not the homeless man way. I wanted to stay in denial and pretend he off tomorrow to get married, but this was probably the last time I would ever see him, and from here on out, no guy would ever measure up to Charlie. Who else this cool would ever help someone like me with a wedding? No one.

Denise rolled down her window. "I'm sorry." She snuffed back tears and hit the unlock button. I got into the back seat and Charlie got into the passenger seat.

"Who was on the phone?" Like I had to guess.

"Kenny. He said he has a new girlfriend. Ashley Kirman. He said she'll be a great mom, and he wants custody of our baby."

"He broke up with you three days ago, because you were pregnant. Now that creepy bag of worms wants custody of Baby Coco?"

"It's a girl?" said Charlie.

I pulled out my phone and dialed Kenny.

"Sheila, don't," Denise pleaded. "You'll make it worse."

"How?"

As Denise considered, Kenny picked up. "What the hell do you want?"

The adrenaline from the past ten minutes pushed its way out of my body and into the phone. "Listen up, you enormous pig's ass. You stay away from Denise and her baby."

"It's none of your business, bitch."

"If you or Ashley get within a mile of her, I'll run both of you over with Denise's car—twice. And then I'll back up over you a few more times, just to make sure you're good and dead. Then I will fling your Frisbee-flat bodies over the Benston Bridge into the landfill and let the seagulls have at you."

"Bold talk."

"I'm tracking your cell phone right now."

He hung up faster than my mom can pocket a stick of cherry-red lip gloss.

Feeling satisfied, I put my phone back in my purse. Up front, Charlie and Denise were chuckling.

"I was serious," I said. "And, if you don't watch it, I'll run you two over too."

Their chuckling turned into laughter.

"I don't get the joke," I said.

"I'm picturing you throwing Kenny's Frisbee body off the bridge," said Denise, her tears turned from sadness to laughter.

Charlie was laughing hard enough he was too was rubbing away a tear. Had I seen him laugh before? I liked it. Although he was probably laughing mostly because he had just escaped death, he needed to do it more. It made him about ten times cuter. Maybe it was adrenaline, the scent of roses, or seeing the two of them enjoying themselves, but suddenly rabid dogs and creepy Kenny didn't seem so horrible.

A car came up behind us and honked for us to move. Denise stuck out her arm and waved it around. The car pulled up beside us — the driver a gray-haired lady holding a well-groomed Pomeranian in her lap.

"I saw what you did," the woman hissed. "You stole Alice's flowers."

"Her name is Alice?" I said. "Good name."

"I'm going to call the police. You're nothing but vile young vandals."

"We're not vandals, ma'am," I said. "We're wedding planners."

Denise and Charlie laughed louder as we pulled away from the lady, sitting in her car with her Pomeranian.

Chapter 29

Even with the windows down, Denise's car smelled of roses, and as we pulled into the entrance of the Wheel In RV Park The "W" flickered festively. We were all in a good mood after taking the flowers without a trip to the ER or the police station.

"I've driven by here a hundred times," said Charlie, "but I've never been in here."

"You've really missed a treat," I said. "Lots of pasty, old dudes without shirts, drinking beer and watering their patches of grass."

I mentally ran through everything Denise and I needed to do that night—make a cake, tell Kevin how to get his ankle bracelet turned off, arrange flowers, and a dozen other things. I hoped there was enough time for me to offer everyone a quick celebratory shot of tequila at the Brew and Suds to toast Charlie off in style. But as we pulled up to my place, all my thoughts vanished.

Swayze and Axel—my tiny security guards—sat in my driveway on their Big Wheels.

"Are those your kids?" asked Charlie, nervously.

"Do I look like the type of person who would leave her children home alone?" I snapped as I opened the door, jumping out.

"What's wrong?" I heard Charlie ask Denise.

"Her mom took her house," said Denise.

I ran up the drive, slipping in the gravel, up to the little kids. They looked so tiny in the empty lot. I shouldn't say it completely empty—the water pipe to the Airstream had been ripped free when mom stole it, and the space I had carved out under the trailer for my wedding supplies was filling fast with water. A dozen or so plastic containers—containing everything from ribbon and fabric to duct tape and spray paint—bobbed about.

"How'd she do it? I took the tires!"

Axel pointed to the Garcias' trailer two spots down. "She stole theirs."

"We tried to stop her," said Axel.

"We got them both with dog poop and the potato gun," added

119

Swayze.

"Both?" I asked as Charlie and Denise joined me.

"She had some big guy with her," said Swayze.

"We're sorry," said Axel.

"It's not your fault. You did your best." I tried to keep it under control, but I wanted to scream. Everything was in that trailer. My supplies. My movies. My clothes. My *Dirty Dancing* poster! My life! Say goodbye to a fabulous monkey wedding. Say goodbye to my chances in *Best Bride*. Say hello to homelessness.

"That wasn't all we did," said Swayze, holding up a tiny pocketknife that looked much larger in a six-year-old's hand.

"You kids shouldn't be playing with knives," said Charlie, stepping up.

"Who is he?" asked Swayze, pointing the knife at him

"A friend," I said. "What else happened?"

"Swayze tried to slash her tires," said Axel. "But the knife was too small. So I shot at them with this." Axel pulled out a flare gun from inside his hoodie. It took both of Axel's little hands to hold it.

Denise gasped. "Where did you get that?"

Axel ignored her. "I hit the truck, but it didn't stop them."

"How long ago did this happen?" I asked.

Swayze shrugged. "I can't tell time yet."

Carla yelled from her RV. "Ten minutes ago!"

"Shit! Shit! SHIT!" I screamed at the bobbing boxes of wedding supplies. I didn't think I was crying, but my vision was blurring, and a few tears slid down my cheeks and onto my halter top.

"You kids see the color of the pick up truck?" asked Charlie.

Swayze put out a hand. "Maybe."

Charlie calmly pulled out his wallet, removed a handful of singles, and knelt down in front of the two kids. "These are yours if you can tell me what the pickup looked like, and if you saw the license plate number."

They snatched the dollar bills out of his hand and held them up to the street lamp.

Swayze turned to Axel. "They're good."

"Sweet," said Axel.

"It was a tan Ford F-250," said Swayze.

"And it only has one license plate." Axel smiled at Swayze.

Swayze stood up, proudly. On the seat of his Big Wheel was the other license plate.

"Did you see which way they went?"

"Do you have more money?" asked Swayze, testing the waters. Charlie shelled out a few more dollars. Axel pointed toward town.

"Let's go," said Charlie. "They couldn't have gotten too far."

Axel and Swayze broke down in a fit of giggles.

"What's so funny, you two?" I asked.

Axel pointed to a few brown bananas scattered about. "They can't go very far. We put bananas in their tailpipe."

I could have kissed both of those little guys, but they were already riding their Big Wheels off to god knew where.

"Thank you!" I yelled at them.

They waved as their little legs pumped the pedals, the plastic tires scraping the pavement.

I felt hope returning. Maybe I wasn't homeless. Maybe the wedding would go on.

We ran to the car.

"How fast can this thing go?" asked Charlie.

"Tonight it can go as fast as we need it to," Denise answered, patting her bump. "Buckle up, Baby Electra."

"Electra?" said Charlie. "That's a terrible name."

Chapter 30

Denise was doing seventy miles an hour on the pothole-filled back road out of Benston. Her '83 Toyota shook like it might start throwing pieces at any moment. Charlie, Denise, and I all scanned the horizon for my Airstream. Nothing. Maybe the banana in the tailpipe was just a myth. Maybe my mom really was going to drive away with my house and business. Maybe I really *was* homeless.

"Don't worry," said Denise, reading my mind. "We're going to find it. And when we do, I'll take the flowers back to my place and get working on arrangements. And you'll start on the wedding cake. We'll be right back on track."

"I know you're right. But right now, can you drive faster?"

She jacked it up to seventy-five. Charlie's face lost a little color, and he grabbed the car door for support.

I tried to calm myself, trying to think about something else other than living out of a box. I pulled out my phone and dialed our DJ, Kevin. He answered on the first ring, and I heard music in the background—a good sign. "Hey, Kevin. You working on the wedding songs?"

"Yeah. But it's not going to matter because I'm still wearing this ankle bracelet."

"Here's what you do. You put your foot in the freezer for an hour. It turns off the bracelet."

"An hour?!" said Kevin. "Won't my foot get really cold?"

"Yeah, but it'll warm back up. It's a foot."

"What about frostbite?"

"Gees, wear some socks or something." I glanced at Charlie and shrugged. Kids.

"What time do you want me there tomorrow?" Kevin asked.

"The zoo closes at 6 p.m. The wedding party is meeting at the back entrance at seven. Wedding at eight."

"OK. See you there."

Knowing one item was moving along gave me a tiny ray of hope. I scanned the road ahead. Still no Airstream.

"That's another felony," Charlie pointed out.

"Driving too fast?" I asked. "You just get a ticket. You don't go to jail."

"Disabling an ankle bracelet. That's a felony."

"It's not a felony if it just gets cold, is it?"

"Well, no, but—"

"He's a really good DJ," piped up Denise, whose car was now hovering around 80 mph. "He makes everyone want to dance. Not just the drunk ones."

"But—"

"This wedding is for *Best Bride*," I said. "We need pictures of a real DJ."

"And this is Cheyenne's third wedding. We need to do it right," said Denise.

"Aren't you two worried about going to jail?"

"Oh my god, if we worried about going to jail every time we did a wedding, we'd never get anything done." But I *was* starting to worry a little. We had a baby on board now. Jails and babies don't mix.

Charlie was about to speak, but then he saw something ahead. "Slow down! Over there."

Denise slowed the car down. There it was. A Ford F-250 was towing my Airstream, but the Ford had pulled off to the side of the road, a tire blown, and lights flashing. Worse, was my Airstream—my beautiful 1973 silver home—on its side, with pieces of aluminum littering the road. The truck must have swerved when the tire blew and causing the Airstream to tip. My chest tightened, and my eyes welled with tears. No CPR was going to help my little friend back to life.

Mom stood on the side of the road by the truck, alongside a huge guy who looked like Kirk Cameron—if he'd spent the last 30 years getting wildly out of shape. They were inspecting the flat tire.

Denise pulled the car over in front of them, and I jumped out. The night smelled like a distillery. Some of Reuben's bottles had broken. They were leaking from the trailer all over the road. My sadness turned to white-hot anger. "You wrecked my house!"

Mom stepped away from the truck, her eyes narrowed. She marched over. She might be crazy, but she was still my mom and knew all my buttons. Heck, she'd created them. I took a deep breath. I was ready.

Mom pointed a bony finger at me. "Just leave now before I call the police."

"So you can report yourself for stealing my house?"

I heard Denise and Charlie getting out of the car behind me. For just a moment, I thought how nice it would be to have a normal mom for Charlie to see. But that was someone else's life.

"You're paying for all this damage," said Mom, waving her hand toward my trailer.

"You stole and wrecked my home! I'm not paying for SHIT!"

Mom smiled through gritted teeth. The fat Kirk Cameron looked up briefly from the flat tire at the commotion then went back at the tire.

"You act so tough, but you're just a spoiled little brat," Mom hissed.

"You left me at twelve years old to fend for myself while you were in jail. That's hardly spoiled. That's neglect."

"You're still holding that against me? Jesus, I left you with a case of Top Ramen and about a hundred movies. You were set."

I looked around to see Denise and Charlie were still there. Charlie stood, mouth agape. Denise was motioning me not to back down. She was right—I had some things to say to my mom, and on the side of the Old Benston Road was as good a place as any.

"A twelve-year-old cannot live for a year and three months on a case of Top Ramen."

"Well, you figured it out. You're tough. Look at you."

"Mom, I looked up the court records. When they arrested you, you never even told them you had a kid. No one was ever coming to help me."

Mom reeled like she'd been slapped. I never told her I knew. Mom took a moment to collect herself. The night was quiet, except for a car that drove by slowly, the passengers watching the roadside drama. Mom and I both flipped them off.

"I didn't tell them because they would have taken you away," she said measuring her words.

"Why didn't you tell *me*?"

"Because you'd feel like you owed me. And you do."

"How do you figure?" I asked.

"Because you didn't spend your life in foster homes. You spent your cushy little life in my Airstream, which I'm taking back now. And you're paying for the damages."

"Dream on," I said.

I saw my mom's hands ball up into fists.

I wasn't backing down. Not this time. "Last warning, Mom. Step away from the Airstream and get out of my life."

Mom just laughed and stepped forward, taking off her rings. I took mine off too and threw them at Denise. We were about fifteen feet apart. Holy shit, I thought, this is on. I had waited years to take a swing at my mom.

Fat Kirk Cameron made a move to step between us, but Mom's glare made him stop cold and step back.

"You're going to lose, old lady." I smiled, trying to show no fear.

Mom laughed again, this time her voice was so shrill, goosebumps rose up on my arms. "You wish!"

She charged, and it all felt like slow motion. Her eyes were crazy, and her hands were stretched out, her claw-like nails aimed at my face. I glanced at the Airstream behind her, picturing the wedding dress, movies, and *Dirty Dancing* poster tucked inside. That Airstream, no matter what shape it was in, was coming home with me. I cocked my arm back ready to let her have it.

My fist flew through the air, but instead of connecting with Mom's face, my body left the ground. I looked down, and there was an arm wrapped around my waist. Charlie swung me around, taking the brunt of Mom's fist with his back.

"Stop this. Now!" Charlie yelled.

Mom momentarily stopped and looked up at Charlie. "Who's this prick?"

******

Charlie had broken up a few fights on the construction site, but nothing like this. He could smell crazy coming off Sheila's mom. He knew Sheila was outmatched, and he could either break up the fight or take Sheila to the hospital. For a moment, he wondered how Sheila could stand up to this crazy woman, when he couldn't even stand up to a sane father. But it would have to be a thought he mulled over later. There was work to be done here, now.

He set Sheila on the ground and turned to her mom. "What's your name?"

"Loretta Lynn, like the singer."

"Loretta Lynn, I'll give you $2,000—everything I've got in my wallet—if you give Sheila the Airstream, and we call it a night."

"Two thousand? How stupid do you think I am? It's worth at least $10,000!"

"A beat-to-shit 1973 lying on its side is not worth $10,000," he said.

"Don't give her any money!" he heard Sheila yelling as she climbed up on top of the Airstream.

"If you've got $2,000 in your wallet, you can come up with more." There was a glint in Loretta Lynn's eye. Charlie wondered if she hadn't missed her calling as a used car saleswoman.

The door of the Airstream creaked, and Loretta Lynn's head whipped around. Sheila was climbing inside.

"You stay out of there!" screamed Loretta Lynn.

"I'm getting the wedding dress!"

"Get AWAY FROM MY TRAILER!" Charlie grabbed Loretta by the wrist to keep her from going after Sheila.

Charlie could feel things were going sideways fast. He turned Loretta Lynn around to look at him. "I've got $2,000 here. That's two grand for a trailer that wasn't worth that before you wrecked it. Take the money and leave."

"Or what?" she snapped.

"I'm going to reach into my wallet and pull out a card for the chief of police, who my family knows very well. You decide."

Loretta Lynn glared at Charlie, his wallet, and the dented Airstream leaking liquids onto the road, then back to Charlie. "Hand me the goddamn money. And it better all be there."

He handed her the cash, which she shoved into her bra without counting. She smiled and lit a cigarette, then walked toward the truck. As she did, she dropped the lit cigarette into the booze leaking onto the road. Her smile widened as a trail of fire raced toward the Airstream.

Chapter 31

I had thrown some of the Febreze out of the Airstream, along with several unbroken bottles of Reuben's booze, and was handing Cheyenne's wedding dress to Denise when I saw the fire racing toward me. "Run!" I screamed at her.

Half my body was sticking out of the top of the trailer, which had been the door before it was tipped on its side. I ducked inside, but not before the flames caught one side of my hair on fire before I made it in

I screamed, swatting frantically with my hands to put it out. Inside, the place was filling with smoke and stink. I had no idea how bad burnt hair smelled. I kept slapping my head, but could still hear the sizzling of hair. Next to my ear, it sounded like an inferno. I saw a future with my face disfigured by fire and a lifetime of ugly wigs. In the smoke, I groped frantically for something to put out my sizzling hair. All I could find was a flip flop and I pounded at my head with it, screaming until I could no longer hear my hair crackling.

Charlie's head poked inside through the top. "Are you OK? Give me your hand."

His arm jutted down through the smoke to help me. I grabbed at it.

"Are you burned?" he asked, lifting me out. We sat on top of the Airstream.

I looked at my hand holding a smoldering flip flop. It was red, but not blistered. My eyes were watering from the smoke, but I could see the fire was out—I guess alcohol burns off quickly. I also caught a glimpse of my mom driving away. I wanted to scream, but I'd lost my voice from yelling while I was burning.

Charlie checked out my head.

"Looks painful, but I think you'll live."

"What do I look like?" I croaked. I dropped the flip flop and reached up and touched my hair. It felt frizzled and wiry, like a Brillo pad, only worse. Like I'd suddenly grown a giant patch of pubic hair on the side of my head.

"Please tell me it's not as bad as it feels," I moaned.

"You're lucky."

"That depends on how you define lucky. Did your mom set *your* place on fire?"

He winced. "Sorry."

"No. I'm sorry." I turned to Charlie. "Can you help me back in there? I need to grab some stuff."

"It's still pretty smoky inside. Maybe you should wait."

Denise stepped up, trying to avoid looking at me. "I've got the wedding dress in my car. I found a few more cans of Febreze on the road that must have fallen out."

"Tell it to me straight," I asked pointing to my hair. "How bad is it?"

"On the bright side, you still have hair," she said trying to smile. "But we should stop by Value Village and pick up some hats."

My world was a disaster. My home was trashed, my hair was fried, the wedding was in less than twenty-four hours, and the coolest guy I knew was not only seeing me at my very lowest moment, he was also leaving to marry freakishly beautiful Julie. It was a new low.

"I called a tow truck to take your trailer into Benston. When they get here and set up upright, maybe you could go in then," Charlie spoke with calm, measured words, like he was talking someone off a building. "Right now it's best you stay clear of a smoldering trailer."

I stared down through the door, now a skylight. He was right, smoke was still curling out. It probably wasn't a good idea to go back in. But what did I have to lose?

"Just one thing," I said, dropping back in. The place was like a fun house, with the walls now ceiling and floor. And my table was sticking straight out of the wall. I tried to get my bearings. Where was my *Dirty Dancing* poster? Was it on the floor? No, wrong wall. It would be the ceiling. I looked up. It wasn't here. Then I saw it—what was left of it.

"NO!" I croaked out.

"What is it?" hollered Denise from outside.

While I was dancing around with my hair on fire, I must have ignited it. The last of the poster was sizzling away, the ashes falling to the floor. All that remained was a piece of Johnny's leg and some movie credits. I couldn't breathe. The poster that had gotten me through countless crappy jobs, crazy weddings, shitty boyfriends, and fights with my mom. The poster that reminded me that everything could be OK, even if you were from the wrong side of the tracks. The poster that told me there was someone out there for me—that romance wasn't dead.

Now it was nothing but black char at my feet. I grabbed the last bit of the poster and blew it out.

"Dirty Dancing is gone. Burned!" My voice was full of tears.

"Oh, no." I could hear real sadness in Denise's voice outside.

"What is it?" asked Charlie.

"We should give her a moment," said Denise.

I sat down on my stove that was now bolted to the floor and cried—big stupid sobs. I pulled out my cell phone and looked at myself. I didn't even recognize me—a face covered with black soot, tear tracks down both cheeks, and a wad of fuzz that was once hair sticking out of the side of my head. I stared at Johnny Castle's leg. I didn't think my life could get much worse.

"Johnny, what are we going to do?" I asked.

Dance, the charred poster scrap said. That's all you can do.

I kissed Johnny's leg, put it in my back pocket, and crawled out of my charred little home.

Chapter 32

Denise, Charlie, and I stood on the side of the road next to Denise's Toyota, which was filled to the brim with wedding supplies we had saved from my Airstream. We were waiting for an Uber driver who should have arrived 10 minutes earlier. Two large trucks sped by and one honked.

Charlie checked his watch again. "Where is he?"

I had a different clock running. It was 9:12 p.m., and we had a wedding in less than 22 hours and 48 minutes.

Denise caught my eye. She was thinking the same thing.

"We need to make the bouquet and centerpieces," said Denise. "And find cups, plates, tables, and chairs."

"Just to be on the safe side, I think you should bring your flute," I said. "I'm not sure Kevin is going to be able to get that ankle bracelet frozen, and you do a nice version of "Here Comes the Bride.""

"You could bring your boom box," Denise said.

"It got trashed in the Airstream," I said.

"Dang. That was a good one too."

"And then there's the wedding cake," I added.

"Did I hear you right?" Charlie asked. "Your wedding is tomorrow, and you're baking a cake tonight?" Those last words he yelled over another semi screaming past.

"It leaves less time for it to fall off a table, or an animal to get at it," I said. "Denise, you remember when you had that cat for a while?"

Denise grimaced at the thought. "Or worse," she said. "Someone could fall into it. Sheila, remember when you slipped and fell into the NASCAR wedding cake?"

Charlie looked confused. "I mean seriously. How do you bake a wedding cake? I saw the oven in that trailer. There's barely room for a TV dinner."

Another semi roared by. I yelled back. "It takes a while. You have to do it in stages."

An Uber driver pulled up in a dark green Subaru. Charlie looked at me, then at Denise's Toyota, and then back at me. "I'm going to regret this. But you can use my oven. I'm leaving in a few hours and won't be using it."

I could have kissed him. But instead I screamed, "YES!" to the night sky and ran to Denise's Toyota for the cake mixes.

Half an hour later, Charlie and I were lugging pans, boxes of cake mix, a couple cartons of eggs, and a gallon of milk into an elevator in his building—a new complex not far outside Benston. It was a three-story, modular thing that looked like someone had designed it with Legos.

"Ricci Construction worked on this building," he said. "It was my first building job after I got out here."

"Cool. Did you design it?"

"We hired an architect. But I had a hand in a few of the features."

The elevator door opened, and we stepped into a hallway that was bigger than my entire Airstream.

"I've got the loft apartment, second door down," he said.

When we got inside and set down the boxes, I was out of breath and my arms hurt, but I barely noticed as I took in the room. "Holy shit. You built this?"

"Well, I had some help."

We stood in a large open room—industrial and modern, but cozy. Tall ceilings, and a wall of windows at one end that looked out over Benston, made the room feel bigger than it was. The floors were made of dark planks, and a thick vertical wood beam in the center of the room looked like it was holding the whole place up. A big leather couch sat in the middle of the room, facing a wall with a flat-screen and an insert fireplace.

I gasped at the open kitchen in the corner. It had a double oven, a stainless steel fridge, and a huge island that also served as a table. And was that a refrigerator for wine?! I didn't think it was possible for Charlie to get even cooler, but he managed it.

"You said you were moving tomorrow. I kind of expected to see this place all packed up," I said.

"I've got movers hired to come in after I leave."

"You've got movers? Cool. So where are your mixing bowls?"

He looked around, like they might be in the living room. "I don't cook much. I'm not sure I have any."

"How can you not have any bowls?"

But he was right. I searched the cupboards and found 12 different kinds of breakfast cereals, a few coffee mugs, and some peanut butter, as well as a wide assortment of condiments, a few plates and a fork, but no mixing bowls.

"Sorry," he said. "I usually order out."

I kept looking and under the sink, I discovered a white bucket. It looked brand new. "Has this ever been used?"

"No. I got it thinking I'd use it for cleaning, but—"

"Let me guess. You've got a maid."

"It's a cleaning service."

"I wasn't judging."

"Sounded like you were judging."

I was. Having money must be nice. Ordering out, having your place cleaned. But then again, I ate at the Brew and Suds more often than I wanted to admit, and I rarely cooked. And cleaning my trailer took about twelve minutes. I decided to cut him some slack.

I grabbed a box of cake mix and emptied it into the bucket.

"You're not going to use that as your mixing bowl."

"You have any better ideas? It's already ten o'clock."

He shrugged. "I guess you'll be cooking out the germs."

"By the way," I said, opening the next box, "I'm going to pay you back the money you paid my mom."

"Consider it an investment in your business."

"That's nice but—"

"Hey," Charlie said, reading one of the cake mix boxes. "The pull date expired two years ago."

"How do you think I get them so cheap?"

"Is it safe to eat?"

"Pull dates on cake mixes are total bullshit. Milk and eggs, they spoil. I made a cake last year with a 2008 pull date. You couldn't tell the difference from the 2013."

"2008. That's over a decade old!"

"Tell me about it. It's the preservatives we should worry about," I said. "That said, I'm not going to tell *Best Bride* about the pull dates. I'm just hoping the budget wedding judges will be impressed when they find out I—sorry, we—made the wedding cake for under twenty dollars."

Charlie looked at the box once more. "You're sure about this?"

"Positive. I'm a professional. Where did you set the eggs?"

He reached over and grabbed the eggs.

"This is how it works," I explained. "We bake up twelve boxes of cake mix—that's twenty-four layers. We stack them up pyramid-style and cover it all with whip cream. If it looks like it's going to fall over, I've got chopsticks in the bag. We just nail it together."

"That doesn't sound so tough."

"Where it gets tough is the decorating. But Denise gave me a barrel of monkeys," which I also pulled out of bag. "So, we're set."

I set him to shaking dry cake mixes into the bucket while I added eggs and milk. In minutes we had a tub of cake batter and the first set of six-inch round cake pans going into the oven. I set the timer.

His oven was huge. It made mine look like an Easy Bake. Charlie looked in at the six pans baking and smiled. "You know, I think this is the first time I've ever used this thing. Nice to see it works."

He reached into a cupboard over the sink and brought out a bottle of tequila.

"I think we need to celebrate. Your wedding cake. And my oven getting used." He handed me the bottle while he got out two shot glasses. The tequila was Gran Patron. I had heard of it but never tasted it. It wasn't something they got a lot of call for at the Brew and Suds. I opened the bottle and filled our glasses.

He held out his shot glass. "To a fantastic wedding!"

"To a great new job in the big city," I added. He nodded solemnly as we clinked shot glasses and tossed the tequila back.

The golden liquid slid down my throat in a warm rush. It was heaven. "This shit is amazing."

Charlie raised a devious eyebrow. "If you're impressed with the tequila, you'll really like this." I followed him into the living room. We stopped in front of a picture painted on black velvet—a big Bulldog dealing cards to a table of cats, dogs . . . and Elvis.

"Pretty nice," I said. It wasn't the sort of thing I expected him to have in his apartment, but as far as black velvet paintings went, it could have been worse.

"Look closer." He nudged me closer to the painting.

I leaned in and looked. My breath caught. "Is that Elvis's signature? THE Elvis?"

He nodded.

"I didn't know Elvis painted black velvets."

"He didn't. My grandpa saw it somewhere. Thought it was funny and had Elvis sign it."

"No way." I reached out to touch the signature. I would be touching something Elvis had touched. Charlie caught my hand before I made contact.

"Are you crazy? You've got batter on your hands!"

I licked it off. "Can I touch it now?"

"OK. But just touch it. You still look kind of sticky."

I gently placed the tip of my finger on Elvis's name and felt a tiny shiver run through me and the hair stand up on my arms. "This is beyond cool."

"Thought you'd like it. You want another shot of tequila? I do."

I nodded.

"Sit down," he said. "I'll get your glass."

I walked over to the big leather couch, thinking Charlie might even be better than Jake Ryan. He loved Elvis. And he was serving me tequila. The good stuff no less. If this kept up, I'd find out he was a closet wedding planner. I sat down, and was instantly engulfed by the soft leather—a far cry from the worn pads in my Airstream. My muscles relaxed, muscles that had probably been tense since running from the dogs earlier that evening.

Charlie came back with the bottle and our glasses and sat down beside me. He handed me my glass and poured.

"We have nine minutes before the timer goes off. Why don't you tell me what's left on your list for this wedding tomorrow."

"You really want to know?"

"I feel like I have a vested interest now."

We tossed back our tequila.

"Well, like Denise said, I need tables and chairs. In the morning, I'm going to call our pastor, and see if he can bring some in his truck. I noticed some old ones from his church out in his demo yard."

"Of course. What pastor doesn't have his own demo yard?"

"I still need to figure out how to get the cake, chairs, glasses, flowers, and booze into the zoo. I mean, I can't carry it all."

"Of course not," he said smiling. "And let me guess, no one at the zoo is going to help you because they don't know they are hosting a wedding."

"Do you know what they charge at the zoo for a wedding? A lot. But we're going to be very good. Clean up everything. And—oh, no!" It hit me. I had forgotten something. Something big.

"What's wrong?"

"The flower girl and ring bearer."

"Maybe you can get by without them."

"Not this wedding. This wedding has to be perfect. And a perfect wedding needs a flower girl and a ring bearer. Shit! Even if I find them, what am I going to dress them in?"

Charlie leaned back, stretching his muscular arms over his head. For a split second, I thought he might casually drop an arm behind me, like a teenager on a first date. But no such luck. He was just stretching.

"When I was five, I was a ring bearer for my Uncle Don's wedding," he said. "I don't remember much. I hear I fell asleep on the altar. They had to wake me up to hand over the ring."

"At least you didn't eat the ring," I said. "I've had that happen."

"No way."

I nodded.

"Have you ever been a flower girl?"

"Once. My job was to throw rose petals. On the day of the wedding, they gave me a basket filled to the brim with real rose petals. I had never seen anything so beautiful and didn't want to give them up, so I hid them behind the garage where they were having the wedding. Then I tore up little pieces of toilet paper and put them in my basket instead. The bride had a cow when I came down the aisle throwing Charmin Ultra Soft."

Charlie smiled. It was a great smile, a relaxed smile. The Jake Ryan smile. The smile of someone who belonged in an apartment like this. His cell phone went off, he glanced at it, and his smile vanished and replaced with something I swear looked like fear. "I have to take this."

He stepped into his bedroom, but before he shut the door, I heard him say, "Hi, honey."

My heart broke a little. His world was so close, yet so far away. The oven timer went off. Luckily, I didn't need my heart to bake cakes. They came out perfect—lightly browned on top and cooked all the way through. I took in a big whiff of warm vanilla aroma. I could already see Cheyenne shoving a piece of it into the groom's face. A messy tradition, but what can you do?

I could hear Charlie's voice, low and concerned, in the next room as I got the next batch of cakes ready to bake.

Chapter 33

I was washing the pans in the sink for the last batch when Charlie returned to the kitchen.

"Your other life calling?" I asked.

"Something like that." He looked at the sink full of bubbles. "I have dish soap?"

"And a dish towel. Grab these pans and start drying. We need to get the next batch in."

He got to work, his arm brushing mine as I washed and he dried. I didn't dare look over at him. I thought he might be able to read my mind, which included throwing towels and cakes aside and doing less-than-sanitary things on the countertop.

"I noticed a lot of '80s movies fell out of your trailer tonight. You must be quite a fan."

"Those are actually my mom's. She used to like them, but after she got out of jail, she was different. But I hang on to them. Growing up, Denise and those movies were my best friends."

"Got a favorite?"

"Dirty Dancing," I said without hesitation.

"That's an old chick flick, right?"

"It's the chick flick," I said handing him a can of Pam. "You spray. I'll pour in the batter."

He took the can and sprayed. "What's so special about Dirty Dancing?"

"Are you kidding me? Understand Dirty Dancing, and you understand women."

"Really? One movie, and that's all it takes. How come we men don't know about this?"

I took the can of Pam spray from him. He was drowning the pans. "Because you ignore the answer to the age old question. Because it's not what you want to hear."

"What answer?"

I handed him a cake pan. "Hold this and focus. I need to pour this in." He held the pan firmly as I poured from the bucket.

"Seriously, what's the answer?"

"A man needs to look beyond the surface to see the real woman inside. He needs to fall in love that beautiful woman—the real one. And if he does, he's golden."

"I'm confused."

"Watch the movie," I said. "And hold the damn pan. I'm spilling this all over your counter."

"If I've seen Titanic, can I skip Dirty Dancing?"

"Nope. He dies in Titanic. That's not romantic," I said, opening the oven and slipping the last of the cakes in. "The last romantic movies were in the '80s: Sixteen Candles, Say Anything, When Harry Met Sally, Pretty in Pink, Romancing the Stone, Roxanne. Hell, even Top Gun is more romantic that anything today. Name one romance today that stands up to those."

"I'm sure there are some." He wiped his hands on his pants, leaving a glob of batter. He grabbed his phone. "I'll find some."

I grabbed his phone from him and hid it behind my back.

"No fair looking it up," I said. "That's my point. You can't think of any. Because there haven't been any."

"Thor was romantic," he said.

"No. Thor was not romantic. You're making my point. Men don't know how to romance a woman today, and women don't know how to be romanced, because it's being sucked out of our lives."

"I can be romantic."

"Really? Show me." Did I just say that?

He stood there for a couple seconds. I couldn't read his thoughts. Then he smiled. "You're on." He set the timer on the oven for twenty minutes. "Before the buzzer goes off," he said, "I'll prove romance isn't dead."

"Do I get to judge?"

"Sure. But you have to be fair."

"I'll be completely fair. Scale of 1 to 10, and you need a 10 to win."

"Fine."

We walked into the living room. Charlie sat and poured us each another shot. I sat next to him, my nerves tingling, and tossed my tequila back. My head was starting to spin a bit. I was going to have eat some real food soon.

Charlie looked into my eyes. "Sheila, you're amazingly beautiful. Your eyes are like . . . brown saucers."

"*Pffft!* I just told you the secret code to women's hearts, and you come up with 'brown saucers?' On a scale of 1 to 10, you get a 2.5. "

He thought hard. "Ok, I'm ready to try again."

He opened his mouth, and I stopped him. "You lose five points for doing anything while sitting on a couch."

"Point taken." He stood and went to his bedroom and came back with a guitar. He strummed it twice. It was almost in tune, and he began an off-key serenade. "Wild thing. You make my heart sing. You make my everything. Wild thing."

I tried not to laugh. He was so earnest. And so sweet. Personally, I would have just attacked him right then. But this was about romance. I stood strong. "I give you a 5."

"A 5?! I sang a song."

"And I gave you five points."

"Do I get another try?"

"You've got until the oven goes off."

He went into the kitchen. I heard things being shuffled around and cupboards opening and closing. "Almost ready," he said.

The anticipation made me feel like a little kid waiting to see what Christmas presents were going to be under the tree. For the first time in a week, I'd completely forgotten about the pending wedding.

Charlie came out carrying a breadboard.

"You've had a long day. And you've got another one coming up. I thought I'd bring you something to eat." He set down the board filled with chocolates, crackers, and cheeses. Just relax and help yourself."

He refilled my tequila glass, and I ate one of the chocolates. It melted in my mouth before I could even chew it. "Oh my god, what are these?"

"Belgian chocolates."

He stepped behind the couch. I turned around to see what he was doing.

"Just stay where you are. I've got this." His hands touched my shoulders, and I jumped. His fingers gently massaged my shoulders and then found their way to the back of my neck. My eyes closed. Stress was evaporating and being replaced by thoughts that were definitely R-rated, bordering on X. It was heaven.

"Feel good?"

"Uh, huh."

He continued the massage for another minute and then came back around, holding out his hand.

"What?"

He pulled me to my feet, then selected something on his iPhone. Music filled the room. It was "In Your Eyes," the song John Cusack played in Say Anything—one of the most truly romantic songs out there. Charlie was getting the hang of the game.

He pulled me close, and we began to sway to Peter Gabriel. Between the massage, chocolate, tequila, and now this, I felt like I was floating in a dream, dancing in Jake Ryan's living room.

Charlie's hands slipped into my hair. His mouth brushed my ear. A shiver ran from my head to my toes. "What's my score so far?" he whispered.

"You're doing OK."

"Just OK?"

"9.5." We locked eyes, our faces close, the music swelling. It wasn't a game anymore. It was the real deal.

We kissed. Not a smash-your-faces-together-because-you've-had-too-much-to-drink kiss, but a real one. A kiss that takes over your body and makes you feel like your feet are lifting off the ground. And mine were. We stopped and looked down and my legs were wrapped around his waist.

I'm sure he was startled with a full-sized woman suddenly wrapped around him.

"I'm sorry," I said. "Every time I kiss, it just happens."

"Don't apologize. I like it."

We kissed again, and I felt us moving. He was taking us toward the bedroom.

"What about the cake," I whispered.

"I turned off the oven when I got the cheese and crackers."

"You just got a 10."

Chapter 34

The bedroom door closed behind us, and clothes were flying off faster than a four year-old ripping open presents under the Christmas tree—and all done without breaking a kiss.

We fell onto the bed, and suddenly I had a moment of clarity.

"Oh, crap. Oh, crap. OH, crap!"

"What?" he asked. "What's wrong?"

"I want to do this. I do. I *really* do. I mean I have fantasized about this forever."

"You have?" He was looking at me, understandably confused.

"Of course. You're like the nicest, sexiest guy I've ever met. I mean, tattoo-your-name-on-my-ass sexy."

"Please, don't do that."

"But I'm a wedding planner. And you're engaged. That is like the worst karma ever. I'm sorry. I can't do this." I couldn't believe I was saying it. Out loud. I wanted to shut myself up, but it was just flowing out. "I should go. I'm sorry."

I tried to pull away, but he pulled me close—so close that every square inch of my skin seemed to be touching his. My breath caught and my stomach flipped a little.

"You don't have to go. I broke up with her."

"When?!"

"A few minutes ago while I was on the phone."

"And you didn't say anything?"

"I thought it might be a buzzkill."

"Not to me."

He laughed. "I see that now. To be honest, I didn't want to ruin my night with you talking about her."

I wondered for a split second again if I had slipped into a coma and the whole evening was just something my mind cooked up to help me handle my new state. I was lying in a hospital bed somewhere, tubes hooked up, with people standing around saying, "Do you think she can hear us?" But everything felt so real—the cool sheets, his warm body, and the smell of wedding caking hanging in the air. I grabbed him by the ears and pulled him in for another big kiss.

"Let's get busy then," I said.

And we did. An hour later, we were sprawled across the bed, sweaty, happy and exhausted, staring at each other.

"I don't usually do this," Charlie said.

"You mean invite a girl over to make a wedding cake and then have wild sex?"

"Yeah, that. But I meant, leaving the next day. I don't know when I'm getting back. I don't want you—"

"Boy, you ARE a buzzkill," I said, punching him in the arm. "I'm not asking you to marry me. We're just having a great evening. A *really* great evening."

"Ow! What are you? Ten years old?" he said, rubbing his arm. "I'm trying to say this is more than just a great night to me."

"Really? It's more than just a great night for me too." I punched him a little lighter this time.

I wanted the conversation to stop, because I was on the brink of blurting out something stupid like, "I want to have your babies." Or worse, "Let's run away, because compared to tonight every day of my life is going to be crap."

He smiled and whispered into my neck. "Let's make this night count then."

I rolled on top of him and stared seriously into his freakishly attractive face. " Buckle up, buttercup."

At 1 a.m. we took a break and staggered naked into the kitchen.

"I'm starved," I said, my stomach rumbling. I should have wondered why it felt so natural to walk around buck-ass naked with Charlie when I'd never felt comfortable being naked in front of any other guys. It just wasn't my thing. I thought I always looked better in clothes and heels. But there I was following Charlie into the kitchen like I did it every evening. I was too hungry to think clearly. I couldn't remember when I'd last eaten a real meal. Was it the Egg McMuffins Charlie had gotten me for breakfast when we left the police station the other morning?

"I'm starved too," he said. "Let me see what's in the fridge."

We stopped when we saw the twenty-four cakes on the counter. Some still in their pans.

"Even though I know they're over ten years old, they still look really good," he said.

"We can't eat them."

"I said they looked good. I had no intention of eating one," he said and headed to the fridge.

When he opened the door, the fridge cast a romantic glow over the kitchen.

"Let's see. I have some sardines, beer, cheese. Some olives. Why do I have olives? I hate olives."

"You like sardines, but not olives?"

"What's not to like about sardines?" he said. "They're little fish."

"Stinky, salty, little fish."

"Delicious, stinky, salty little fish."

We pulled everything out, and I found some Ritz crackers next to the Cocoa Puffs in a cupboard over the sink. We laid it all out on the counter like a weird picnic, and dug in.

"I didn't know rich people bought Cocoa Puffs," I said.

"What's wrong with Cocoa Puffs?" He shoved a handful in his mouth and washed it down with some beer.

"Nothing. I love Cocoa Puffs. In fact, these are the best puffs I've ever had." And they were. To be honest, I was so hungry, the Formica counter would have tasted good.

I cut off a chunk of cheese and tossed it in my mouth, followed by a Ritz cracker. I was too hungry to take time to stack them.

We looked at the sea of cakes.

"That's a lot of cakes." He shoved another handful of Cocoa Puffs in his mouth.

"Let's put it together," I said.

"Right now?"

"Yeah, it'll give us something to do while I get my strength back," I said.

"It seems a little, I don't know, unsanitary to do it . . . naked."

'It's not like you're going to be decorating them with your junk."

He considered as he grabbed another handful of Cocoa Puffs. "Ok, I'm in."

"Great," I said. "I'll get the chopsticks."

I realized we had a problem.

"Shit."

"What's wrong now?" he asked.

"We don't have a base for the cake. What am I going to haul it out of here on?"

"I know what to do," he said, popping open one of the Reddi-wip containers I'd brought to decorate the cakes. He squirted some whip cream onto his finger and drew a smiley face on my stomach.

"How's that supposed to help?"

"It doesn't. But now I have a snack for later." I watched his naked butt as he crossed to the far side of the kitchen and pulled out a breadboard that was built into the countertop. He brought it over and set it on the counter in front of me.

It was perfect—three feet wide and about three feet long. I arranged four cakes on the board. Charlie moved to squirt them with Reddi-wip.

"No!" I said, grabbing the can. "Reddi-wip melts. You have to wait until right before the wedding."

He grinned. "I learn the weirdest things hanging out with you."

"Well, now you're going to learn how to build a wedding cake. Grab four more cakes," I directed.

He stacked them on top of the others. "I wonder how many health code violations we're breaking," he said.

"Next time I'll make sure to bring hair nets."

He laughed as we continued to stack. After the fourth layer, the whole cake started to lean. I handed Charlie the chopsticks, and he slowly inserted them to straighten and secure the cake. He was an expert; all his construction experience had paid off.

As he worked, it was my turn to play with the cream. I squirted some on my finger and drew a smiley face on his back. Charlie's skin was warm. I added ears, hair, and a beard as an excuse to keep touching him.

He inserted the last chopstick. "Now what?"

"Tomorrow I take it to the wedding, slather it with Reddi-wip just before the guests arrive, and then I add these. I showed him the Barrel of Monkeys (the kid's game that is literally a plastic brown barrel full of little monkeys that link hands to form a chain).

We stepped back, taking in the naked cake. "Not bad for a ten-year-old cake," he said.

"I know." I grabbed my phone from my purse and took a shot for *Best Bride*, thinking maybe they might like before-and-after shots. I took extra care to make sure there were no naked parts of Charlie or Cocoa Puffs in the shot.

I set down the camera down and glanced at Charlie. He was gazing at me with a wicked grin. "Come here."

He lifted me up and over his shoulder.

"What're you doing?"

He grabbed a container of Reddi-wip.

"I'm going to practice my new caking decorating skills."

Chapter 35

I woke up in Charlie's bed. It would have been better if he had been in it with me, but you can't have everything. I looked over at the empty spot and rolled into it, trying not to be sad he was gone—just enjoy the glow of an amazing night.

It was monkey wedding day. Time to get my head together. I grabbed my phone off the bedhead and checked my text messages. Three from Cheyenne, one from Topeka, four from Denise. And one from Charlie. I checked Charlie's first.

Thank you.

Seriously? That was it? A wild, cake-filled night together, and I get a generic thank you? And what for? The conversation? The sex? The Reddi-wip?

Chill, I told myself. He's on a plane to another life. You're lucky to get the thank you. Now you're on your journey too. Get your shit together. Don't feel sorry for yourself. But there was a little tear in my eye. I wiped it away with his incredibly expensive duvet and got out of bed.

I checked myself in his bedroom's full-length mirror—something I didn't have in the Airstream. I grimaced. I didn't look too bad from the neck down. But my head . . . my head. Oh my god! The short, burned hair on the left side of my head stuck out like an angry rat's nest, and the other hair stuck out, stiff with Reddi-wip. My mascara was smeared, and there was a little lipstick on my chin.

And what else did I see in the mirror?

"AHHHH!" My scream filled the silent the room.

Standing in the doorway behind me, was a short, muscular man, in overalls, his mouth the shape of an 'O'. I grabbed the duvet and spun around.

"Who the hell are you?"

"I'm the mover," he said. "I wasn't told there would be someone here."

I'd totally forgotten about the movers! Who could blame me though after an evening like last night?

"Can you come back in about 20 minutes?"

"Sure."

"No, wait!" I said. "How are you at moving cakes?"

"We don't."

"You do today."

"Mr. Ricci didn't mention a cake," he said.

"If you call him, I'm sure he will tell you he just forgot," I said with confidence, or as much confidence as a deranged-looking woman wearing a duvet can have.

And that's how I got the cake and myself moved to Denise's.

Denise stood there in a pink robe, a little surprised when I, followed by two men and a cake, entered her place at 8 a.m., but she adjusted quickly, moving stuff off the kitchen table to make room. Her parakeet, Archie, chirped wildly as the men set the three-foot tall cake down, sighing with relief.

"Thanks," I said. "Any chance you guys can come by at six to move it to the wedding?"

"You're on your own lady," the short one who had seen my naked said.

"I had to ask." I searched in my purse for a tip. I found two dollars—my last two dollars—and handed them to him. "Thanks. I really appreciate it."

He looked at the tip, rolled his eyes, and shoved it in his pocket. With that, he and his partner were gone.

"Wow, last night must have been a heck of a night," said Denise, taking me in.

"How can you tell?"

"Your outfit for starters."

Oh yeah, I'd forgotten. I had cleaned up my makeup and hair, but I wasn't putting on my mini skirt and halter-top from the day before—they were stained and smelled like smoke. So, I had slipped on a pair of Charlie's briefs, which did wonders for my ass. I also threw on one of his button-down shirts, a pair of running shorts, and a baseball cap to cover my disgusting hair. The only thing of mine I was wearing were the heels.

"It was incredible. Beyond incredible. It was like being on a zip line all night. A wild, romantic, zip line."

"I've never been on a zip line."

"Me either. But I've imagined it. And this was better."

"While you were getting your zip line on, I was working." She pointed to the living room of her small, pink apartment. In the corner next to the TV was a box of leis made of ivy. On a coat hook hung a stunning bridal bouquet with a magnificent white rose in the center. Over on the rocking chair were four of corsages, and the banana centerpieces sat on the floor.

I let out a low whistle and patted her baby bump. "You and baby Alexis, went above and beyond."

"Isn't that the name of that computer thing?"

"No, Alexis is the name of a car. A nice car."

"We are not naming her after a car." She pulled off my baseball cap and gasped when she saw my hair. "Holy shit. It's worse than I remembered."

"I know."

"The shower is yours. And you can raid my hair products and my closet."

"You're the best friend ever."

"I know."

I looked around the room one more time. I couldn't help but smile. It was a wedding explosion. "I think we're going to crush this wedding today."

"Don't say that. You'll jinx it," Denise said.

Too late, I already had. My phone rang. It was Cheyenne.

Chapter 36

"I can't find him anywhere," cried Cheyenne.

Denise and I were standing on the porch of the bride's family's doublewide, which was in a high-end trailer park in Benston. Cheyenne was a total mess, with mascara dripping down her cheeks. Topeka stood beside her sister, slamming her fist into her hand so hard I was surprised she wasn't breaking bones.

It appeared the groom had been out of touch since the night before. Cheyenne was scared he'd gotten cold feet and it was more bad luck. I had seen grooms go missing before, but most of the time they showed up.

"He's probably under a pile of strippers," said Topeka. "I'll kill that little bastard when I find him."

"Let's kill him after the wedding," I said, trying to bring down the tension. "I'm sure we'll find him. I've seen—"

"Shut up," snapped Topeka.

"You shut up. You're just making everything worse," I back turned to Cheyenne. "We need to think of where he likes to hang out."

Topeka's eyes narrowed. "Didn't you used to date him? This is probably your fault."

God, I hoped this was Cheyenne's last wedding. I hated Topeka.

"I only dated him once in high school. It wasn't even a good date. No offense, Cheyenne. We just didn't hit it off like you guys did."

She nodded and sniffed back tears.

"You're probably seeing him behind her back," said Topeka.

Cheyenne gasped.

"Tony? No way. Gross."

"Gross?" wailed Cheyenne.

"See what you've done," said Topeka. "We should just fire you now."

"Cheyenne, he's not gross. What I meant was, the idea of dating someone I'm working for is gross. I'd never do it."

"Just admit it. You're a shitty wedding planner. We want our money back."

Maybe it was my aching heart now that Charlie was gone. I was hurting more than I wanted to admit. Or maybe, it was Topeka's tooth-challenged grimace, or maybe it was that I was going to do anything it took to get this monkey wedding in the pages of *Best Bride*. Maybe all of it caused me to square off in front of Topeka.

Denise grabbed my arm. "What are you doing?"

I shook Denise off, looking Topeka eye to crazy eye. "If you want to do something useful, go find Tony. If not, just shut the hell up."

"You little bitch." Topeka took a swing, I ducked, but I wasn't fast enough. The lights went out—fast.

I woke up in the passenger's seat of Denise's car. A light rain splattered the windshield, and my head felt like someone had taken a baseball bat to it, which was close to what happened.

"Did I win?"

Denise patted my leg as she drove. "You did quiet everyone down. Topeka even helped get you into the car."

I pulled down the visor to look in the mirror.

"Holy shit!" I touched my eye. "Oww!"

"Yeah, it's not pretty."

That was putting it mildly. My eye was swollen almost shut and turning a nice shade of smoky blue. And the other cheek had a scrape, probably where I hit the porch. It was going to take a buttload of cover-up and some big-ass glasses to hide this mess.

"Is Tony still missing?"

Denise handed me a list. "Got this from Cheyenne. It's the list of Tony's hangouts. She wants us to check them out."

I looked over list, basically the scummiest dude spots in town. "Seriously? Tits and Bigger Tits? She's going to marry a guy who hangs out there?"

"Look at the bottom one."

"No way."

"I can't go in there," said Denise. "Not with Baby Heidi on board."

"First, I need some ice and aspirin. My face is killing me. Second, Heidi sounds like some country bumpkin that runs through the hills yodeling."

"How about Heidi Klum? She's not a country bumpkin."

"Bet she yodels."

"We better agree soon. I don't want to have a nameless kid."

"We'll think of something."

I pulled a bottle of foundation from my purse. I wished I had my bridal makeup case. I carried twelve shades of cover-up in it. With my throbbing eye starting to turn shades of blue, I was going to use up the one in purse pretty quick. I tried to dab a bit, but it hurt so bad I stopped when both eyes watered so bad I couldn't even see from the good one.

"I need ice."

"We can get it at the first stop," said Denise.

We pulled up in front of Big Bangin' Babes, the worst strip joint in Benston. And that's saying something. Benston knows a thing or two about strip clubs. For a while, I think Benston held the record for the most strip joints per capita in the state. They ranged from little mom-and-pop pole dancing dives, to disgusting places like Big Bangin' Babes, which on a Saturday night was a pulsing hive and probably carried more diseases than patrons. A friend of mine worked there one night and quit. She said no one should go in without Kevlar.

Even at ten in the morning, there were a dozen cars outside. What kind of assholes need to see a stripper at 10 a.m.? Tony, I guess.

"Wait here," I told Denise. "Keep the car running and the doors locked. "

"Be careful!"

I approached the front door of Big Bangin' Babes, which resembled a black box. The only thing that gave it away as a strip joint was the name and some graffiti—a spray-painted sex doll. The graffiti wasn't half bad. Someone had talent.

I opened the door and stepped inside and let my one eye adjust to the dark. It looked like a disgusting storage facility. All metal and open spaces, except for a long bar and a stage in the middle. A gal about my age, wearing only a Daniel Boone hat and a G-string, was grinding to something she was listening to on her ear buds.

The place smelled like old booze and something rank I wasn't going to try to place.

There were three tables of guys spread around the empty room. I headed for the closest table, stepping over someone on the floor— hoping he was sleeping it off and not dead.

With my good eye, I checked out the four guys at the table. No Tony. Just sorry, half-drunk, purvey-looking assholes

"You seen a guy named Tony Lopez?" I asked. No one answered, but a wiry guy with greasy hair slapped my ass. I kicked him in the shin, hard. He yelled out, and his friends laughed as I moved on.

Wanting to avoid having my ass slapped again, I went to the bar. The bartender was a woman who looked as old as my mom, with her hair piled high on her head. She was wearing a lace teddy, which I noticed was frayed around the edges. Tips must suck here, I thought.

"I'm looking for Tony Lopez. Have you seen him?" I asked.

"You buying a drink?"

"No. I'm busted right now."

She shrugged and went back to cleaning a glass.

"Give me a break, will you? I'm a wedding planner. And we lost the groom."

She started laughing. "And you're looking here? Must be some wedding."

"You seen him?"

"Yeah. He and his friends were here earlier. Drinking pretty hard. Must have been a bachelor party."

"When did they leave?"

She rubbed a glass hard, trying to remember. "It was after Candy Cane danced, but before the police raided the place, so it must have been around 2 a.m."

"Thanks. And any chance I can have some ice?"

She wrapped some ice in a bar rag. "Who did this to you? Someone here?"

"No, it was the bride's sister."

"Maybe you should get into a different type of business," she said. "We've got a bartender opening."

"Thanks. I'll keep it in mind."

Wow, this day was hitting a new low.

For the next two hours, we hit every joint on the list. After the Big Bangin' Babes, we stopped at Big Tits, Two Tits, Big Titty, and Tits Galore (there is a serious lack of creativity in Benston). Tony and his friends had been to almost all of them at some point during the night, but they had moved on.

I climbed into Denise's car, applying new ice from the last bar. The swelling had stopped, but my eye was officially swollen shut.

"Think we should check the morgue?" asked Denise. "They drank a lot last night."

My head and eye throbbed. I popped a couple of Tylenol. "Why doesn't he have a cell phone like everyone else in the world? Seriously."

"Cheyenne said he had one, but he accidentally dropped it in a lake when he thought he saw a monkey."

"Of course he did."

Chapter 37

Charlie sat in the backseat of the company car, hurtling from the airport to his family's offices in downtown Manhattan, Charlie was on the phone with his sister, Camella, but he wasn't focused on the conversation. All he could think about was the previous night, which now seemed like a big blur—a beautiful, sexy blur. Like if you mixed Christmas, your favorite ride at the fair, and hot dogs into one, only better.

Camella's voice sounded intense, but he knew whatever she was saying he didn't want to hear it, because it meant he was now in New York City and would not be returning home any time soon to the life he had made for himself out in Benston. He wanted to bask in last night's blur as long as he could.

"Are you even listening to me!" yelled Camella.

"Sorry, sis. I missed a little of that."

"How much did you miss?"

"Umm . . . "

"Wake *up!*" Camella yelled even louder. "I know you broke up with your supermodel fiancé last night. But you have to focus."

"How did you know?"

"She called me and cried for an hour asking me to get you two back together. You know how I hate that."

"Sorry. I should have warned you."

"That woman is a self indulgent nightmare."

"I thought you liked her."

"Mom and Dad like her. You can do better."

"Thanks. I appreciate that. So, what is it that's so important?"

"What is it?! Everyone has been texting you."

He glanced at his screen. There were twelve texts and five unanswered messages. "Shit."

"You got that right."

The car was pulling up to the Ricci building. "I'm getting out of the car right now. I'm on my way up."

Charlie stared up at the Ricci Building, a twenty-five-story monument to his family. It was modern, with clean lines and lots of glass. Charlie's dad had a hand in designing it, and Charlie always thought it looked a little like him—short and powerful amongst the taller downtown buildings.

Charlie tipped the driver as he got out.

"You smell like cake," said the young driver.

Charlie smiled. "I do, don't I?"

Charlie climbed the steps of the building and pushed through the thick tinted glass doors into a massive lobby with marble columns—something that also reminded him of his dad, hard and cold. Two beefy guards stood inside the door. At the reception desk he was greeted by two receptions. He recognized the older one, Sharon, who was about his mom's age and also a skinny, no-nonsense type, and who had been handling the desk since Charlie was a boy. She pointed a bony finger toward the elevator. "They're waiting for you, Mr. Ricci, in the conference room. Eleventh floor."

"Thanks, Sharon."

Charlie walked toward the elevators trying to imagine what could be so important for all those messages. A corporate takeover? The death of a board member?

He noticed a little glob of cake batter had dried on the cuff of his pants. He knocked it off, thinking he would never look at cake the same again. A piece of his sleeve was stiff from dried tequila, which he hoped no one would notice. He had thought about putting on a suit that morning before he left Benston, but he didn't want to wake Sheila up. She looked so peaceful. Instead, he slipped on the casual clothes he had worn the night before.

Charlie ran his fingers through his hair. It would have to do, he thought as he opened the door into the company's conference room.

The conference table was surrounded by a sea of dark suits—the Ricci Company board of directors. His dad sat at the head of the table. In his jeans, cowboy boots, and button-down, sans tie, Charlie looked like the maintenance man.

"Charles, finally!" His dad, said. "Thought you might take an earlier flight."

All eyes turned to Charlie. "Long night—long story. I'm here now. What's going on?"

Camella sat at the other end of the conference table farthest from the door. She rolled her eyes and pointed to a free chair beside her. He quickly walked over and took a seat.

Camella had taken to the corporate life like Indiana Jones took to treasure hunting. It was in her blood. Charlie never understood the appeal, but he was proud of her. And she was super smart. She had skipped a couple of grades in school and earned her law degree by the time she was twenty-one; she had been legal counsel for the company for years. The siblings loved each other, but Charlie had known how very different they were since he was six years old and offered to teach her how to ride a bike. She had turned him down because she was playing office with her friends and was expecting some important calls.

Camella leaned in and whispered, "Dad had some heart issues last night. They've scheduled surgery and are admitting him into the hospital in an hour."

"Surgery?! Jesus, Dad. Why didn't you say anything?"

"We tried. You never picked up your goddamn phone."

"Sorry," Charlie looked sheepishly around the room. The Ricci board was staring back at him, disgusted, especially his uncle, Martin Ricci, and Martin's idiot son, Garrett, who his dad most certainly did not want to take over the company. Charlie felt small, out of place. He wanted to run out of the room and back to his regular life, where there was a woman, probably still asleep in his bed.

Charlie's dad broke the silence. "I've briefed everyone on the hospital visit and that I want things in order, with you at the helm, as of this moment. Just in case anything happens."

"Happens? How serious is this surgery?"

"Quadruple bypass," answered Camella, sliding a large document in front of Charlie. "The board voted unanimously to approve you last night. I drew up the paperwork. Uncle Martin and Garrett will witness."

Camella handed her brother a pen. "Just sign the last page."

Charlie tried to make sense of what was happening — his dad's surgery, the document, the board's judgmental stare.

He heard his father say, "Son, you're the CEO now. Don't let me down." When his dad smiled, Charlie could see the unhealthy stress around his eyes. He knew his dad had planned to be at his side, showing him every step to running the successfully family company. Things weren't turning out like either of them had wished.

With sweaty hands, Charlie took the pen from Camella. It was the sleek, ivory and gold pen his dad always used. The saying was right, he realized; the pen was truly mightier than the sword. This pen was going to change his life forever.

Chapter 38

Time was ticking away quickly. It was 2 p.m., and Denise and I had stopped at every bar and strip joint in Benston, as well as two funeral homes and a county courthouse, and we still hadn't found Tony, the groom. We decided to give up for the moment. Hopefully he would show up. We were running out of time, and there were lots of things left on our to-do list.

Denise and I sat in her apartment, putting our final game plan together.

"We need to head back to my place," I said.

"You don't have a place anymore."

"I know. But I need some stuff that was under the trailer." I slipped out of Charlie's shirt and gave it one more big whiff before I set it aside and traded it for one of Denise's pink lace tops.

My cell rang and Denise answered it. "Hi, Cheyenne. It's me, Denise." There was a long pause as Denise listened to what was undoubtedly a freaked-out bride. "We just got back from looking. You don't have to worry," Denise lied while giving me a "we're screwed" look. "We're on top of it. No problem. See you soon."

Denise hung up. "Cheyenne wanted to know if we found Tony and who we got for a flower girl and ring bearer. Do we even have a flower girl and ring bearer?"

"Crap. I forgot *again*!" I grabbed my little red book to add another note. "Do you know any little kids?"

"Renee has a couple, but all they do is set fires."

"What about Mandy's two kids?"

"They're in high school."

"No way. They can't be that old, can they?" I said, pulling off Charlie's running shorts.

"Do the math," said Denise. "We graduated ten years ago, and she got knocked up our freshman year and—are you wearing Charlie's underwear?"

"Yes. But look at how good they make my ass look! I'm never taking these off."

"Your ass does look great. Do they feel weird?"

"They feel amazing. You should try them."

"No thanks. You look ridiculous," said Denise.

The phone rang again. This time I picked it up. I could hear the screaming on the other end before I even put it to my ear.

"My foot! It's dead! It's DEAD! You killed my foot."

Denise handed me a pink-and-white cotton miniskirt, and I slipped it on over the briefs. "Kevin, just calm down," I said. "What happened?"

"I put my foot in the freezer for an hour, and now it won't work. It's like . . . frozen."

"Does it hurt? Can you drag it?"

"I can't feel a thing. I took my sock off, and two of my toes are blue. Like the color BLUE!"

"Relax. Those are just the first signs of frostbite. I looked it up on WebMD. You're fine."

Denise mouthed, "You looked it up?" I shook my head.

"Are you sure?" Kevin's voice had dropped a frantic notch.

"I'm sure. You'll be just fine. What about the ankle bracelet?"

"I think it's frozen too. The light's off."

"That's' great. That means it's not working. We'll see you at the zoo. Come in the back way."

"OK."

I dropped my phone into my purse. "Let's get going. I think I know where to find a ring bearer."

Chapter 39

The sky was overcast, and it was raining lightly when we pulled into the entrance of the Wheel In RV Park. I had checked the weather report earlier. There was supposed to be no chance of rain that day. I don't even know why we have weathermen in the Pacific Northwest. They suck.

I looked at my watch. It read 3:21 p.m.

My trailer lot looked like it had been the site of a tiny concert— empty except for a muddy mess of litter strewn about. The water had been turned off some time after my mom ripped the Airstream from the pipe, but now my boxes of supplies that had been stored under the Airstream sat in the muddy pool. A few brown bananas were scattered around like tiny body parts. The box that contained all my orange and white feathers from a parrot-themed wedding last year had broken open. The feathers floated around, catching in the wind and mud. In the center of it all, Pastor Bee's ape-hand birdbath reached to the sky.

"This is kind of disturbing," said Denise.

"Most people get regular moms. Why did I have to have a monster?"

Denise put a hand on my shoulder. "Some people just aren't meant to have kids. I hope I'm a good mom."

"You wouldn't steal your daughter's home, would you?"

"Never!"

"Then you'll do fine."

I patted her bump, which seemed to have grown overnight. "OK, kid, watch and learn," I said.

I kicked off my heels and waded out into the muck. "Denise, I'm going to pull out the boxes. You drag them to the car."

Denise nodded. Within half an hour, a dozen boxes were all lined up beside her car, and we were checking their contents. It was still drizzling, and our hair and clothes were plastered to our bodies.

We took what we needed—the box with the paper plates, plastic cups, and silverware, the box of vases, and the one with the few remaining banana centerpieces that hadn't gone bad. We also took the box full of true wedding essentials—a hammer, nails, duct tape, drills, and such. We left the boxes of past issues of *Best Bride*, one with fabric samples, two of decorations, one of candles, and a miscellaneous box of cat toys.

"I don't remember a cat-toy themed wedding," said Denise.

"Me either. Weird."

"They're mine," called Carla from inside her trailer. "I ran out of room. Don't touch them."

I was about to ask her how long I'd been her storage facility, when I heard the patter of plastic on cement. Swayze and Axel pedaled their Big Wheels up beside the car and peered out from under their damp hoodies.

"Sorry about your house," said Swayze.

"It looks terrible," said Axel.

"How'd you see it?" I asked.

"Duh. We pedaled down to the tow yard," said Swayze.

"That's at least two miles away," gasped Denise.

They shrugged and stepped off their Big Wheels in unison to check out the carnage. Axel grabbed one of the brown bananas.

"You two don't know a couple kids your size that would like to be in a wedding, do you?" I asked. "I need a flower girl and a ring bearer."

They looked at each other, then to me.

"We can do it," said Axel. "We can go with you right now."

"You can't," I said.

Swayze pointed a half-eaten banana at me. "Why not? You just said we're the right size."

"First, you are two boys, and I need a girl and a boy."

"Swayze's a girl," Axel said, grabbing her hoodie and pulling it off. Like magic, there was a beautiful little girl, with messy blond hair.

Denise stepped back. "You *are* a girl!"

"Of course, I'm a girl," said Swayze. "Why would you think I was a boy?"

"Are you a girl too?" Denise asked Axel.

"No!" Axel pulled off his hoodie. The two weren't identical, obviously, but they were definitely twins. Axel's hair was shorter and darker—and looked self-cut—and his eyes were a little darker than Swayze's.

"We're perfect for the job," said Swayze, taking another bite into her brown banana.

Still reeling from the Swayze revelation, it took a moment for me to answer. "You're perfect. I just need to get permission from one of your folks."

Axel spoke from behind a mouthful of banana. "They're at work."

"What's their number? I'll give them call them?" I was already wondering what it was going to be like talking with whoever raised these two.

"No," said Swayze. "It's impossible to get them."

"Because they check for mines," said Axel.

"They don't let you have phones when you do that," explained Swayze "Could get you blown up."

"Your folks are hunting for landmines in Benston. Seriously?" said Denise.

"There are lots of them," said Swayze.

"It's a big secret," said Axel. They both nodded gravely.

"As much as I would love for you two as my flower girl and ring bearer, it can't happen unless I talk to your landmine-hunting folks."

"Why?" asked Swayze.

"Because it's illegal to just pick up kids and take them somewhere."

"Even if it's a wedding and we said OK?" said Axel.

"Yes, even then," I said. "You know me. I don't mind breaking a few rules for a wedding. But kidnapping? Police are real serious about that one."

Axel and Swayze shared a deep stare. An unspoken conversation was taking place.

"Where's the wedding?" asked Swayze.

I wasn't taking the bait. "Too far for you guys to Big Wheel it,"

Axel, still thinking, picked up another brown banana and peeled it. "What's your number? We could have our mom call you."

"That works." I gave him one of my soggy business cards I found in the mud. Then I walked over to one of the plastic boxes we were leaving behind. Inside was a gallon of soapy liquid and a bubble machine I'd gotten off Craigslist.

"All yours," I said, handing it to the twins. "Someone's probably going to steal it today anyway. Mostly likely you two."

The kids' eyes lit up. "Really? Ours?" they squealed in unison. They splashed through a puddle to get to it.

Denise and I drove away, watching them duct tape the box with the bubble machine onto one of their Big Wheels. I should have been happy to watch them pedal away with their loot, but something was bothering me. It felt a little déjà vu.

"That was nice of you to give them that," said Denise. "You're going to be a great aunt for Tina Fey."

"Tina Fey isn't bad."

"You like it? Really? Did we just agree on a baby name?"

"They are going to shorten it to Tina, though."

"They can't," said Denise, the joy draining from her voice.

A girl named Tina used to bully Denise in grade school. Tina was huge and came from the rough side of Benston, which was saying something. Every day Tina would push Denise into someone or something. Why she did it was anyone's guess.

Denise spent third, fourth, and most of fifth grade on edge, ready to be tipped over by the giant girl. You'd think Denise could have avoided Tina, being that Tina was huge and should have been easy to spot, but Tina was stealthy. She could sneak up on you in an empty hall. Probably a weird survival skill she had picked up living on the sketchy side of town. It finally stopped when Tina's family moved to Seattle. I heard Tina joined the army. I always picture her now sneaking up on tanks and pushing them over.

"Thanks for ruining another name," said Denise.

"It wasn't me. It was Tina who ruined it."

"Good point," said Denise. "Where are we headed?"

"To the Airstream. I need some dry clothes and makeup. I forgot to get them last night."

"Was there any more of Reuben's booze left in there? We only got four bottles," added Denise. "That's not enough for Cheyenne's family."

"There might be some in a box next to the fridge. It was hard to tell with all the smoke."

My cell phone buzzed. I didn't recognize the number, but answered anyway. The voice on the other end coughed a couple times before saying, "Hello, is this Sheila?" Although it was a decent attempt to sound like an adult, it was definitely a little kid. I put my phone on speaker so Denise could hear.

"Is this Swayze?"

"No. This is Swayze's mom. I'm calling to let you know that Swayze and Axel can go to the wedding and be a bride girl and ring boy."

I played along.

"Thank you for calling Mrs. . ."

"Smith. My name is Annabelle Smith."

"Annabelle, I would love to have your kids at the wedding this evening. I'll need a note though."

"What does the note need to say?" asked the person who was clearly Swayze.

"I give authority for my children to be flower girl and ring bearer at Sheila Johnson's wedding."

"We can do that."

"We?"

There was only the slightest hesitation. "I meant me and my husband . . . Rocko." I heard Axel whisper, 'Good job' in the background.

"Where should I meet you to get that note?" I asked.

There was a longer silence. "I'll leave it on top of the ape hand, where your trailer used to be. Thank you. Goodbye. I have to go hunt for some more bombs."

They hung up and Denise looked at me, "Where do you think their mom really is?"

"No idea," I said, having a strong sense déjà vu again. "We still need kids though. We have a wedding in four hours. Keep thinking."

Chapter 40

We decided to swing by Denise's place, where we changed out of our wet clothes. I threw on pink leggings, pink running shoes, and her pink T-shirt that read, "Who's Pete Sake?" I was going to wear her pink cut-offs, but Denise is about two sizes smaller than me and my ass hung out too much for a professional wedding planner.

I grabbed some cover-up off her dresser and tried to hide my black eye, which was still throbbing and too swollen to see out of. While I dabbed on the makeup, I thought about Charlie out there somewhere, already living another life. Doing something corporate. The night before already felt like forever ago.

I tried to put him out of my mind and focused on Swayze and Axel. Something felt off with those two. I couldn't quite put my finger on it. Not like anything was normal about them, but there was something else.

I walked into the kitchen and was overpowered with smell of roses and Bamboo Febreze, which Denise was using to spray a box of handmade ivy leis while she talked on the phone.

"We hit all the clubs," she said to someone. "Sheila even got punched!"

Denise hit the speaker button, and I could hear Cheyenne crying on the other end.

"Cheyenne, Sheila here. You need to stop crying. Everything's going to be fine."

"But Tony is gone!" The words were hard to make out between the sobs.

"Take a deep breath. Are you listening to me? Deep breath."

I heard a jagged intake.

"Good job. Keep breathing and listen to me. This is your wedding day. *Your* day. This evening you're going to look beautiful, and Tony will be there. Your family is going to be there. Everything is going to be stunning. And you're going to be gorgeous, standing up there in front of those monkey cages. And afterwards, you and Tony will leave, to spend the rest of your lives together."

"You really think?"

"I don't think. I know. All weddings look messed up right before the big moment. Remember your last one, when we had to bail Topeka out of jail for robbing Home Depot?"

"She wanted to get me that microwave for a wedding present."

"And that all worked out. Right? This one will too," I said. "You just relax. Enjoy the day. Because you need to look fabulous in a few hours for your wedding."

The crying had stopped. There were just a couple hitched breaths.

"Do you believe me?" I asked.

"Yeah. I do."

"Good. Now go take a long bath. Relax. Do your hair. And if you hear from Tony, let me know."

"I will."

I hung up and Denise put a hand on my shoulder. "You really believe all that? That everything is going to be OK?"

"Absolutely. All we need to do is find Tony—who is probably dead in a ditch somewhere—get the booze out of my trailer, break into the zoo, and set up a wedding while not getting thrown out or arrested before they say "I do"—all while I get some great pictures for *Best Bride*. Piece of cake." I reached into my purse to see if there was any tequila left in my flask.

"Why are weddings always so difficult?" asked Denise.

"I don't know. You got more Tylenol? My eye is killing me."

Denise went into the bathroom. I opened the flask from my purse and took a sip. The liquid slid down my throat. It was the good stuff! Charlie's good stuff. I had missed the note taped to the bottom. I pulled it off and read, *Good luck. I think you'll need this. XOXO Charlie.*

I tried to smile, but two tears were busy chasing each other down my cheek.

Chapters 41

Denise drove us to the wrecking yard. At least it was close—about three blocks behind the Beer and Suds.

It was two acres filled with every type of mangled car, truck, and SUV. They were missing doors, windows, bumpers, hoods, and engines, like they were in the process of being eaten. I guess, in a way they were, by guys in dirty T-shirts and jeans who parted them out.

At the gate, we looked in and spotted my poor little Airstream. There was an immediate lump in my throat. It was alone there, with black streaks from the fire up one side. They had propped it upright, but the left side—the side that had connected with the street—was bashed in and scraped, and two of the windows were broken. Sticks and dirt hung from the wheelhouse. My little home, which had taken care of me since I was twelve, looked back at me forlornly. I wanted to say, "It'll be all right. We'll get you back together, good as new," but that wasn't going to happen. Men with crowbars would eat my little home piece by piece.

"It looks so much worse in the daylight," said Denise, her lip quivering, close to tears.

"I know," I said, trying to ignore the lump in my own throat.

We buzzed to be let in. A grimy guy, about 35, who looked like he lived on a diet of cigarettes and beef jerky, walked over. He wore overalls that were probably orange at one time, but were so covered with grease they were more of an autumn brown. If he took them off, I'm sure they'd stand up on their own. He lit a cigarette.

"Is that a good idea?" said Denise, putting a hand on her belly to shield the baby. "You look . . . kind of flammable."

"I haven't gone up yet," he said. "What do you two want?"

"I need to get some things out of my trailer over there," I said.

"You mean my trailer."

He had the upper hand, since he was on the other side of the locked chain fence. "That's my house. My mom stole it last night. I just need to get some of my things out of there. Have a heart."

He looked us over. Denise took a little side step behind me.

"Two hundred," he said.

"Dollars?! Are you shitting me? That's *my house*."

He smiled. "Don't look that way to me."

"Well, I don't have $200."

His grin got a little wider. "How about a date?"

"In your dreams." I couldn't believe it. In a matter of hours, I had managed to go from being romanced by Mr. Amazing to being propositioned by Mr. Greaseball. It was like going from a steak dinner to dog food. Not even good dog food.

"I'm just making a deal," the man said. "I let you in here for a half hour to grab some things, and you go out with me." He motioned to my eye. "I can tell you like the rough stuff."

"I *don't* like the rough stuff. I'm a wedding planner."

He smiled, showing off nicotine-stained teeth that were almost the same color as his overalls. "Sweetie, whatever you say. You'll find I'm pretty charming once I'm out of my suit here."

I looked back at Denise, who was shaking her head ever so slightly.

"Can you let me have a moment with my friend?"

"Be quick. This deal ain't going to last long." He lit another cigarette with the stub of his last one.

I backed up a few steps to talk to Denise, who looked like she was close to throwing up. "You can't go out with that man," she said flatly. "He looks like he belongs in a penitentiary—at least."

I looked back at Mr. Greasy, who I saw had a big old scar on his left cheek I hadn't noticed before. He smiled, pointing to his watch. "Tick-tock, ladies."

"I need my clothes and makeup. And we gotta have that booze," I said. "What if I just do a coffee date?"

"He doesn't look like the coffee date type."

"Got a better idea?"

"Maybe rethink your profession."

"What am I thinking? I know what to do. I'll just give him my address," I said, and marched up to Mr. Greasy.

"OK, big boy. You and me, next Saturday. Now let us in."

"I pick the date. Tomorrow. "

"Tomorrow." My stomach lurched at even standing next to this man. "You know, you need a better way to pick up women. Blackmail is not cool."

"I work with what I got," he said.

Within twenty minutes we were filling Denise's trunk with five more bottles of Reuben's moonshine, my two makeup cases, my favorite perfume, and a sack of smoke-scented clothes and shoes. Mr. Greasy watched from his office doorway.

"I couldn't find the *Dirty Dancing* DVD," said Denise, helping me put things in the trunk.

"I saw it smashed on the road last night," I said. "But I found something better."

I held out another piece of the *Dirty Dancing* poster I'd found in the sink. It must have flown off when it caught fire. The piece was maybe three inches across and two inches tall, and you could see Johnny's hand around Baby's waist, and even a tiny bit of the "y" from Patrick's signature.

"Cool, huh? I think it's a sign things are looking up," I said, tucking the piece safely into my little red notebook.

"Things are *not* looking up. You gave that creep your address."

"I gave him the address to Big and Bigger Tits. I'm not going out with that freak."

"Oh, thank god," she said, and gave me a little hug.

I checked my phone. No message from Charlie. He was gone. Really gone. Off on his new life. Denise was right, things did suck a little at the moment, but what didn't suck was the night before. I would just have to relieve that memory when things got bad.

"Hey, this ain't your address. I know this place!" yelled Greaseball. "What're you pulling?"

"Let's go!" I yelled to Denise.

Chapter 42

Charlie and Camella sat alone in the conference room. After Charlie had signed the document making him CEO of the company, all the suits had marched out of the room behind his dad, just like well-dressed robots. He could imagine them all standing around the operating table with blank faces as the surgeons worked on his dad.

"Are they going to follow me around like that?" asked Charlie. "I don't think I could handle it."

His sister laughed. "Don't look so scared. I'm here. And you know my firm's motto, 'We clean up what Dad screws up.' All I'm doing is switching names."

Camella was wearing her signature outfit—a black pantsuit, white shirt, and pearls, and Charlie knew she was the meanest and smartest person who had been in the room—that included their dad. "I like the name Camella," she would tell clients. "It rhymes with Cruella."

At least a hundred times, Charlie had brought up that he thought Camella should be the CEO of the company. She could run it so much better than him or dad. Her response was always the same. "Run that boy's club? God, no."

She enjoyed brutal litigation. The bloodier, the better. Charlie imagined one of her past lives was that of some Spartan warrior, screaming into battle with a smile on her face, dead bodies in her wake. Throughout his life, whenever he got into trouble, she was the one he looked to. Like the time one of his construction guys got drunk, stole an excavator, and drove it into the side of a Safeway. Her law firm stepped in and handled things so quickly, it was as if it had never happened. But what he really admired was how she stepped in as a sister. Like when his senior prom went south. He had gone to pick up his date, Annie Waters, only to find out she had already left with an asshole named Arthur Cooley, a senior from a neighboring school. Charlie sulked back to his car and called Camella, trying not to sound devastated, but doing a terrible job.

"Get your ass over here," said his sister, who although younger than him, was already a junior at NYU.

169

He drove to the campus, ashamed and defeated. He knew he was shy when it came to girls. What could Camella do but confirm what he already knew? He was going to be a dateless wonder forever. Twice he thought about turning around and going back home, but Camella knew him well. She texted him nonstop until he drove into the university parking lot. There she was, all dressed up in a little black dress and makeup, her blonde hair spilling over her shoulders.

"I didn't know you had something going on," said Charlie. "I can go back home."

"Don't be stupid, you little sad sack." She took him by the hand and led him to her dorm room where there were five beautiful girls, all equally as dressed up. "We're taking you out for a proper prom," she said.

It was a night of dreams. Six gorgeous college women escorted him into his high school prom. They surrounded him wherever he went, even on the dance floor. After making a suitable appearance in front of his classmates—and most importantly, Annie Waters—they took him clubbing. Everywhere they went, people stared at the beautiful girls and the dorky guy—his sister leading the way, ordering drinks with a fake I.D., and orchestrating the entire evening.

At the end of the night, Camella and the girls dropped him at his car. Camella smiled, ruffled his hair, and kissed him on his cheek. "I texted you a few pictures of everyone dancing and grinding. If you want some real closure, send a couple of these to Miss Annie What's-her-fuck."

It was one of the best nights of his life, and probably one of Camella's too—she was absolutely in charge, crushing the evening and cheering up her little brother all at the same time.

She would have to come to his rescue again, because he knew he was in way over his head as a chief executive officer. Leading a corporation would be a far cry from running a construction company.

"How serious is this thing with dad?" asked Charlie.

She shrugged, but Charlie read his sister's shrugs like the blind read braille.

"That bad, huh?"

"Valve replacement is risky because his blood pressure is out of control. Mom is freaking out. As soon as word got out about his condition, the company stock took a drop. Everyone is looking for someone . . . " she pointed at him, "to stand up and take charge."

Charlie felt a wave of nausea. Life was spinning way too fast. The scent of Sheila's perfume still hung on his clothes, there was still dirt from construction work under his nails, his dad was rolling into surgery, and he was sitting in a conference room that would probably become his new home.

His heart beat hard in his chest, causing a ringing in his ears.

"You're not going to pass out are you?"

"I don't think I'm ready for this."

"No, shit. You should have been preparing yourself instead of playing with your Tonka Toys."

"Good thing you didn't go into medicine. Your bedside manner sucks."

"If I had a nickel for every time I heard that . . . " Camella said, leaning in. He thought she was going to kiss him on the cheek, but she sniffed his shoulder instead. "You smell like birthday cake and cheap perfume."

Charlie smiled for the first time since the plane had touched down.

"Has my big brother fallen in love? That must be why you dumped that vapid little manipulating bitch."

"You're good. Mom's going to be pissed. She loves Julie."

"Mom can marry her. What's this woman like that's stole my brother's heart?"

"A little like you. Goes after what she wants. Tells it like it is."

Camella nodded. "So far, so good. What's she do?"

"Is this an interview?"

"Maybe. A little," she said smiling.

Charlie wasn't sure how to put the next piece, so he just laid it out there. "She's a wedding planner and works at the minimart."

Camella's mouth dropped open ever so slightly. Charlie tried to read her expression. but couldn't. Finally, she blinked, then smiled. Then laughed. Not a little snicker but a big, full laugh that echoed in the empty conference room.

"I can hardly wait to meet her," Camella said. And he could tell she meant it. There was nothing but love there.

"Mom's going to hate her."

"Probably." Camella grabbed her brother's shoulder and squeezed it gently. "Let's go see how Dad is doing and tell his entourage to take a hike."

"Or, maybe I could make Garrett CEO and go back to my Tonka Toys?"

"I'd kill you in your sleep," she said.

Chapters 43

I stood in the vacant lot that was once my home. Residents of the Wheel In RV Park had confiscated every last thing on my lot, even my plastic box of Christmas decorations. All that was left were a few banana peels. A light rain continued to fall. Droplets rolled off leaves overhead and hung from my nose. There was no Axel or Swayze in sight.

My neighbor Jim opened his door and stepped outside. "I tried to stop the neighbors from taking your stuff," he said, "but they wouldn't listen."

"Really? Because you're wearing one of my groom's hats."

He touched the brim of a green bowler. It had been a Scottish-themed wedding. "This? I've had it for years," he lied.

"Have you seen Axel and Swayze?"

"Not for a while."

Denise rolled down the window, her car still running. "What are we doing here? We need to get going."

"Let's try the laundromat," I said. "I've got this terrible feeling."

"We have to be at the zoo in two hours."

I hurried back to the car. "We'll make it. First, let's just do a quick check for them."

We drove around the laundry facility. Nothing. Denise drove around the far side of the Wheel In. I scanned the trailers with my one good eye, between slow sweeps of the rainy windshield. No one was outside. The place looked deserted. Probably because they were all inside their trailers checking out all the shit they stole from me.

"STOP!" I screamed.

Denise hit the brakes, and I launched forward, smacking my forehead on the dashboard.

"Damn!"

"Well, if you wouldn't scream 'Stop!' I'd brake slower."

But I barely heard the words. I was already out of the car and running toward a piece of shit, green trailer that made my burned-out Airstream look upscale. I had spotted two Big Wheels parked in a dead bush out front.

The trailer was a super-old model, propped up on cinder blocks, and over the years, it had developed quite a tilt. A few side panels were missing, and the insulation was bleeding out of the gap. I ran up to the front door, which hung ajar.

Denise was climbing out of the car, opening up a magenta umbrella. "Whose place is this?"

"I don't know. I didn't even know anyone lived back here."

"Are you OK?" Denise said.

I wasn't OK. I was frantic. Every internal alarm I had was going off. I felt like I was on the verge of a panic attack—but I wasn't sure why.

I climbed the wobbly front steps made of plywood that looked like they had been gnawed on by dogs. I scanned the area. No dogs. They'd probably moved on to better porches. I pushed open the door a little. "Swayze? Axel? It's me, Sheila."

"Axel!! Swayze!!" I yelled into the trailer. Nothing.

I listened hard. Still nothing.

"No one's here. Let's go," said Denise.

"Their Big Wheels are here. I'm going inside."

"Are you crazy? This place looks like an abandoned meth lab. I'm not taking Baby Blanche in there."

"Get back in the car and keep it running."

I took one step inside. It smelled like old cigarettes and burned bacon. With the shades drawn, it was difficult to see anything. A bead of cold sweat trickled down the back of my neck.

I turned on my phone flashlight and shone it around. The room was filled with worn boxes. I yelped when I bumped my shin on something hard. It was the end of a kid's slide. I found a light switch, and the room lit up. No surprise—it was dirty and run down, and water stains covered the walls and ceilings. Even so, the room had a magical feel. It was the biggest kids' fort I'd ever seen. Boxes were piled two and three high, with doors cut out and pictures drawn on the sides. It reminded me of Peter Pan's fort, if he had lived in the ghetto.

"HEY!" yelled a voice from outside.

I jumped, spun around, and banged my shin again.

Axel and Swayze stood on the bottom step, their wet hoodies shadowing their faces. "What are you doing here?" demanded Axel.

"Looking for you two." I walked out and jumped off the rickety porch. I wanted to hug them—thrilled to see they were alive and well— but Swayze and Axel took a step back.

"Your eye looks worse," Swayze said.

"Really? It looked pretty bad before." I grabbed my phone to check it out. "Good lord!" They were right. It was worse than horrible. Besides the swollen, purple eye, my makeup had run down my face in the rain.

"Bet it would hurt if I poked it," said Axel.

"It would, so don't touch it," I said backing out of arm's reach.

Denise, still under her umbrella, was looking from the trailer to the kids. "You live in there?"

"Yeah," said Swayze. "Want to come in?"

This time Denise took a step back.

"We heard from your mom," I said. "You two still want to be in the wedding?"

"Yes!!" they yelled.

"On one condition," I said.

The two little smiles under their hoodies turned into frowns.

"You have to tell us where your parents are. Really."

The twins shared a long look, the serious and silent conversation taking place.

"It's OK if they aren't around," I said. "My mom left me when I was a kid."

"Your mom is terrible," said Swayze. "Ours was good."

"Oh my god. Is she dead?" I squatted down to their level, hoping Denise's tight, pink skirt wouldn't rip in two.

"She didn't die," said Swayze. "She went to stay at a hospital for people who cry a lot. She's getting happier."

"She sent us a postcard," said Axel.

"Where's your dad?" I asked.

Axel shrugged. "Uncle Richie is taking care of us."

Denise was now at my side, squatting in the mud. "And where's Uncle Richie?"

They shrugged.

"How long has he been gone?" I asked.

"A long time," said Swayze. Axel nodded.

"OK, guys," I said, standing up. "Grab some clothes. You're coming with us. And we're stopping by McDonald's on the way."

Denise and I watched the two gleeful kids run into the busted-up trailer for their things.

"Did you just take on two little children?" asked Denise. "The woman with no house or car? The one who is probably going to be living with me?"

"Holy shit, I think I did."

"Shouldn't we call Child Protective Services?"

"Later. First, I'm leaving a note for Uncle Richie. Then we've got a wedding to get to."

I scribbled a message to Uncle Richie on the back of some junk mail I found on the table. It was simple: If you ever get back, call me. I put the note on the refrigerator door using one of the dozens of magnets stuck there. I chose the one with a cowboy boot stomping on a pile of horse shit. *Fancy.* I already hated Uncle Richie.

When I stepped out of the trailer, Denise was arguing with the twins.

"No, you can't," she said firmly.

"All we need is duct tape," pleaded Swayze.

"Then we can just stick them on top," said Axel.

And that is why we arrived at Denise's apartment with two Big Wheels duct-taped to the top of Denise's car.

Chapter 44

We had one hour to be at the zoo. I scanned Denise's closet for something to wear to the wedding. I normally wear one of my "wedding coordinator" dresses. I have one for the summer and one for the winter. The winter one is black and classy, with a scooped neck, a plunging back, and silver sequins around the waist. The summer dress is more nondescript—an off-the-shoulder design, in a red floral print with a stretch bodice and a hem that hits me about mid-thigh. Unfortunately, neither dress made it through the fire, so I was pulling on one of Denise's bright pink nightmares, with a lace bodice and a crepe-like skirt.

When I walked out of Denise's bedroom, Axel gasped. "You look like a scary ballerina."

Swayze smiled from behind the Big Mac she was wolfing down. "I think she looks like a pirate that had a fight and lost. The other pirate stabbed her in the eye."

"Shut up and get those flowers in the car," I said.

I looked in the mirror. I didn't recognize the woman looking back at me. Her hair was burned off on one side, one eye was not only swollen but also a horrific shade of purple—the color purple that makes you think of bad fruit and dead bodies. Then there was the red blotch on the other side of my face, from being burned the night before.

"Here. Take this." Denise handed me a bottle of concealer. "You can cover that all up again on the way over."

"I don't think I can cover all this."

"Try. You look terrible. And I have a pink summer hat in the closet. It will hide the hair," she added.

Denise spoke firmly to her bump. "Winona, when you grow up, do not pick fights, or you could look like Aunt Sheila."

"Tell her it's important to stand up for yourself," I said as we both picked up armfuls of Bamboo Febreze. "And I'm not a big fan of Winona."

"Big shock," she said as we walked out to the car. "Winona Ryder had a big comeback. I think it's a strong name."

"They will shorten it to Wi, though, and that will be weird."

"Why do you always have to shorten them?"

"I'd call him Captain Avenger," said Axel, who was already coming out with a second load of flowers.

"It's a girl," said Swayze. "It should be Bertha Big Booty."

The twins cracked up, their laughter filling the air. I couldn't remember ever hearing them laugh before. It was a nice sound.

As we piled our flowers into the trunk, the Fast Food Fast Gas van pulled up and Monte stepped out. He looked at my face. "Doll, you need to hide them peepers."

"Thanks. It's in there," I said, pointing to Denise's apartment.

Denise looked at me, confused.

"I told him I'd do an extra shift next week if he moved the cake for us."

"Sweet," she said.

I turned to Denise, Swayze, and Axel. "OK, everybody. It's countdown. Grab your stuff and get in the car. We've got 45 minutes to get to the zoo, and we still need to get some clothes for you two."

Chapter 45

We were driving 75 miles an hour to Value Village when my phone rang. It was Cheyenne. For a quick moment, I thought about not answering. All brides are a hot mess before a wedding. But most at least knew where their grooms were.

I answered, trying to sound cheerful. "Hi, Cheyenne! You ready for the big moment?"

I heard nothing. "Cheyenne, you there?"

There was a big gulping sob. "He's still not here. He stood me up."

"Did he tell you that?"

"No."

"That's good news."

"What if he didn't tell me because he's . . . DEAD!?"

"He's not dead. The police would have called you."

There was a loud wail from Cheyenne. The conversation was taking a bad turn.

I wished I still had some Valium from last year's root canal. Dentists scare the crap out of me, and I had gotten pretty worked up beforehand. My dentist gave me a prescription for Valium—two pills later, all fear had evaporated. I could have faced down ten root canals without the slightest care.

It was then that I realized this drug was a bridal miracle. The next three weddings, I slipped a Valium into a glass of sparkling cider that I gave to the nervous bride as a toast. The brides all relaxed perfectly, and my work was a dream.

Since then I've been trying to get another prescription from my dentist but he's been extremely stingy. Even when I told him I was having flashback nightmares about my root canal—dental PTSD I called it—he said he wasn't buying it.

As I listened to Cheyenne's uncontrollable sobs, I imagined how her swollen eyes were going to ruin the pictures for *Best Bride*. I wondered if I had any more teeth that needed work. I'd jot that down later on my "to do" list in my little red notebook.

"Cheyenne, I want you to listen very carefully to me. You need to wash your face, reapply your makeup, and I'm going to go get Tony."

"You know where he is?"

"Yes, I got a text from him right now."

The sobs stopped. I could almost hear the tears evaporating on her hot cheeks. "Oh, thank god!"

Topeka grabbed Cheyenne's phone. "You tell that turd he's got some explaining to do."

"I'll pass that along. Just get Cheyenne cleaned up and at the zoo back entrance in the next half hour."

I hung up. Denise stared at me, confused. "Tony texted you?"
"God no. I just had to get her to shut up. If she didn't stop crying, she was going to be a mess for the wedding."

"She's going to cry a lot more when he's not there."

My good eye started to twitch, an obnoxious reaction I have to stress.

"Oh no, not your eye thing," said Denise. "That creeps me out."

Swayze yelled from the back seat. "Let me see!"

"Me too," chimed in Axel.

I turned around. "It's nothing. It'll go away in a minute." It better, I thought.

Axel laughed. "That is SO gross."

"Like *The Exorcist* gross," said Swayze.

"You two have seen *The Exorcist*? I'm going to have to talk to your Uncle Richie."

Minutes later we were running down the kids' aisle of Value Village to find outfits for Swayze and Axel. Axel picked out a camouflage jacket.

Denise hung it back on the rack. "Ring bearers wear a black suit."

"What do flower girls wear?" asked Swayze.

"A nice dress."

Swayze grimaced.

Denise grabbed a little black jacket off the rack. "See if this fits."

Axel shrugged it on. It hung to his knees. But it did look kind of cool with his Cookie Monster T-shirt. Denise rifled through the rack for more.

Swayze pointed to something red, white, and blue.

"That's a Wonder Woman costume," I said. "That won't work."

"How about that one?" she asked.

"Little Red Riding Hood?"

She nodded, and I took it down. If we removed the red cape, leaving a white dress with a black sash, it wasn't too bad. And it came with a basket for petals. Bonus!

"It's yours," I said, looking for something for Axel, who was pulling on a camouflage vest. I spotted a Prince Charming costume. If I could pull off the sash and little fringes on the shoulders, it could work.

"No way I'm wearing that," said Axel. "How about this one?"

"No, on the Ninja Turtle," I said.

"Then this one."

Denise shook her head. "That's a SWAT outfit. Think wedding."

"It might work," I said. "It does come with black pants."

Axel nodded. "Yes!"

"If we take away the gun belt, and lose the police hat and SWAT vest, it's just a white shirt and black pants."

"Then it's stupid," said Axel.

"You can have the rest of the outfit after the wedding," said Denise. "Now everyone to the car."

Denise and I looked at each other. She smiled. I tried not to because my face hurt. "Did you hear that?" she said. "I sounded like a real mom right then."

"I know. You got this."

I looked at my phone. We had fifteen minutes to get to the zoo.

Chapter 46

The zoo's back entrance looked a lot like it had a couple of days before. I rolled down the window, hoping the rain had at least removed the stink. The mostly empty parking lot now just smelled like wet animal poo.

I called Reese, Denise's zoo pooper scooper friend and put the call on speaker so Denise could hear. Reese picked up on the first ring. "Yeah?"

"It's me, Sheila. Can you come down and open the gate?"

"What do you mean?"

"I mean, can you open the gate? We're in the back parking lot. We're here for the wedding."

"Damn, didn't I tell you?"

"Tell me what?"

"I got fired yesterday. I'm home playing Halo."

Denise gently beat her head on the steering wheel.

"So, how do we get in?" I tried to keep my voice calm, but I could feel a mean edge to it.

Swayze leaned over the seat. "Your eye is doing that freaky thing again."

"You can't," Reese said.

Denise took the phone. "There has to be a way. Do you hear me?! We have people arriving in five minutes, and we need to get in. Now!"

"Jesus, calm down," he said. "The only way you can open the gate is to push the numbers on the keypad on the other side."

"What numbers!?"

Five minutes later, I was climbing that stupid fence again, but at least I knew the terrain a little better. Denise, Swayze, and Axel watched.

"Be careful," said Denise. "That's one of my best dresses."

"I'm doing the best I can."

I was perched on the top when I felt the gate slowly open, just like last time. I grabbed on with both arms.

Swayze laughed. "Good one."

I looked down, and Axel had crawled through the fence and typed in the code.

"Why didn't you tell me you could get through before I climbed up here?" I yelled.

"Because this is more fun," said Axel. "Swayze, climb up, and you can ride too."

"No!" I yelled as I climbed down. I felt something on my back. I spun around and saw nothing but then felt the same thing on my face. It took a moment to figure out what it was. Warmth. The sun was peeking through the grey clouds. It was clearing up!

I quickly thanked the wedding planner gods, and Patrick Swayze, who was probably up there somewhere helping out.

Monte's Fast Food Fast Gas van pulled up. Monte stuck his head out the driver's window "Is this where the doll's getting hitched?"

"This is the place," I said so received I could kiss him. "You got the cake and the Reddi-wip?"

"In the back of the heap." He gestured to the back of the van with his thumb.

"Can you give Denise a ride up with the flowers?"

"Sure," he said. "Jump in Toots."

Denise and I loaded the flowers, some booze, and the box of paper plates and cups into the back next to the wedding cake, which I was amazed to see Monte had already covered with the Reddi-wip. His van was refrigerated, so it all held into place perfectly. It was a beautiful mountain of white, with monkeys around the base, hand in hand, and two monkeys on the very top. Monte had even thrown in a couple of bananas on the second layer.

As Denise got in the passenger seat next to Monte, I ran up to his window.

"That cake looks amazing! Thank you."

"Kitten, I'm a sucker when it comes to weddings." He gunned the van and took off.

I took a deep breath. This was it. The wedding was under way. I was closing in on the Monkey Wedding of the Century—the wedding that was going to blow *Best Bride's* mind. All this work, the black eye, my beat-up Airstream, and my reeking zoo entrance—it was all going to be worth it. If we could find the groom, that was. Too bad Charlie wouldn't be here to see it. I brushed the thought aside.

I checked my little red notebook to make sure I hadn't missed anything. Pastor Bee seemed to be running late, so I dialed him as I yelled to the kids. "You two grab the Febreze and spray the shit out of those leis." The kids jumped on it.

Pastor Bee finally picked up. "I'm getting there. The traffic has been hell and—"

"Hold on," I said. "I'm getting another call."

It was Kevin, our DJ. "I can't make it."

"You have to make it!"

"I can't walk. My foot's frozen."

"Solid?"

"No. But when I try to walk on it, it doesn't move. It's like it's asleep or something."

"Hold on."

I switched to the other line. "Pastor Bee. Can you pick up Kevin? His foot's frozen."

"He still live with his mom, on Proctor?"

"Yep."

"I'm on my way."

I hung up as the first guests drove up. It was a couple I didn't know. They looked like Cheyenne's family, though. The whole clan was kind of tall and skinny and looked like they had just stepped out of a rodeo.

They parked and walked to the entrance, both dressed in denim. The woman, about 45, even had a denim scrunchy pulling back her stringy brown hair.

"Welcome," I said, placing a couple of Febreze-doused leis around their necks. "I'm Sheila, the wedding planner. You are . . .? "

"We're Cheyenne's Aunt Mindy and Uncle Thomas. You don't remember us? We were at both the other weddings."

"Oh, yeah. Hi!" I lied. I handed them a bottle of Reuben's moonshine and two plastic glasses. "Please walk on through those gates and up to the right. When you get to the monkey cages, you're there."

"Monkeys. Really?" said the man, an older, skinny dude in cowboy boots, not at all excited about the theme.

"The groom likes monkeys." I smiled, trying to make it sound normal.

"Well, I like monkeys," said Aunt Mindy.

As they walked through the gates I heard Uncle Thomas tell Aunt

184

Mindy, "If one of them throws shit at me, I'm out of here."

Oh Shit! Monkeys do throw shit. How had I not remembered that? Suddenly I imagined pictures in the pages of *Best Bride* of a bride walking down an aisle, petals under her feet being pelted by turds. I tried to breathe evenly, but my eye was twitching faster than ever.

Two more cars pulled up with Cheyenne's dowdy relatives. I threw leis on them, handed each couple a bottle of booze and some glasses.

I turned to see Swayze and Axel, who were spraying a tree and some bushes with Febreze. "Hey, don't waste that stuff."

"But it stinks here," said Axel.

"Spray some on your hands and rub it under your noses," I said.

I heard Pastor Bee's truck before it arrived. It sounded like a tailpipe might be failing, and possibly dragging on the ground.

My phone buzzed. It was a text from Denise "Where are the chairs? We have people wandering around, drinking and daring the monkeys to throw shit."

"Almost there. Hold on," I typed.

Pastor Bee's truck pulled up. He popped his head out. "Whew! Smells like a carnival back here—but without the cotton candy and just the dung."

Chapter 47

When I reached the site with the last of the wedding guests, I got nervous. Cheyenne was pacing, and Topeka was tossing back a shot of Reuben's white lightning, giving her some stern advice that I'm sure was bad-to-horrible. The guests were either restless or three-quarters of the way to shit-faced. Even the monkeys looked nervous and were screeching at the guests. Worst of all, there was no groom.

I tried to look at the bright side. At least the rain had stopped, and the sun was setting over Puget Sound. A majestic Mount Rainier was in the distance, surrounded by frothy clouds, like whip cream on a sundae.

Cheyenne's wedding was hardly my first rodeo. I could put a wedding together faster than Topeka could throw a punch. I saw Pastor Bee's truck parked to the side and flew into action. I put Denise on guard to warn me if any zoo employees came. Pastor Bee unloaded and set up chairs and tables. Kevin limped off to set up his boom box. Swayze and Axel were in charge of putting banana centerpieces on the tables, with strict orders not to eat any of the bananas.

Of course, Cheyenne's family just stood around like a lazy bunch of slackers, watching, getting drunk. Not that I expected anything else.

Once a table was in place by the monkey cage, Monte set the wedding cake on the table.

"It's perfect," I said. "Thank you."

"Nice cheaters," he said, motioning to my sunglasses.

I lifted them slightly to show him the black eye. He took a step back and let out a low whistle.

"Going to find me some hooch," he said. As he sauntered away, I looked at my phone. It was a new record. I had set up a wedding in under seven minutes.

Kevin limped up to me, his foot wrapped in a towel and duct-taped. "Got the music ready."

"Maybe play something quiet and . . . soothing. We're still waiting for the groom," I said.

"You don't have a groom?"

"How's the foot?" I said, changing the subject.

"I froze two toes, thanks to you."

I pointed to the towel. "Are they bleeding or something?"

"It's for the cold pack. Got worried my ankle bracelet might warm up, so I wrapped it in cold packs."

"Good thinking."

A finger tapped lightly on my shoulder. I turned to find Cheyenne, looking wonderful, except for some smudged massacre. She was crying again.

"Topeka said you're lying. He's not here."

"He texted me. He's on his way. If I had five bucks for every wedding where the groom was late, I'd be rich."

But real fear was settling in. Maybe Tony really was dead somewhere. Grooms aren't late. They bail. I'd only had two other weddings where the groom was this late. One was because he got a ticket speeding to the wedding. The other groom went to the wrong house, was attacked by a dog, and called us from the hospital where he was getting twenty-six stitches.

Cheyenne wanted to believe me. She straightened her hair, which was piled higher on her head than I had ever seen it. It worked for her, but with her heels, it made her like six foot four—she'd be towering over Tony, if he ever showed up.

"Why don't you go over to Pastor Bee's truck," I suggested. "Your bouquet is in there."

I checked my texts again. Nothing from Tony. The minutes were ticking by. It would only be a matter of time before the zoo employees figured out we weren't supposed to be there. Where was that guy? He was odd, for sure, but he just never struck me as a sprinter.

Denise ran up to me. "There's someone here I don't know, taking photos."

"Where?"

Denise pointed to a gal in her 20s, wearing stylish black pants and a tailored white shirt, snapping pictures with a very expensive camera. One of Cheyenne's uncle was trying to hit on her, and she was trying nicely to extricate herself.

"Do you know her?" Denise asked.

"Think it's some detective?"

Denise nodded. "That's what I thought. But why would she come to a wedding?"

"Look around," I said. "Half these people look like they're on parole or should be in jail."

Denise glanced at the guests. With the exception of an elderly couple who looked pretty harmless, sitting in plastic chairs getting hammered, it was a sketchy crowd at best. Like an aging outlaw gang form the west, minus the horses.

The ache in my eye was traveling to my temple. This wedding was feeling doomed. I approached the chick with the camera. She was sweet and all smiles.

"Hi," I said. "Are you with the wedding party?"

"Not really," she said.

"I figured. Can you hold off arresting anyone until after the ceremony?"

"Arrest? My name's Tracy. I'm a photographer. Charlie Ricci hired me to come take photos. He said you needed some for a bridal contest."

My heart warmed. "He's so romantic."

"If you say so. Do you have any specific shots you want me to get?"

"The bride and groom—when he gets here—in front of the monkeys. And make sure you get the dress," I said. "And the cake! And, if you could try to avoid some of the sketchier guests, that would be great."

"I'm on it. I've done a lot of weddings. You go take care of your bride. She looks upset."

I turned to see Cheyenne throwing a paper plate and yelling at Topeka. Not good. I wanted to help Cheyenne, but I also didn't want to get too close to her right-hook-swinging-sister. I needed what sight I had left.

An older guy, maybe forty-five, slapped the photographer on the ass. She jumped and let out a little scream.

"Who's this little number?" he asked as fumes from Reuben's brew rolled off him.

"Get your hands off her," I said. "You're drunk. Hit on your own wife over there."

"With cute little fillies like this here?" He gave me a sloppy wink.

"I'm serious. Keep your paws off the girls or I'll beat the crap out of you with your own shoe."

He looked at me confused. "How did you get my shoes?"

I pushed him off in the direction of his wife and turned back to

Tracy. "Sorry about that. I wish we could control who comes to these things."

She nodded. "When are you expecting the groom?"

I wished I had an answer.

"I'm HERE!" yelled a male voice. I spun around. Finally! I thought with relief. But my heart sank when I saw who it was. Kenny.

"Denise, where are you?! I want you to sign over custody of our unborn baby, right now!"

Chapter 48

Kenny stood by the wedding cake with his new girlfriend, Rita. I knew her—she lived in the Wheel In RV Park too. She was nice enough, and even had a cute figure. She worked at the Diamond Casino, where I hear she got great tips, The thing is, she had a face only a mother could love, and by that I mean if her mother was a possum. Her features were long and pointy, her hair always seemed to strike out in different directions, and her eyes were beady and black.

Rita smiled at me, giving a "What can you do?" shrug. I gave her a "You can take your asshole boyfriend the hell out of here is what you can do," look back.

Cheyenne stopped talking to Topeka and turned to watch what was about to go down. In fact, the whole wedding party had stopped to watch. The only sounds were of "Hey, hey, we're the Monkeys" playing on Kevin's boom box. I had to hand it to him, he'd done a nice job of finding themed music.

As the wedding planner, it was my job to handle this. I marched up to Kenny, feeling myself almost shaking with anger. If there was a man I could kill with my bare hands, it was him. And if there was a crowd I could do it in front of and get away with it, this was the one. Hell, they would probably cheer me on.

Kenny's breath stunk of beer and cigarettes. Big shock. "You're not on the guest list," I said, trying to keep it together. "You'll have to leave. Right now."

"I'm not leaving until I see Denise."

My phone buzzed. Denise was texting. "Hiding in the bathroom. Get him out of here!"

"She's not here," I said. "Now get lost."

"Or what? You'll call the police?"

Axel and Swayze were suddenly at my side. They were so small and cute in their outfits, but they still looked a little lethal. It was probably the loaded slingshots they carried.

"We can help," said Swayze. She pulled back her slingshot, which held a stone the size of a golf ball.

"We have lots of rocks," said Axel.

Kenny looked down at the kids. "You don't scare me."

I nodded to Swayze. "Aim for the thigh."

She squinted, aimed, and let her slingshot go. The rock tore through the air and smacked him right in the nuts.

"AHH!" His scream was high-pitched, like a girl's, as he doubled over in pain. "My junk!"

"Kenny, maybe we should go," Rita said, then turned to me. "I'm sorry. I tried to tell him this was a stupid idea, but he just wouldn't let it go."

Kenny's eyes watered as glared at me. "Bitch."

"My turn," said Axel. He let his stone fly. The rock hit Kenny's ass hard enough that it ricocheted off and landed back at Axel's feet.

Axel and Swayze grinned as Kenny let out another girly cry and fell to the ground.

"Stop!" cried Kenny.

Rita took his arm. "Honey, let's get out of here. Seriously, this is not a good time." She shook her head at me. "Men. What can you do?"

I leaned in and whispered to Rita. "You don't know where Tony Lopez is, do you?"

"I did see him earlier. Where was that?"

"At least he's alive." I looked around to make sure Cheyenne hadn't heard that.

"I can't remember where he was, but I'm sure his friends would know. They were with him." She pointed to a couple of guys leaning against the monkey cage drinking.

"I think the kid broke my dick," whined Kenny.

"Thanks, Rita," I said. "I really appreciate it."

"You're welcome. You know, I've been meaning to tell you, there's an opening at the Diamond Casino, if you're interested. Cocktail waitress." She turned to Kenny. "Come on. We still have to climb over that gate."

"Tell Denise this ain't over," said Kenny, as he slowly hobbled off leaning on Rita.

"Next time, bring a cup," I yelled back.

I texted Denise, "Coast is clear," as I ran up to Tony's friends. I knew them from back in high school. We used to call the duo Jock Itch behind their backs. They were dumb as a bag of socks and played any sport with a ball. Now they worked at Tony's dad's used car dealership. Jock was about six-foot-two and 280 pounds, and he looked like he could disassemble the monkey cage with his bare hands. Itch was about as tall, but balding, and had clearly let his high school physique go to hell.

"OK guys. Where's Tony?"

"How would we know?" said Jock.

Itch smiled and lit a cigarette.

I grabbed the cigarette out of his fingers, dropped it in the dirt, and smashed it out with my heel.

"I don't have time for this."

Jock smiled. "Oooo, you going to bring out the little kids? Rocks don't scare me."

Itch looked down sadly at his smashed cigarette. "Damn. That was my last one."

I'd had enough. Time was running out. We'd been lucky not to have the zoo staff catch us. It had been almost half an hour, and we were now on borrowed minutes. If I didn't have a wedding soon, I wasn't getting the pictures. If I didn't get the pictures, I wouldn't have a chance at *Best Bride*. If I didn't get into *Best Bride* and get some better paying weddings, I was going to be working at The Shits or the Diamond Casino for the rest of my life.

I grabbed Itch by the balls and squeezed. "Where?"

"Hey! Ow. Let go."

Jock pulled me off as we saw Cheyenne walking our way. Jock dropped his voice so only I could hear. "We're his friends. We're not letting him marry her. She's bad luck. He'd be her *third* husband. If he marries her, who knows what would happen? He could get hit by a truck!"

"Or worse," said Itch.

"Are you guys high?"

"No. Just looking out for our friend," said Jock.

Cheyenne stepped up, tears brimming again. "Where's Tony?'

Jock shook his head. "He said he was sorry. He's long gone."

Cheyenne's face went slack. Then the tears fell. Her mascara was ruined once more.

Denise ran up. "What's going on?"

"He's not coming," Cheyenne wailed. "Tony left me at the aisle. I'm bad luck!"

I love weddings. But brides? Why can't *they* be the ones late to the wedding? They're just a big, emotional wreck in a nice dress. My patience was gone. I could feel one eye throb as the other twitched worse than a hyperactive Chihuahua.

"Cheyenne, he's coming," I said firmly. "They're just pulling your leg. Denise, please take Cheyenne. I need a few more words with these guys."

"Come on. Let's get you fixed up again," said Denise. Then she turned and whispered to me, "I'm out of mascara."

I reached in my purse and tossed her a tube of waterproof ultra lash. You're not a professional, if you don't have at least three or four in your purse.

Kevin was playing "Shock the Monkey" as I grabbed Jock by his T-shirt. "Start talking."

"Or what?"

"Topeka," I called out, "I need some help!"

Jock's eyes widened as Topeka strode over.

Chapter 49

I never thought Topeka was good for anything but starting fights and drinking beer, but it turns out she got Tony's friend Jock talking in sixteen seconds flat. I made a mental note to add her to my red notebook—Topeka's services could come in handy for future weddings.

She had one of Jock's arms pinned behind his back and his face planted in the dirt. With his good arm, he was trying to point to something beyond the monkey cages. "He's in the barn," he finally squealed.

Topeka started dragging Jock toward the cages. Pastor Bee, now in full pastor attire, and I ran alongside. At the bottom of a knoll was the barn, which most of us would have called a big, ugly shed with one small window. As we ran down to it, I felt a little guilty leaving Denise to handle the sobbing Cheyenne. It was the harder job. Even if Topeka intended to use me as a battering ram to break down the barn door, I would still have the easier job. The only thing worse than a crying bride, in my opinion, was possibly a full body wax.

"Tony said they keep the monkeys in here that they don't want in the big cages," said Jock.

"You put him in with the monkeys?"

"We figured Tony would have a good time, since he likes them so much," said Itch.

The door was padlocked. And the only window was tinted.

"Where's the key to the lock?" demanded Topeka.

"We don't have it," said Itch. "We found the lock inside and used it."

While Topeka contemplated whether to kill them right there in front of the shed, I peered in the window. I couldn't see much, but my vision was kind of impaired with only the one good eye. I pounded on the window. "Tony, you in there?"

"I'm here. Somebody get me out!" Tony's voice sounded desperate and a little hung over.

"Are there monkeys in there?" asked Topeka.

"Just a few," said Tony.

Topeka turned to me. Was that fear I saw in her eyes? "I'm not going in," she said. "I've heard a regular-sized little chimp is ten times as strong as a grown man. And they can rip your arms off. Not like dislocate. Off."

Pastor Bee was trying to pick the lock with no success.

"We're going to get you out of there," I said. "You've got a wedding to go to."

"Is Cheyenne pissed?" Tony asked.

"Just worried," I said. "I think we have to break the window to get you out."

"OK. But you might let one of the monkeys out. That window goes to her cage."

"Then we are NOT breaking the window!" said Topeka, turning to Jock. "You stupid dumb asses. Now we're going to have to call security."

"No we aren't," said Pastor Bee. "I've got some bolt cutters in my truck. They'll go through that lock.

"Go. GO!" I yelled.

Pastor Bee took off up the hill toward his truck, which was parked behind the public restrooms.

My phone buzzed. It was Denise. "Tell Cheyenne Tony is on his way. His idiot friends stuck him in the monkey barn"

"I think security is coming," she said.

"Shit. Stall them. We'll be right there." I turned to Topeka and Jock Itch. "We don't have much time. I'm going to get everyone set up. As soon as Pastor Bee springs Tony, get everyone up there ASAP. Got it?"

Topeka nodded. "Got it."

I sprinted back up the knoll, panting like a dog, sweat trickling down my back. As I took a second to catch my breath, I checked out the situation. No security yet. Most of Cheyenne's family members were three sheets to the wind. Her Uncle Robert was peeing at the base of a maple tree. One of his cousins was talking to a monkey. Others were leaning against whatever would hold them up. It could have been worse.

Cheyenne stood to the side, still looking a little mascara-challenged, but not bad. Where were my ring bearer and flower girl? I spotted them—EATING CAKE.

"Get away from the cake!" I ran over and pulled them away.

"We got hungry!"

"You just had McDonald's."

"Like an hour ago," they said.

"Go get to your spots. We're ready."

There was a nice big hole at the bottom of the cake. I carefully turned it around so it faced the other direction, then quickly spread some of the Reddi-wip frosting over the hole with my figure to make it less obvious. It wasn't great, but it would have to do.

I turned to the wedding guests. "Places, everyone! Tony's coming. And we have to do this fast before security gets here."

"Security? I gotta get out of here" said Kevin.

"Relax," I said. "It's not the police. Just zoo security. They don't care about your ankle bracelet." At least I didn't think so.

Tracy, the photographer raised her hand. "Where would you like me?"

I pointed toward a circle of rose petals and several banana/rose arrangements near the large white monkey cage. "Stand over there. That's where they're going to say their vows. And snap those shots fast. We're not going to have a lot of time."

Tracy scrambled into position. "Oh, my! This is exciting."

Denise stepped up beside me. "I can see the security car coming. Where's Tony?"

I could feel my panic meter rising. I took a long, deep breath. Someday I would write a book about the time management issues wedding planners have to deal with. It's unreal the restraints we often have to work under.

I released the breath, took another, and screamed, "Get to your seats. NOW!"

People scrambled to their chairs as the security car pulled up. Two security guards stepped out, wearing grey uniforms with a big zoo emblem on the breast pocket. I was relieved to see they weren't the same security guards I'd talked to the day before. One guard was a little heavier than the other and reminded me of Chris Pratt before he lost all the weight. The other was a smaller guy, with dark glasses and darker hair, chewing on a toothpick.

"What's going on?" asked the Chris Pratt-esk security guard.

I was suddenly glad that Charlie wasn't here to see how many felonies I was about to commit.

Chapter 50

Chris Pratt and his sunglasses-wearing partner took in the scene.

I tried to see what they saw. A group of semi-average people sitting, waiting for a wedding. And hopefully, since they were sitting, he couldn't see how drunk they were. They also saw an elegant bride, fixing her makeup, a white monkey wedding cake, and a very perplexed photographer standing next to a flower girl and ring bearer carrying slingshots. Slingshots? I thought I told them to put those away. *Best Bride* wouldn't understand

I tried to block the security guards view of Pastor Bee running toward the monkey barn.

"Hello, gentlemen. As you can see, we've got a wedding going on here. We're just waiting on the groom." I hoped they couldn't see my twitching eye through my sunglasses, because it had evolved into a full-on spasm.

Chris Pratt pulled out a sheet of paper from his pocket. "We don't have a wedding on our schedule."

"There must be some mix-up. We've had it scheduled for months," I responded sweetly. "We were worried we might have to cancel because of the rain, but aren't we lucky? The sun finally came out." I adjusted my sunglasses to make sure my black eye was covered.

"Is that your priest running over there?"

"Yes. Pastor Bee. He's giving some last-minute advice to the groom."

The little security guy grunted. Chris Pratt interpreted, "My partner wants to know what happened to your hair."

I reached up and touched my head. The hat must have come off while I was running up the knoll. My burnt hair was sticking out at an odd angle. "Curling irons," I said. "You guys are lucky you don't use them. When they fritz out, they can really damage your hair."

Chris leaned in. "Jesus. It burned your hair right off!"

I tried, unsuccessfully, to pat down the scorched patch. "Sure did. But you know, the bright side is that it will grow back. Always does."

Chris's partner grunted again. I thought I made out a word, but I wasn't sure.

"My partner thinks something's fishy. Can you show us your event permit?"

"Of course, I've got it by the cake. Let me go get that."

"That would be great," said Chris Pratt.

As I casually made my way back toward the cake. Cheyenne grabbed my arm, her long nails digging into my skin, and whispered, "Do something!"

"I'm trying."

There was a crash at the monkey barn. The little security officer perked up.

"What was that?" asked Chris Pratt.

"It better be the groom," said one of Cheyenne's relatives. "We've been sitting here forever. I've got my shows to watch."

Both officers started to walk toward the commotion.

I waved to the security guards to get their attention. "While I'm getting the permit, would you two officers be so kind as to take a picture with the bride? I think this will make a great photo—the security officers who crashed the wedding."

I looked to Denise and Cheyenne silently pleading for help. Cheyenne got it immediately. She sauntered toward the men. As she passed me she whispered without moving her lips, "We don't have a permit, do we?" I shook my head.

Cheyenne pinched my arm — hard — then focused on the two men, turning on the sex appeal. The little officer's toothpick fell from his mouth when Cheyenne took the little man's hand in her hers. "Oh please, please, *Pleeease*. I'd love a picture with you guys"

The little officer, face-to-boobs with Cheyenne, nodded eagerly.

"My buddy seems OK with it," said Chris Pratt.

As the photographer snapped some pictures, I ran to the knoll and looked down the hill. The barn door was open and Tony was coming out, but holy shit so was a monkey. Not a little monkey like the type that sits on your shoulder and begs for peanuts—but a full-sized chimpanzee. The chimp held Tony's hand and gazed at him with an expression of what anyone could see was true love.

I watched in horror as Tony, hand-in-hand with the chimp, ran up the hill, followed closely by Pastor Bee and Jock Itch, with Topeka lagging behind.

I turned to the crowd. "Everyone ready? Kevin, cue the music."

The bridal march filled the evening air. Maybe it was because this was Cheyenne's third wedding and people knew the routine, but suddenly—despite the officers and the monkeys and the drunk wedding guests—it started to come together.

I would love to take credit for moments like this, but every wedding has a life of its own. I think of a wedding as a tiny bird. A tiny bird you hold in your hand, trying to protect it—while also trying to keep it from pecking the crap out of you. Finally, when the moment is right, you open your hands and let it fly.

Over the knoll came Tony, like Prince Charming looking for his princess—if that prince was barefoot, wearing a dirty black T-shirt and jeans, and holding hands with a chimpanzee).

Family and friends gasped, but were too drunk to do much else. One of Cheyenne's drunk uncles whispered to his wife, "I knew the groom's family was ugly, but Christ!"

"Oh baby, you're OK," said Cheyenne.

"I am. And I want to marry you."

Cheyenne nearly swooned.

"And this here is Daisy," he said, nodding to the chimp. "I'll explain later." Tony and Daisy walked to the circle of rose petals.

Pastor Bee took his place outside the circle of roses.

The two security guards stared, stunned and confused. The little guy pulled off his sunglasses to make sure he was seeing correctly.

"Is that one of our monkeys?" whispered Chris Pratt to me.

"We rented him for the ceremony. The groom is a trainer. He knows what he's doing."

The little guy grunted.

"He doesn't think we rent our monkeys out."

"Of course, you do. We paid good money for her. Now be quiet, the ceremony is about to start." I hoped my voice oozed confidence, because if my heart beat any harder I was going to swoon myself, from a heart attack.

I pointed to Axle and Swayze, "You're on. You know what to do."

They dropped their slingshots and grabbed the basket with flower petals and the little pillow with the rings. Swayze skipped along throwing petals on the ground, but also at the audience and on herself. Axel followed behind, holding the rings high over his head, showing them off to the crowd. I made a mental note to give better instructions next time.

The two stopped at the circle.

It was finally Cheyenne's time to shine. She took Topeka's hand, and they walked down the aisle together. Topeka glanced nervously at the chimp and it gave her a little wave. Topeka's eyes widened in horror; she shoved Cheyenne toward Tony and backed up, standing a safe distance from the couple.

Fat Chris Pratt turned to his buddy, "Dude, that chimp doesn't even have a leash."

Denise tapped Chris Pratt on the shoulder. "Shhh! This is a wedding. Whatever it is, it can wait."

They quieted. Denise would make a great mom, I was sure of it.

Jock and Itch stood next to Tony as his best men—although with the monkey there too, I wasn't sure who officially had the honors. Topeka was trying to stand next to Cheyenne, but also as far away from Daisy as possible.

It was a beautiful evening. The sun cast an orange glow over the waters of Puget Sound. Mount Rainier seemed to glow pink in the setting set. Even Daisy seemed to be taking in the perfect moment.

The photographer snapped pictures as Pastor Bee said the sacred words. "Do you, Cheyenne, take this man to be your lawfully wedded husband?"

"I do." Her face beamed.

"And do you, Tony, take this woman to be your lawfully wedded wife?"

Tony smiled at Cheyenne. "I do."

"Then I now pronounce you man and wife. You may kiss the bride."

There was drunken, wild applause and whistles from the audience as Tony and Cheyenne leaned in for their first kiss as husband and wife. As their lips met, Daisy screamed out in jealousy.

It was at that moment, I should have run.

Chapter 51

Charlie, Camella, and their mom waited outside the hospital room as their dad barked orders at his suited minions inside.

Charlie could tell Camella was about to tell them to leave when a male nurse stepped in. He was large enough to play center for the Seahawks. And he worked out. Charlie had seen tree trunks smaller than the nurse's arms and would have offered him a job on his crew if it were a different place and time.

"Sorry gentlemen, he's being prepped for surgery," the nurse said in a deep, commanding voice. "This can wait."

Charlie's dad pointed a finger at the nurse. "I still have—"

"No, you don't."

Charlie liked this nurse. A lot.

The nurse grinned at Charlie's dad, while pushing the men out of the room. "Mr. Ricci, I'm sure these men have it in hand. You are due in surgery shortly."

As the men quickly filed out, the linebacker-nurse motioned for Charlie, Camella, and their mom to enter the room. "We've given him a sedative. He will be getting sleepy soon."

Charlie's mom went to her husband's side, squeezing his hand. "You're going to be fine, dear. Just relax."

"How the hell am I supposed to relax? They're going to cut my goddamn chest open."

"You've got a point, Dad," said Camella. "You should definitely worry right up to surgery." She leaned over and kissed him on the forehead. "Make sure they give you the good drugs when you come to."

Charlie watched his dad yawn, thinking how only twelve short hours ago, he was in bed, watching Sheila stretch and yawn , before she fell asleep in his arms. He glanced at his watch. She was probably right in the middle of her wedding, having the time of her life—eating cake and dancing to some monkey tunes. He could picture her, turning up the volume, grabbing some guy and dancing in the grass under the monkey cages. He felt a stab of jealousy. Or was it just longing to be back there with her?

"Charlie. Charlie!" Charlie looked up. His whole family was staring at him.

"Charlie, your dad is going to have major surgery, and you're off daydreaming?" his mom scolded.

"No, I was just . . . Dad, how are you doing?"

Charlie's dad motioned to his wife and daughter. "Can you give Charlie and I a couple moments alone?"

"Sure thing. See you soon." Camella squeezed his hand and stepped out.

Charlie's mom gently kissed her husband on the lips. "Love you."

"Love you too, sweetheart."

As his mom reluctantly left the room, she pinched his arm and glared at him, whispering, "We'll talk about Julie later."

Charlie shut the door behind them and turned to his dad, who wore a goofy grin. The drugs were kicking in.

"I know you didn't want to come back home," his dad said. "You've got a place out there. Maybe even a girl too"

"I do. How did you know?"

"Because that's what Ricci men do. We sow our wild oats."

"Our oats?"

"I had a few women before your mom. Great gals. Big round asses and—"

"Really, Dad? That's what you want to talk about?"

"You're right. I think the drugs are messin' with the mind." He thumped his forehead with his finger, smiling, then took his son's hand. "Thank you. Thank you for coming home. I can go into surgery knowing you're here."

"Of course, I'm here."

"Staying here and running the company is a big job. I got worried you wouldn't make it, and your cousin Garrett would step in. That boy is dumb as a box of hair." His dad yawned again.

"I know," said Charlie.

"You'll do great. And later, it will be you and me working together. I've dreamed of this, son. Since the day you were born."

He squeezed Charlie's hand as he drifted to sleep.

Charlie took a moment to watch his dad peacefully slumber. It had taken a heart attack and strong narcotics to get him to reveal the gentler side Charlie always knew the old man had. Although Charlie figured he'd probably never see it again, it was nice to know it was in there.

Charlie gently laid his dad's hand on his chest. "Good luck, Dad."

In the quiet room, his next thought was to run for the window, jump, and take off for Benston. Unfortunately, his dad's room was on the twenty-third floor.

Chapter 52

I thought the wedding had a rocky start without a groom, but nothing prepared me for Daisy's reaction. Her monkey shriek sounded like someone was tearing off a limb. And who could blame her? Cheyenne and Tony were ripping her heart out. It was the cry of emotional agony. Any woman would have recognized it.

Denise grabbed my hand with one of hers and clutched her baby bump with the other. Fat Chris Pratt dropped his phone.

Daisy climbed up Tony's torso, held onto his head, and kicked Cheyenne away with her feet. Cheyenne fell backward, and Topeka caught her.

"Daisy, please be good," said Tony. Daisy did settle down, but she stayed pressed to Tony's chest with her arms wrapped lovingly around his neck.

"What the hell happened in that monkey barn?" said Denise.

"How are we going to pull that thing off him?" I said.

"We?! I'm pregnant."

I turned to Chris Pratt. "You guys need to help me take care of this."

"We don't handle monkeys," he said, staring at Daisy. He was sweating profusely. "I don't even know who does."

Cheyenne's family watched in horror. Even Jock and Itch kept their distance as the monkey yelled and batted everyone away from her and Tony.

Chris Pratt's partner stepped up. "Leave her to me." He strode calmly toward Tony and Daisy.

"We aren't supposed to handle the animals," said Pratt, chasing after him.

The little guy took Daisy by the hand. "Hey, girl. Come to daddy." The chimp jumped from Tony onto the little security guard's head and screamed louder. I'm not exactly sure what happened next, because I turned to everyone and yelled, "RUN FOR THE GATE! NOW!"

As if on cue, the zoo's security alarm went off. Damn it. That's all we needed. More chaos.

I looked around for Swayze and Axel and found them up to their elbows in cake again.

"You guys go with Denise," I said. "Hurry!" They each grabbed an extra handful of cake and took off after Denise who was waddling toward Pastor Bee's truck.

Most of the wedding party was already sprinting down the path toward the back gate. The ones in the lead I assumed were the ones on probations, including Kevin who was limping on his frozen foot.

I surveyed the madness. Daisy was still screeching and standing on top of the little guard, who was planted face-down in the grass.

"Let's calm down, folks," said fat Chris Pratt. "That alarm just means there's an escaped animal. Which is probably this chimpanzee." It was then that I noticed the bracelet on Daisy's ankle—not much different than Kevin's tracking device. We were screwed.

Cheyenne's Aunt Freda fainted, and the handful of people who had still remained, took off running.

Tony clasped Cheyenne's hand, and they ran across the green grass. I chased after them. I was still the wedding planner. My duty was to get everyone out safe and shut the gate with the love-crazed chimp inside.

I needed to get the gate before Tony, Cheyenne and Daisy.

Chapter 53

I learned that blaring zoo security alarms and a screaming chimpanzee will double your sprint time. Or at least that was my experience, I can't speak for everyone. With arms and legs pumping and my chest burning, I managed to get to the zoo's back entrance ahead of Tony and Cheyenne.

I turned and saw the couple sprinting over the last knoll. They looked like Indiana Jones and his bride, outrunning the natives in *Raiders of the Lost Ark*— until Cheyenne tripped on her wedding dress. She tumbled and rolled. Tony grasped at the gown's train to stop her. They both landed in a heap.

That's when the screaming, lovesick monkey came racing over the hill.

"Get up. Run! She's coming!" I screamed.

Cheyenne got to her feet, took one step, and fell again, "My ankle!"

Just when you think a wedding is a complete disaster, that your bride may be torn apart by a crazed monkey and your career as a wedding planner may be finished, something beautiful can happen. (Not that this wedding was going to be saved—it was a total bust.)

Tony gathered Cheyenne in his arms, and like the scene from *An Officer and a Gentleman*, ran with her to the gate. I could almost hear the movie's theme music. But there was no time for pictures because this was going to be close. I needed to close the gate after they got through, but before Daisy did. And Daisey was gaining, fast.

"Come on, come ON!"

Tony and Cheyenne were only ten feet from the gate, but Daisy was only twenty feet behind. Daisy was so close I could see her face, and it was filled with desperation and anger. My heart broke. I knew that look. She might be strong enough to rip a human's arm off, but I knew her pain. She had experienced a few fleeting hours with the man of her dreams, and suddenly, he was taken away from her. A man who was from a different world than hers—so different he might as well be a different species.

Daisy and I both knew how it felt when that perfect guy left your life. You want to chase after them. Cry. Scream out, "Come back! I love you!"

Goddamn it. I had more in common with the monkey chasing the bride than with the bride herself.

As Tony and Cheyenne reached the gate, I pushed them through. Daisy didn't slow. I could tell she was going to climb the gate, and I knew what I had to do. I braced myself and slammed the gate shut, still standing inside. As Daisy leapt for the gate, I threw myself in front of her with my arms open wide.

The impact of a 120-pound chimp running at full speed brought us both to the ground and knocked the wind out of both of us too. When I recounted the event later for the police, I explained that it was like being hit by a very large, hairy bowling ball.

Daisy stood first, a bit dazed, and walked toward to the gate. I was close behind and a bit more dazed—the whole zoo swimming in and out of focus as I fought to stay conscious. Daisy grabbed the gate and was almost over it when I reached out and grabbed her foot. She pulled me off the ground at least six inches and screamed. My heart stopped. I knew that scream. It was the heartbreaking cry of love lost.

"I know. He's gone," I said, trying to comforted her. "I would have given him to you if I could. But it wasn't in the cards."

Daisy stared down at me — her eyes filled with sadness, ager and fear.

"We're women," I said feeling my own tears well and making Daisy a watery, hairy image. "We're strong. We have to let him go. And have a happy life."

She turned and looked through the gate, watching Tony pushing Cheyenne into and car and getting in. Daisy looked back at me. Were there tears in her eyes?

"It's hard," I said. "But we'll make it. We will."

Daisy let out one last sob. And so did I. I let go of her foot and held out my hands. "We need a hug."

She hesitated, then climbed down and walked slowly into my embrace, wrapping her strong arms around me. I could feel my tears falling, landing on her hairy shoulder. I knew we were thinking the same thing, "Why don't they want us?"

Chapter 54

It wasn't the first time I had finished up a wedding in a jail cell, but this time it seemed worse. The cell wasn't all that different from the monkey cages at the zoo. It was five a.m., and fifteen women of all sizes and shapes were snoring and sleeping it off. I recognized a few from the wedding party.

Every inch of my body was sore and bruised. Denise, head resting on my shoulder, snored peacefully. The police had charged us with unlawful entry, trespassing, property damage, littering, failure to obtain a permit, animal endangerment. There may have been more, but I was still a little loopy from having a head on with Daisy. They said they would have to wait until the following day to sort it all out.

I looked down at Denise's baby bump and fought back tears. What had I done? My best friend, who would have followed me anywhere, was sitting in a jail cell as an accessory to my crimes. Who gets a loyal and very pregnant friend thrown in jail? Me. That's who.

The baby bump moved. Seems I wasn't the only one awake. I ever-so-gently placed my hand on the bump and felt her little foot push against my fingers. Denise groaned a bit in her sleep.

"I'm sorry," I whispered to the bump. "I thought I was a wedding planner, and look what I've done. You aren't even born yet and you're a little jailbird. It's all my fault. I had to be in *Best Bride*. Who am I kidding?" "I'm no wedding planner. I'm a homeless gal with a job at Fast Food Fast Gas."

The little foot moved against my hand. I had to assume it was in agreement.

"And Axel and Swayze? I thought I could help them, and I endangered them."

The little foot kicked my palm again.

"I know. I've got to give up wedding planning before I kill someone. As of today, I'm done. I'm getting a second job, and I'm going to be there for you and Axel and Swayze."

Suddenly I was tired—tired to the bone—and every square inch of my body ached.

"I love you," I whispered to the bump.

"I love you too," whispered Denise. She sat up slowly and smiled. "And you can't stop being a wedding planner. You're incredible. Tony and Cheyenne are happily married thanks to you."

"But— "

"But nothing. And something else."

"What?"

"I picked a name," said Denise. "You'll like it."

"Baby Jailbird?"

Denise placed a hand on each shoulder and faced me, smiling. "I'm naming her Baby. Like in *Dirty Dancing*."

I was speechless.

"I know. It's a good one, huh?"

I hugged Denise even though every muscle screamed in pain. "It's perfect." I put my hand on the bump. "Do you hear that? Your name's Baby."

"And her middle name is Sheila," said Denise.

"You don't have to—"

"I do. Because when Baby is older, and she gets scared, I'm going to tell her, 'You don't have to be scared, because your middle name is Sheila. You're named after the bravest woman I know. She faced a chimpanzee head-on for true love.'"

"Some people might call that stupidity."

"I want her to grow up as brave and as driven and as amazing as you are," said Denise.

I hugged her tight. "Thank you. I love you."

"I love you too."

There was a smattering of applause. We looked around. Most of the women in the cell were awake now, and had been taking in the show.

A female officer entered the room. "Someone is here for Sheila Johnson and Denise Brown."

"Who is it?" I asked.

The officer shrugged as she walked toward the cell.

"Maybe it's your folks," I said to Denise.

"God, I hope not. If they had to come back from their trip to Reno for this, they're going to kill me."

Then I heard the music from outside. It started quietly, but I recognized that beat. It was "The Time of My Life" from *Dirty Dancing*.

The volume was turned up, and I could hear the lyrics that I knew by heart:

You're the one thing
I can't get enough of
So I'll tell you something
This could be love.

The police officer shook her head. "I told him. 'Don't you dare play that.'"

I turned to Denise. "Oh, my god. It's him!"

I yelled out beyond the wall, "Charlie is that you!?"

"It's me!" he called back over the music. "No one puts Baby in the corner."

"You watched the movie!" I screamed.

"Of course I did. Get out here!"

The cell door opened, and I ran. I ran past the guard, past security, and into a cinder-block waiting room. There was Charlie on the other side, holding up his cell phone, playing "The Time of My Life."

He set down the phone and held out his arms.

I nodded and ran. As I got to him I leaped with my arms out. He caught my hips and lifted me up. He spun me around to the music once, then twice, and then he slowly set me down like in the movie—my body gliding against his.

"You smell horrible," he said, kissing me.

"It's a combination of monkey and jail cell," I said kissing him back.

The police officer broke us apart.

"I don't know what kind of weird shit you two are into, but you need to take it outside."

Chapter 55

It was a beautiful summer morning in Benston. The sun was rising over the McDonald's sign as Charlie told the Uber driver to take the drive-through. Denise sat up front with the driver, and I snuggled next to Charlie in the back.

As soon as the car stopped in front of the take-out sign, Denise was yelling out her food order. "Three Egg McMuffins, a coffee, a Coke, two hotcakes, and a breakfast burrito. And make it quick. Really quick."

"Wow," I said.

"I haven't eaten since yesterday. This morning, I ate my cherry-flavored Chapstick."

"Ewwww."

"I know," said Denise.

"Order whatever you want, said Charlie, taking my hand and giving it a little squeeze. I squeezed back, maybe a little too hard. I still couldn't believe he was here, and I wanted to make sure he was real.

We all wolfed down our fast food like it was our last meal while the Uber driver drove us to Denise's place.

"As soon as I drop you off, I have to go back," said Charlie. "I wish I could stay, but I left while Dad was in surgery. They have *me* running the company.

"I understand. I'm just glad you came back," I said. "You didn't have to."

"I wasn't going to leave you in jail."

"By the way, how did you know we were in jail?" asked Denise.

"I kind of guessed." He wiped his hands on his pants and pulled his phone out of his pocket. "You went viral last night."

On his phone, Denise and I watched a shaky video of me running through the zoo, with a screaming wedding party, toward the back gate. It showed Cheyenne falling, Tony carrying her valiantly through the gates, and then me throwing myself in front of Daisy. The video ended with Daisy and me in a big sloppy hug, crying on each other's shoulders.

"Not one of my best moments."

"Are you kidding? You're amazing," said Charlie. "What other wedding planner would go to those lengths? I mean, look at that hit you took. Holy shit. That must have hurt."

The car pulled up to the Wheel In RV Park.

"Dude, I'm not driving in there," said the driver. "I heard the last guy that drove in there came out with only a steering wheel."

"That's a total lie," I said. "He left with everything BUT his steering wheel. Whole different thing. Anyway, it doesn't matter because you drove to the wrong place. Denise lives on Steele Street."

Charlie handed him a hundred-dollar bill. "We need to pick up a couple things. Keep driving."

The driver took the hundred and begrudgingly drove in.

"By a couple things, do you mean Axel and Swayze?" asked Denise. "They should be with Pastor Bee. I gave him specific instructions to take them to his place, and we'd pick them up later."

The driver swung around to my lot and parked. There were Axel and Swayze, on two new Big Wheels, next to Pastor Bee, who was standing in front of a beautiful new thirty-foot Airstream.

"Is this for real?" I gasped.

"I couldn't leave you homeless. You've got weddings to plan."

Denise stepped out of the car in shock. I turned to Charlie. "You don't need to rescue me."

"I know. But you rescued me first."

"How so?"

"You don't see me marrying Julie, do you?"

"No," I said smiling.

"You showed me that we are in charge of our destiny—or at least we can die trying."

"You still didn't need to buy me a new home."

He leaned in and whispered into my neck, "Yes, I did. I love you."

I wrapped my arms around him and gave him a long, deep, and thankful kiss. He kissed me back, and a wave of heat ran all the way to my toes.

He finally broke the kiss. "I'm sorry. I have to get back to New York."

"Call me and let me know how your dad's surgery went."

"I will. Have that eye looked at. It looks worse today."

I laughed, as a tear fell from my good eye.

Charlie leaned in and kissed me on the forehead. "I'm going to miss you."

"I'm going to miss you too." I slipped out of the car and waved goodbye. I was still waving as the car pulled around the corner and out of sight.

I turned around when I heard Swayze and Axel pedal up on their new Big Wheels. "Look what we got."

"Sweet."

Pastor Bee filled in some details. "Charlie called me this morning. Asked if I could help get it moved in."

"Does the shower work? I smell like a chimpanzee."

"You're all set up."

As I took all the new changes, I saw something I hadn't noticed before. I had a family. There were two little kids racing around the Airstream, who were going to be looking to me as sort-of a mom. A mom who was there when you needed her. Not like mine. And there was Denise, who would need me to be strong, and not stupid. It made me feel good—Christmas morning good.

Denise put a hand on my shoulder. "I'm sorry Charlie had to leave again."

"It's all good," I said. "Really."

I received a text on my phone. It wasn't a number I recognized, but when I read it, my heart stopped. I felt my knees start to give.

"Is it something bad?" asked Denise.

"It's *Best Bride*. They saw the video of the wedding last night. They want to know if we're available to be in their new reality budget wedding show."

I read it again. "We did it, Denise. Oh my god. We did it!"

Denise patted her bump. "Did you hear that, Baby? We're going to be famous!"

CPSIA information can be obtained
at www.ICGtesting.com
Printed in the USA
LVHW031451100120
643107LV00013B/43/P

9 781087 852157